STILL SHE WISHED FOR COMPANY

STILL SHE WISHED FOR COMPANY

Margaret Irwin

PENGUIN BOOKS
London

First Published by William Heinemann, Ltd. - 1924
Reprinted by Chatto and Windus - - 1932, 1935
Published in Penguin Books - - - - - - 1937

Made and Printed in Great Britain for Penguin Books Limited,
by Wyman & Sons, Ltd., London, Fakenham and Reading.

SINCE
THERE IS NONE NOW LEFT
TO REMEMBER HER,
MY APOLOGIES
FOR THE LIBERTIES TAKEN IN THIS BOOK
ARE DUE ONLY TO
JULIANA

TIME IS

PROLOGUE

THROUGH the early summer dusk in Hyde Park, three children ran shouting down the hill and by the water-fall garden. There they stopped a moment, suddenly silent, to peer through the railings at the miniature lake just beyond their reach. Pale yellow flags and rushes stood deep in the dark water, stirring very slightly now and then.

The smallest child stretched out her grubby hands through the bars to the rabbits that were feeding so tamely on the slope of the further lawn, their white tails clear in the twilight. The biggest child suddenly emitted a piercing yell: " Look at the bunnies, Ada, just look at the bunnies ! " Not a rabbit moved nor pricked up its ears.

The children joined hands and ran on again, until their light-coloured frocks became lost in the moving darkness of the crowd that passed slowly, persistently, up and down the Row.

The drone of traffic in the streets beyond sounded clearly in the still air.

Two soldiers came down the path. They stopped to lean their elbows on the railings and watch a moor-hen scud jerkily across the tiny lake.

A chain of girls, linked arm in arm, swung jauntily along in step to the scraps of music that floated down from the band. They also loitered a moment, their frocks and hats making shapeless splashes of orange and pink and scarlet in the dusk. A shrieking titter went up from first one and then another, the soldiers became quickly and noisily enlisted in their company and all passed on. But the moorhen, paying no attention to their voices, darted in and out of the rushes close to the railings.

Workmen came by with heavy, slow steps, a man and woman with a perambulator, both silent and tired, a tall man with books under his arm, shuffling clumsily along as though he were a tree walking, a woman whose sunken eyes seemed to burn in the shadow of her hat, a thin, weary clergyman, two Indian students talking in staccato voices.

Nearly all stopped as they went by, some for an instant, some for longer, to glance at the garden behind the railings, where creatures, usually shy and wild, went about their business, indifferent and unperturbed by the noisy crowd of humans so close to them. They were secure and isolated, as if in an impenetrable solitude.

It seemed to Jan Challard, who had been there for the last ten minutes, that she was looking into a garden removed from her, not by a row of iron railings, but by an immeasurable distance. She wished that she were there.

Jan's father, in a flight of fancy consequent on the reading of ballads, had had his second daughter christened Rose Janet, and called her this in full. The rest of the family, who were in more of a hurry, called her Rose, but a succession of housemaids, all goddaughters to that flower or the violet or lily, gradually rendered this unbearable, and the first syllable of her second name was adopted instead, greatly to the relief of its owner.

Beside Jan and a little behind her stood Donald Graeme who was silent because she was.

He looked at the top of her hat, and wondered if Jan had " gone away " again. It was a phrase he used only to himself about her, for he had not let her know that he was aware of her occasional absence of mind.

Usually he thought her full of life and laughter, all on the spot, however fagged out she might be by the daily grind at the office. He hated her to be at that office. He was sure it was too much for her, that she hated it too, in spite of the fun she made of it. But if she *were* fagged, he wished it would not take the form of this sudden silence and forgetfulness of his presence, when it was the last evening they would have together for weeks. Nor was it for the first time that evening.

They had met after work and dined at one of the cheaper Soho restaurants. His work at the architect's atelier had kept him too late to get a table by the window, and they sat by the fireplace in a crowded room on the first floor.

He had pointed out that the high chimney-piece of painted wood had a carved scroll-work running up the side which was probably of Adam's date, perhaps even Adam's own work. It should have been a beautiful design of grapes and vine-leaves with a ram's head at each side, but it had been defaced in some parts and almost obliterated. Jan ran her fingers over it and pulled off a long piece of dirty yellowish paint that had cracked and was peeling off. Underneath it, the wood was seared and blackened. The carving had clearly been defaced by burning, and seemed to have been done deliberately with some red-hot instrument that had made deep scars in the wood.

They had examined it, joking over their guesses as to how it had been done and why, until they were interrupted by the next course. Then they had talked nearly all the time of the extra long holiday Jan was to have after one more day at the office. To-morrow, the 1st of May, she was to go to Helen, her married sister, who had taken a cottage for the summer at the village of Barton in Berkshire. It was to be a real rest for her ; she was to prowl about country lanes and do practically nothing for five long weeks, perhaps even longer. He was sure she would find it dull.

"Yes, Helen says there's nobody to see, except perhaps the Vicar. There's a big house and park near which takes up so much room that there are hardly any other houses round, and the Harrises, its owners, are deadly, bought it some years ago and don't know what to do with it, just keep it as a secret store-house for their lost h's. They've grown too grand for their own friends, poor dears, and are shy of anyone else, but they are leaving quite soon I think.

"Bored ? Don dear, I long to be bored. There's nothing so dull as a perpetual rush. I'd like to sit in a lovely garden and a lovely frock and be beauti- fully bored for ever."

"Couldn't I be there to help bore you ? "

"But are you quite sure you would, Don ? "

It was just after this promising question that her eyes wandered back to the burnt scar under the peeling paint of the chimney-piece, and she never noticed his answer which he flattered himself was really rather apt, nor the devouring gaze that accompanied it, but became abstracted and forgetful, answering him at random or not at all.

At last he recalled her attention sharply and asked if she were again wondering about the burnt carving, but she said no, she had been thinking about something quite different and quite unimportant, she didn't know why, and it wasn't worth telling.

He did not want her to tell it, he wished to discuss

their engagement and plans for the future. Apparently he did not regard Jan's refusal to consider herself engaged to him as much to the point.

This evening she did not put forward this objection, but listened to him with docile attention tinged with both admiration and mockery.

But Donald Graeme noticed neither. His mind was concentrated on his subject, and he had leisure only to observe how brilliant Jan's eyes were when she smiled, but that when the smile passed they looked tired and heavy. Poor lass, it was high time she got that extra long holiday.

Now, as he stood with her by the railings of the waterfall garden, he said it again to himself, but with a touch of annoyance.

He began to speak, and Jan turned suddenly, looking at him in surprise. It was, he thought, as though she had expected to find someone else beside her, not him. The fancy, or rather conviction, struck him most unpleasantly, but he did not let his mind dwell upon it at the moment.

Jan had not noticed what he had begun to say, for she remarked hurriedly that if they waited till the band stopped the buses would be crammed for getting home.

" Wait a bit," said Donald slowly, still conscious of that slight shock he had just received. " What was it you were thinking about at dinner ? "

" Good heavens, Donald, how should I know now ? "

That was just like Donald to wait a couple of hours to refer to something that he had never appeared to notice.

" But you do know," he replied.

Jan at once capitulated, knowing it was the quickest thing to do.

" You mean when I was staring at the chimney-piece

and the burnt bit. I was thinking of the face of a man in a picture, an eighteenth-century portrait, that's all. I suppose it was because you'd said the chimney-piece was of that time, and we'd been wondering if it was some young rip of the period who'd burnt it when he was drunk. You know how one wanders on. I'd suddenly remembered some words : ' Tell me where all times past are,' but I didn't know I'd ever heard them before. Do you know where they come from ? "

" It's in a poem of Donne's. But you've got it wrong. It's ' Tell me where all past years are.' "

" No. I know it's ' times past.' "

" I tell you, I remember——"

" And I tell you, I *didn't* remember. I thought of it for the first time as though someone had just said it to me, and it came like that."

" The edition I had at Saint Andrews," pursued the dogged Scot, " was the latest and most correct and it had ' years.' "

" I don't care. It's times, times, times. Time is, time was, time will be. And I believe I actually do know who said that—Francis Bacon, unless it was Shakespeare wrote Bacon. Brrr ! Why am I shivering ? "

" Jan, you're cold. That thin frock——"

" No, it was only someone walking on my grave. What on earth, or off it, are we talking about ? Do let's get back to something comfortable."

" What is the picture you were thinking of ? "

" Oh, a portrait called a ' Gentleman Unknown.' It had been reproduced in the ' Connoisseur ' and I stole it in my first term at school—the only theft I ever committed, and I never had a twinge of conscience. I believe I liked it all the better for having stolen it. We were allowed to look at the improving magazines with pictures in Miss Bisley's drawing-room for a few minutes after tea on half-holidays, and I used to go back to that face because it looked at me as though it knew me, and none of the faces at school did that. You know what a blank it is—the first term at a boarding school.

" Then one day I noticed that the page was quite loose, and I pulled it out and popped it into my large hymn-book with tunes and looked at it all through the service, and ever afterwards I kept it very carefully in my desk or pigeon-hole, whichever was safest from inspection at the moment, and used to look at it in secret, and the face looked back at me, very watchful and amused as though he shared my secret and enjoyed it."

" And have you kept it ever since ? "

" Rather. It's pinned up in my room under the gas bracket, getting a bit torn at the edges. I might have run to a frame and glass by now. But then he's not as good company as he was, of course."

" What do you mean ? "

" Oh, well, at school, there isn't so much else to amuse one as now. I used to peep at him under the lid of the desk and pretend that if only I were quick enough I should just catch him winking at me. And of course I made up stories about him in lessons, and it gradually became a habit to read anything about his time that I could find in the school library. But does all this interest you ? "

" It concerns me," corrected Donald, " since what concerns you, concerns me. It does anyway," he added sharply, " whether you marry me or not."

She looked quickly at him and saw an obstinate line about his mouth.

" Don," she said, " you are not jealous, are you, of a Gentleman Unknown ? "

He wished he could think of something to say that

15

would be sarcastic and yet admiring, and easy and charming and witty all in one breath. But his expression only grew a shade more sullen and he mumbled: " Jealous ? What rot ! "

He knew, however, that he was jealous, in a fashion that was never effected by Jan's casual flirtations, which she generally imparted to him with much ridicule and laughter.

But when he was unable to hold her attention, or, most of all, when he sometimes caught in her a look of delighted expectancy, a look that was surprisingly radiant, sparkling and intimate to herself, then he felt jealous of her thoughts, whatever they might be, that could withdraw her so securely from him. She was genuinely fond of him, she was occasionally in love with him, but he was not the chief thing in her life, not even for the present moment.

He wondered for a little what was this chief thing, since it was not himself, nor anyone she liked better (he knew she had always played straight with him as she did with everyone) nor her people, though she was very fond of them. But she was different from them, anyone could see it, and see that they felt it so, though you could not tell if Jan felt it herself.

He would not ask his question. She should tell him of her own accord or not at all, and he stalked stiffly beside her down the path so that her high heels had to patter very fast to keep up with him.

" Oh, Don, I'll believe your legs are as long as stilts without your striding on like that. If you keep ahead of me, you may look round to find I'm gone."

" Gone where ? " He slackened his pace.

" How should I know until I'm gone ? Why are you cross with me ? But crossness becomes you. Oh, dear, now you are really angry. Don, I like you better than anyone I know. Isn't that enough ? "

"It doesn't seem to be," he replied after a pause, "since it's not enough to make you promise you'll marry me."

"No. I would rather wait until I like you better than anyone I don't know. It would be a pity to marry you and meet my ideal just after."

"I thought only sentimental schoolgirls talked about their ideals," he replied, uneasily conscious, but just too late, of the extreme surliness of his tones.

"Then I'm a superannuated sentimental schoolgirl. It's a destitute situation."

They had turned into the Row and become part of the slowly moving crowd that jostled them, stared at them, or walked intertwined in oblivion of them and everyone else. Perversely, Donald now wished to make all the more pleasant remarks that he might have made to greater advantage in the comparative quiet by the waterfall garden.

He inwardly cursed the crowd, his recent sullenness and Jan's flippant detachment. If they could only have more time together, and space, they would get to understand each other. But she had so many distractions beside her job—her friends and dances and theatre parties and week-ends in the country where she was asked down "for a rest"; and, on his side, he had the work to which he must give every possible moment if he succeeded as he meant to do. He squared his shoulders as he thought of it, and was exasperated to find himself remembering Barrie's words, quoted in Jan's softly laughing tones: "Mon, it's a grrrand sight to see a Scotchman on the make."

"There isn't room to move—or breathe," said Jan below him. "For that matter there's no room in this world to live, and barely room to love."

It was what he had been thinking, but he was annoyed that she should say it. She should not let herself be

17

influenced by trivial circumstances, she had not enough
strength of purpose, not enough vitality, she did not
know what she wanted, she undertook a job that was
too hard for her, flirtations which quickly became
distasteful to her ; she was too daring yet too fastidious,
too fanciful, too fragile for work or pleasure, or, he
doubted, for a marriage that was bound to be poverty-
ridden at first ; she was a frivolous, uncertain creature
that he could pull to pieces in his mind as easily as a
butterfly in his hands.

But, as he did it, he noticed the point of her chin
beneath her hat, the delicate curve of her neck where
it set into her thin shoulders, and wished painfully
that he could protect her from the laughing disillusion-
ment that pursued her own escapades—yes, and from
her responsibilities and her necessity to work, whether
now or later when married to him. This was
inconsistent in Donald, who considered responsibility
and work two of the chief motives of existence.

There was already a small crowd waiting for the
bus at Hyde Park Corner. Jan and Donald caught
it running, but their superior strategy was only half
rewarded.

" One on top only," roared the conductor. " Full
up now, full up, full *up* ! " He had ruthlessly separated
Jan from her attendant swain, who had to spring off.
She mounted on top to find that even " One on top
only " was incorrect. There was no seat for her. She
stood at the back, looking up at a clear pale sky where
ragged strips of cloud were racing fast.

" 'Ere, you can't stand up 'ere," snapped the
conductor, appearing as suddenly as a Jack-in-the-
box.

" You said there was a seat," said Jan, clinging
weakly to what she knew to be a desperate position.

At the same time she clutched the rail, for the bus was lurching furiously.

"Can't 'elp that. Thought there was, but there ain't. Sorry, miss, but you'll 'ave to get orf."

"All right. But I'll be getting off at the top of Park Lane. Couldn't I——"

He banged the bell relentlessly.

"Can't be done, miss. I might get into trouble. If yer lives in Park Lane why don't yer go 'ome in yer broo-um?"

He grinned good-humouredly, and Jan with the greater good humour of the vanquished, grinned back.

A final lurch of the bus pitched her forward on to his chest as she was beginning to go down the stairs.

There was no use attempting another bus from here. She would walk up to Oxford Street and get the Bayswater bus. And as she was going up Park Lane she might as well branch off into the quiet side streets, and strike Oxford Street a little higher up. It was only three steps longer and so much nicer. How stupid she had been not to walk with Donald, across the Park at any rate. And she had had to leave him without saying good night or anything pleasant, after he had been so cross, poor dear. It irritated her to feel pity for him. He was so much steadier and more sensible than herself, and yet she often felt that he was helpless in her hands. She did not want her midge bites to hurt him, but what were people for, if not to laugh and give cause for laughter? Oh dear, how tired her feet had got in these thin shoes, and what heaven it would be if she actually *could* jump into a taxi!

She was in Hill Street when it began suddenly to rain. It was as violent as it was sudden, and she dashed for an arched doorway. No cloak, no umbrella, a thin frock whose colours, she had discovered, "ran" even in cold water, and her new *suède* shoes which were such a pretty shape but cheap, and certain to spoil. She had put them on for Donald who was not a connoisseur in shoes nor even in feet. Damn that conductor ! She might have got a seat inside the Bayswater bus by now.

Repeated taxi whistles pierced the air, some close to her ; there was the scurrying, skidding sound of rubber tyres on the wet road as a huge car sped past ; a huddled, shrunken form ran splashing through the rivulets. The rain made a din in the streets like the furious beating of kettledrums.

Jan had pressed as far as possible into her doorway. She watched a small torrent rush down the gutter and the huge drops leap up from the pavements in a thousand tiny fountains. " Fairy thimbles " her mother had called them when they were children. Was this fairy rain ? It seemed to have fallen all at once out of a clear sky as though it were an unnatural storm raised by witches.

As a child she had been afraid of rain as many people are of thunder. And that, no doubt, was on account of a funny little verse and still funnier picture, in a large book of her father's, which she had thought was addressed to herself as she was then called Rose :

" O, Rose, thou art sick !
The invisible worm,
That flies in the night
In the howling storm,
Has found out thy bed
Of crimson joy,
And his dark secret love
Does thy life destroy."

Whenever she had had a cold or a headache her father had an irritating habit of remarking " O, Rose, thou art sick ! " which was quite enough to make her shiver in bed when she heard the rain on the roof at night, and wonder if the invisible worm were even now flying through the storm to seek her out. She laughed now as she thought of it huddled in her doorway.

The straight, severe old houses that she liked so well looked blankly at her and offered her no welcome. They had been standing here a hundred years, far more than a hundred years ago. There would have been coaches rumbling down this street then, and sedan chairs hurrying through the rain and link boys running and calling. Perhaps one of them would be calling for *her* coach—did they do that ? She had the haziest idea of the duties of link boys. The old inn of the " Coach and Horses " at the opposite corner, now dark and silent, would be full of life and bustle as some traveller's coach arrived for the night. A gentleman from the country—no, a gentleman newly arrived from France. That sounded nice.

The face of the " Gentleman Unknown " in her room had again flashed into her mind, and she now imagined it looking at her from the window of a coach. She could fancy the horses champing and steaming in the blurred light of torches in the rain, the footman jumping down from the box and swinging open the door, and the exquisite beruffled hand that would first appear, as the " Gentleman Unknown " stepped down into the street and—perhaps—turned that half-quizzical, half-flattering gaze on her.

She had begun to hum a song from the " Beggar's Opera " :

> " Youth's the season made for joys,
>   Love is then our duty,"

and stopped as she noticed for the first time the tall

figure of a man in the shadow of a neighbouring doorway. He was watching her ; she wondered how long
he had been doing so, how long he had been there. He
walked out into the rain with a long, careless stride,
and came towards her. He wore an opera hat and a
monocle, and a white silk scarf beneath his coat. There
is a faint resemblance in the dress to the dandyism of
an earlier date ; Jan noticed it now as she had often
done before.

" Getting wet ? " he asked and took up his stand
beside her.

" Not very," said Jan, without much conviction,
for the wind at that moment was beginning to blow the
rain into their corner.

" You'll get drenched," he observed.

She was silent. What was the use of his making
remarks like that unless he offered her his coat like
Sir Walter Raleigh or Saint Martin ? And even that
wouldn't protect her precious new shoes. But he was
silent too. He seemed to be considering something.

" Better get a taxi," he said at last, " I've whistled
half a dozen times for one. What direction are you ? "

So that was it. It was not the most polite way of
making the suggestion, but she liked his low, monotonous voice. There was a note in it of command,
not intentional but instinctive. She liked, too, his
well-cut, inexpressive face and the hard, rather dull
eyes—at least, she found them interesting. They
were not like any eyes that she knew.

But why hadn't he asked her straight out ? Probably
he was shy. It was certainly rather bold, and he had
evidently been considering, hesitating. His manner
was constrained, though pleasingly unlike the constraint
of the men at the office, who were often a little shy of
her. It was an adventure, and Jan could generally
manage adventures in her own way. She felt chiefly

22

an amused interest as she looked full into the heavy eyes and replied :

" I live in Bayswater—Norham Road. Are you suggesting we should share a taxi ? " She did not draw her pay till to-morrow and hoped she had enough in her purse.

" No, certainly not ' share ' it," he replied, " it is for my pleasure."

" And for my convenience," said Jan.

" Your convenience," he answered, " is my pleasure."

He laughed as though he had been rather absurd, but Jan laughed delightedly. Any flickering doubts of the proceedings were dispelled by such a phrase. It was quite like " Love is then our duty."

" Thank you," she said, " it's very nice of you, but I shall think it still nicer if you let me share, without any fuss. You see, don't you ? "

A man who could turn a sentence like that *must* see. She was filled with a sudden hope. Was this at last her ideal, the man she had always dreamed of ? A hitherto wholly unreal man, composed chiefly from her casual glimpses in the library, that last year at school, of La Rochefoucauld's Maxims, Lord Chesterfield's Letters, Congreve's Valentine, Lovelace without his insatiable vanity ; a man of easy ironic wit, assured composure impossible to ruffle, and yet of fancies as fantastic as her own.

This man had more of the air and bearing of her ideal than anyone she had ever met. He would look magnificent, though a trifle heavy, in the graceful dress of the latter half of the eighteenth century. This was a test that Jan was apt to apply with failure. Donald, unwittingly, had been considered to disadvantage in powder and ruffles, though he would look very well in a kilt.

The man did not seem to have noticed her late request.

He was looking intently at her and said presently :
" I'll go up to the corner. It's impossible to get one
here."

The words were spoken so low as to be almost
muttered. He added, equally low, but forcibly :
" You will wait."

He suddenly lowered his head as though to look
at her the more closely. Jan met his eyes squarely,
with a certain surprise. She had felt so sure that she
liked him a minute ago, and liked him to the point of
feeling quite hopeful and excited. Now she was not
so sure. That hard, mask-like expression seemed to
have opened for a flash, and she did not know what
it was she saw beneath it. But in the same instant
he had turned and was striding away up the street,
his head bent low against the driving rain.

No sooner had he gone than she hoped he would not
get a taxi, would not come back. Was she being a
reckless fool ? Donald had said she had no idea how
to take care of herself. But why should she ? It was
so dull to take care of oneself, so tiresome to imagine
it was always necessary.

A taxi came down the next street, turned the corner,
was coming fast behind her, went past a little way.
The door was ajar, and a man's hand, thrust through
the window from inside, was holding it so. The taxi
slowed down, began to turn round. As it backed into
the pavement, Jan darted out from her doorway and
raced up the street. In a few seconds she had left
Hill Street behind her and was making for Oxford
Street.

Three-quarters of an hour later, she plunged,
bedraggled and dripping, into a small room where a
worn-faced woman sat at a sewing-machine among
a quantity of heterogeneous articles. A tall, largely-

24

built girl who sat on the floor, half covered with stockings, got up clumsily, scattering them in all directions,
and flung herself on the intruder with the eagerness
of a prisoner who has seen a chance of escape. The
escape was from a quarrel with her mother which had
been in full progress a minute before.

" Oh, Jan, your frock ! Your shoes ! "

" They're done for," said Jan. " I couldn't get a
bus the whole way."

She took off her shoes and held them up, letting the
water run on to a plate on the crowded table ; they
looked like two small drowned rats.

" What wicked extravagance," wailed the woman
at the sewing-machine, " if only you'd got a sensible
pair as I told you."

" Oh, mother, I know. But I do so love pretty
shoes."

" We can't afford pretty things if they're not sensible,
and it's bad taste to dress as though we can. I wonder
you don't feel that," said her sister, peeling off the
stocking she was darning from her arm and hand.

" I do, Barney, I do. But you're so much younger
and wiser than I am. I recognize that my taste in
conduct is deplorable, but my taste in shoes—come,
you will grant that, though a little damped by present
circumstances, they have an elegant shape ? "

" She's talking nonsense again," murmured their
mother wearily. " Jan, do you really hope to go
straight down to Berkshire to-morrow after the office ?
I don't see how you can do it. It's terribly late now,
and there won't be a moment to pack in the morning
before you start. Do go upstairs quietly. Father
has had a bad day and is very tired. That frock you
began to make—I did mean to help you finish it, but
there's not been a moment. Tim and Johnny simply
had to have these shirts."

25

"It's all right, mother. I'll just shove in one or two things to-night. I don't mind a bit about the frock or anything. I'll live in my old coat-frock all the time, and my sensible heavy-soled shoes. Alas, *these* shoes lie heavy on my soul to-night!"

Brandishing the drowned rats in her hand with a tragic gesture, she left the room and seemed to leave a dull emptiness behind her. Her mother sighed. "It will be nice for Helen to have her," she said.

Barney swept armfuls of stockings into the large mending-basket, very hastily lest her mother should resume the quarrel, kissed her goodnight as hastily and with exaggerated cheerfulness, and ran upstairs to the room she shared with her sister. It was poorly lit by a gas jet that gave out a pale blue flickering glare. Jan was lying on her bed, as motionless as if she were asleep.

"Jan, you perfect ass, in your wet things! Get out of them at once! Do you want to be up packing all night? If you don't hurry up, I'm damned well not going to help you. Where on earth can I put the suit-case if you don't get off your bed?"

Jan rolled slowly off it, looking a trifle dazed.

She had been thinking of Helen's cottage which she had not yet seen. Half asleep, she had forgotten that it was a real cottage with tiny rooms and windows, likely to be rather a squash with the baby and the nurse-maid and the addition of her brother-in-law each week-end, and had seen herself looking out of French windows on to a wide lawn, wandering through spacious rooms and gardens, never in a hurry, never having to make decisions, living through long days of placidly busy leisure in which she could do all the things she had always wanted and never found time to do at home.

She would sit in a large, silent room and read musty

old books (Jan loved the smell of old books) she would make pretty bags and absurd, charming little sewing aprons for herself and her sisters, she would try to write down some beginnings of stories (she could never make up more than beginnings) she would lie in the sun and do nothing at all.

She shook herself, rubbed her eyes, said aloud : " What a fool I am ! " and began to pull clothes out of the chest of drawers where all hers and Barney's things were mixed up together. They had been meaning to tidy them for months, but there had not been a moment.

She rummaged for all the letters she would now have time to answer. Bobby, in Cologne, nice, but dull, good only for dancing and revues ; poor old Alice who was having such a deadly time teaching in that school ; Kitty and Iris who were wealthy and had a lovely time, with nothing to worry them, but made up for it by going nearly demented over their successive love affairs ; dear, stiff old Mr. Arnold who lent her books that she never had time to read properly ; that queer man whom she had only danced with once or twice but who kept on writing letters from India— " Barney, Barney, *have* you seen any letters with an Indian stamp on them ? No, not that one—where *is* the last ? "

Suddenly she sat down on a heap of clothes and declared that she would put the alarm at half an hour earlier and finish packing in the morning. It was no good going on looking for things in this beastly light with her head swimming.

As they undressed, she told Barney about the man who had wanted to take her home in a taxi. But she could not tell why it was that she had run off at the last minute in that silly melodramatic way. Barney thought it neither silly nor melodramatic. At nineteen she had all the air of an elder sister to Jan at twenty-four, whom she yet admired as much as she deprecated. It was Jan who, through her grit in sticking to a job she loathed, combined with odd irrational flashes of cleverness, had got on the best of her rather feckless family, and Barney respected her accordingly. But she was a fool to behave like this. " You *said* that when he looked at you just before he went off you thought his face looked beastly."

" Yes. I thought that afterwards as I was coming home. I didn't at the time—I just wondered what it was that made him look like that. Now I know that it looked brutal—a sort of coarse, stupid brutality that wouldn't have cared a bit what I felt about anything—wouldn't have known, even. But it wasn't till that moment—I liked him up till then."

" Why ? "

" He had never had to bother. He was easy, assured, accustomed to get what he wants."

·" Exactly. There you are."

" Oh, shut up, Barney. Why should we assume that all men want is to kiss girls in taxis ? "

" Well, then, why did you run away ? "

" I tell you I don't know, or at least I can't tell. It wasn't because I was afraid of him—it hadn't dawned on me then that that look was beastly. I was afraid of something else, and in quite another way—it was awful. A creepy sort of fear, as one used to have of the dark—of that street and the rain and that if I stayed there another minute I might see it all quite different. I wanted to, too, but I had a sort of panic—I *can't* explain. It frightens me now to think I could have been such an idiot."

" You're just tired," said Barney. " I wish you'd marry Donald and let him look after you. You need a home."

"A *home!* Another! Haven't we enough of a home as it is?"

But Barney persisted in considering the advantages of an alternative home. Of course it would be a grind at first, but Donald would be sure to get on in time. "And you know, Jan, it's something to be able to marry anyone now. Lots of girls can't. And you work and live so hard——"

"That I'm not likely to last well. So that I ought to make haste and secure a husband while I've got the chance? Lord, what a rush it all is!"

"I don't believe you're seriously in love with him a bit."

"I am a bit in love with him, but why seriously? Is love always serious?"

"It is with Donald."

"Yes. And that's where the gallant had such an advantage over the lover. His mind was free to cultivate all the graces and none of the inconveniences of an ardent passion. Barney, do you not also sometimes regret that love is no longer an art?"

"I regret that you *will* talk such rot, and just like a book, too. I can't think where you get it from as you hardly ever read."

Jan yawned suddenly and reached over to put out the gas, but stopped, with her hand outstretched, to look beneath it at the picture she had stolen from the "Connoisseur" of the "Gentleman Unknown." How peculiarly bright those eyes were, even in that cheap reproduction. They had fascinated her as a child, had drawn her back again and again to look at them. As she looked at him now, the half-smiling, half-questioning lips seemed to be repeating her last question. It was not the first time she had caught him listening to their conversation.

Barney, already in bed, pursued her thoughts.

"After all," she observed in her reflectively calculative way, as though she were engaged in a process of mental arithmetic, "we mayn't have as good or as easy a time of it as most of the girls we know, but you do come in for a lot of funny experiences. That man *might* have been quite nice, a new friend—perhaps even useful. You've made some real friends almost as oddly—look at those delightful people you met in the train. It's a pity, in a way, that now you will never know——"

"Barney, *don't !* "

"What's up ? Do you feel you regret it ? "

"Yes, of course. One always regrets everything one hasn't done. But it's not that. I can't bear totting up what one gets or doesn't get out of life as though it were a commercial proposition."

"Surely one must try and get the most out of life and not miss any chances," Barney replied, in the voice of one who states the first article of a religion.

"Chances ? " Jan teasingly considered a few of these. Tony, the emptiest man in London, with nothing to marry on but his money ; the earnest young man from Bloomsbury who had preached on her moral obligation as an adult female to love for the sake of experience, his offer of an opening course being, no doubt, actuated by a sense of duty to his neighbour ; or was there more solid business value again in the senior partner's strictly honourable proposal across a luncheon table at the Pall Mall ? True, he had neither looks, nor charm, nor even youth, but then he could offer a house complete with servants, and surely that was enough to justify his asking for her with the dessert and with as complacent an air of security.

Jan's laughter did not conceal her disgust nor her obvious regret that she had never received " a really decent proposal," whether honourable or otherwise.

30

Barney was sure that Donald couldn't have proposed like that.

"Donald never proposed at all. He just assumed I was going to marry him."

She threw herself on to the bed, twisting her two plaits of hair tightly together under her chin so that it formed a close brown cap round her suddenly eager face.

"Barney, I didn't want to go with that man. I was afraid of disappointment and I know now I should have been disappointed. He was so nearly right— that walk, that unconscious air of authority, that—that touch of hardness. And 'Your convenience is my pleasure'—pretty, wasn't it?

"But he *wasn't* right, Barney. He was stupid, really, and gross. He'd have had no more penetration than the senior partner. That crispness was only an echo, a chance likeness."

"Echo—likeness—what of?"

"Barney, Barney, I wish I knew! Barney, I'm always just on the point of remembering something— something very interesting and delightful, but I never can quite. Do you ever feel like that?"

"Never. You don't know what you want, Rose Janet, that's what it is."

"Yes, I do. But I know now that I'll never meet him because he can't exist in an age that hurries and scrambles and pushes. It's a kind that's died out."

"The clothes have, that's all. You're so absurdly romantic. Human nature's just the same at any time."

"*Is* it?" exclaimed Jan with sudden savagery. "Can't you remember when Mother was not 'just the same' as now?"

There was silence for a minute. Both girls had known, in their early childhood, a mother whose air

31

of repose and gentle distinction had long since been frittered away by the swarm of small cares that crowded, cramped and jostled her and her household.

Jan, now in bed, pursued her advantage. "Would I behave like a 'gamine,' or you calculate our opportunities of 'useful' friends, if we'd been brought up as she and Granny were ? "

But Barney was here on safer ground. "What rot ! You know you'd hate to have been 'brought up.' I'd like to see you, of all people, putting up with any real authority ! "

"But where there is authority," said Jan sleepily, "there is a chance of rebellion."

Barney meditated throwing a pillow at her, but reserved her energies instead for jumping out of bed and putting out the light, as Jan had apparently given up all intention of doing so. She looked round with her hand on the gas bracket and had a glimpse of Jan's face on the pillow, a laugh at some unspoken thought flashing across her lips and eyes. Barney turned off the gas, then switched it on again so hastily that it re-lit of itself, and the familiar untidy room, the half-filled suit-case on the floor, the motionless figure on the other bed, all flashed again out of the darkness that had engulfed them.

"I'm still here," said Jan drowsily. "Why did you turn it on again ? "

Barney did not know. She put out the light firmly and finally and got back into bed remarking that it was a pity Donald couldn't get out of work to-morrow in time to see Jan off. There was no sound in the darkness. She wished Jan would answer her.

TIME WAS

B

CHAPTER I

On warm days when the air was still, Juliana Clare would walk down through the terraced gardens of Chidleigh House, through the wrought-iron gates three times her height, and into the drive of beech trees that stretched for two miles in a straight line across the park. This drive, together with most of the house and gardens, dated from the time when Henry VIII had rebuilt Chidleigh as a holiday residence for his delicate son. Juliana always walked more slowly when she entered the drive, for she liked to linger in it and think how it had looked when the young prince and his gorgeous retinue came riding down to Chidleigh between those rigidly straight lines of trees. But that was in the days of the Tudor kings. In this dull year of grace, 1779, nothing pretty and romantic ever happened.

Presently the drive went over a bridge with low stone parapets, and Juliana always paused there to look down at the fishes in the small, clear stream below. Sometimes, especially on very hot days, she would sit for a time at the side of the drive, near to the bridge, and look up at the cool green arches overhead, for the upper branches met and formed a vaulted aisle that stretched away till nothing could be seen but greenery.

Sometimes she would turn aside by the stream and follow it through the park till she came to the lake, and there she would lie on the stone seat that her father had had made on its shore ; lie looking downwards at the dragon-flies that darted here and there above the smooth and shining water, or lie looking upwards at the many chimneys and turrets of her home. They rose from the summit of a wooded slope, and looked from the lake like the towers of a fairy city rising above the trees.

Often Juliana carried a book or a piece of embroidery or some drawing paper or, lately, the fat manuscript book, bound in calf and fastened with brass clasps, which her mother had just given her on her seventeenth birthday.

" If you write in it the events and industries of each day," said Lady Chidleigh, " it will, I hope, encourage application. You are sadly idle, my love, but I think that when you are accustomed to see for yourself how you have ordered your time you will be more careful to employ it well. It would surely shame you to write down ' This was an empty day.' "

Mamma always spoke so beautifully. Juliana was fired by her eloquence into a burning desire to employ profitably every moment of her time. She wrote carefully on the first page, in a delicate, pointed hand :

Juliana Clare—Her Journal,
February 15th, 1779,
Chidleigh.

Then she drew up a time-table, composed, as nearly as might be, on the rules laid down for herself by Clarissa Harlowe, the peerless heroine of Mr. Richardson's great novel, rules that should serve as a pattern of perfection to young ladies through all the centuries.

" *February* 15*th :* I will allot my first three morning Hours to Study in my Closet," wrote Juliana, " and five Hours every day to my Needle, Drawings, Music, etc."

She debated with herself the next item of "One Hour to Visits to the Neighbouring Poor," to give them "brief instructions and good books." There were no neighbouring poor at Chidleigh, owing to the extent of the park, the nearest village being nearly four miles off. Nor, were they more accessible, could Juliana imagine what instructions, however brief, she could give them.

It was true she visited Nurse's cottage in the drive nearly every day. It stood half-way to the park gates, the only break in the drive, except for the bridge over the stream, and its bright patch of garden glowed like a many-coloured mosaic set in that endless straight expanse of green trees.

It made a convenient reason for a walk, and Nurse was always so happy to see her, and never too busy for a chat. She was so fresh and round and rosy that she looked almost as young as her eldest daughter, Molly (now maid to Juliana), although she had been Nurse to all the present generation at Chidleigh and now had a great family of her own. Little William, the youngest, was an angel, and Juliana generally contrived to find some treasure to bring him in her bag, while Nurse on her side never let "little miss" depart without some flowers or their first pear or plum or strawberry, or a taste of the new jam or elderberry wine or cowslip tea that she had been making.

But in trying to consider Nurse as a substitute for the "poor," Juliana could not but feel guilty of a mean evasion.

As compensation she decided she would account for moments that the peerless Clarissa had not mentioned.

"In employing the time while Molly does my hair,

by learning my Geography or History Cards—one Hour each day."

And to crown all and leave no possible room for subterfuge in the matter, she wrote at the end in very firm characters :

"And I *will* not allow a single Hour to pass in Dreaming and Idling."

For the rest of February and March the journal was so closely written, and accounted for each hour of the day so minutely, that it seemed Juliana must be the most persistently occupied person on earth. She embroidered an apron, she painted flowers, she drew fanciful figures to illustrate some classic fable, she practised the harpsichord and some new songs, she studied the European rivers from Guthrie's maps, she read French memoirs and plays with Mamma, and English history to herself, and, on Sundays, Blair's Sermons on the Government of the Heart and the Necessity of Order in Conduct. Moreover, when the dressing bell rang at three o'clock, the hour appointed for all to be put into " full dress," she ran at once and first fetched a book of poems or the history or geography cards, and sat with them on her lap during the elaborate process of having her hair brushed, dressed and powdered. If she did not always succeed in learning much, that was because Molly was such a chatterbox, not she.

Quite a large proportion of time had to be allotted " to the writing of my journal," and she found also that the frugal heroine on whom she modelled herself, appointed no hours to carriage exercise, riding abroad, or excursions to friends. But there had not been so many of these since Fanny, her eldest sister, had married

Mr. Daunt nearly a year ago, and gone to live in his London house in Hill Street.

Juliana was the youngest of the family, and Fanny, who was seven years older, had always petted her and treated her with a mixture of patronage, protection and adoration, as though she were a favourite doll or her own baby. Juliana, for her part, had a deep veneration for her sister, as well as a clinging affection.

And when at the end of March dear Fanny came to pay a visit of some weeks at Chidleigh, Juliana's delight was too ecstatic to record her doings with the same length and precision in the new journal. Often the single entry under some date was " A happy, happy day."

Nor would the doings have made such an edifying record of industry as before. The sisters made up parties with their cousins, Charlotte and Sophia Clare, and the numerous Miss Hilburys from the Grange and their schoolboy brothers, and rode and drove, played, sang and danced, laughed and chattered together, all day and often half the night. There was no end to the joys and surprises that Fanny provided— Fanny's dresses, Fanny's little presents, Fanny's new, modish maid, Fanny's gossip of balls and the opera and witty gentlemen and pretty ladies, and a shocking affair of a duel fought by one of her acquaintance on account of a well-known beauty, a notable toast, whom Fanny had met and declared to be as lovely as an angel but with surprising bold eyes. Fanny was not herself a beauty, except in as far as a charming, unconscious air of dignity and sweetness could make her so.

Once when Charlotte and Sophia had stayed the night, the four girls sat on the great bed in Fanny's room and talked so late and made so much noise that in the middle of the night, well after midnight in fact,

Mamma herself had come along the passage and tapped on the door to bid them go to sleep. How startled they had all been—startled into complete stillness, their open mouths suddenly silent, their eyes very round and large, much like a nest of young birds gaping and staring !

But even those delightful weeks, so long because so full of incident and variety, came to an end, and towards the end of April Fanny went back to the town, taking Sophia with her for a visit. She wished to take Juliana, but Lady Chidleigh considered her daughter too young to make her first experience of the town without the watchful care and guidance of a mother as well as a sister, and she could not arrange to leave Chidleigh herself at present. In reality, she feared lest anyone so young and impressionable might form some " unfortunate attachment," and had, therefore, decided that she should not go to London until she was safely married.

On the day that Fanny and Sophia had left, Juliana pulled out her journal again from the drawer in her black japanned writing table, and sat bolt upright in a chair at the table with the great green china inkstand close in front of her, and wrote :

" *May* 1st. This Morning they all drove off in the Phaeton, Coch, and Vis-a-Vis, back to the Town. My brothers ackompani'd them on horseback as far as Windsor."

Here she came to a long pause and tapped her ebony pen against her small white even teeth. She could think of no more to write, and considered that though there would now be plenty of time to write in her journal, yet there would be nothing to write about for many weeks. It would be so dull to fill up the

40

book again with her occupations—those occupations that she now had no wish to resume. So she continued to tap her teeth and look out of the new French window of her " closet," a pleasant, low room, as big as many drawing-rooms of a later date. Her father, Robert Clare, the late Lord Chidleigh, had had these French windows put in in all the rooms downstairs.

Outside, the brilliant green of the wide lawn lay bathed in sunshine, and the shadow of the great cedar made a deep purple pool in the middle of it. It was unusually warm for the beginning of May, enervatingly so.

Juliana sighed, then yawned, then sighed again. She had a slender shape, unformed but graceful, though the proper carriage of her " back-bone " was the despair of Lady Chidleigh. Her small oval face was of the exquisite complexion that has never faced wind and weather. Her mouth drooped a little ; it gave her an expression that was pensive and languid ; not discontented. She had no particular features except for her eyes, which were large and lustrous, and in the language of her day would no doubt have been described as swimming. They were certainly swimming now, for they were full of tears that did not fall but remained caught on her long lashes.

" Nothing to write about," repeated Juliana to herself, and her mouth drooped almost piteously by now. On a sudden impulse she dipped the pen into the inkstand again and wrote : " I have felt very low ever since my dear, dear Fanny left."

One of the tears, as though it had been encouraged by this admission to a greater boldness, fell with a large round plop into the middle of the page.

" Oh ! " cried Juliana. It had made the ink run just at the top of the first " dear," and though she at once unscrewed her minute sand-castor and sprinkled the page, yet even when it was dried it left a crinkled round. She consoled herself by remembering her resolve that not a soul should ever see her journal but herself.

It was extremely warm, even in this cool room. She would take her journal out of doors and fill up some of the blank pages she had left for the past weeks, writing in pencil. It did not matter, since no one would ever see her journal but herself.

She put on a wide straw hat to shield her complexion, and tied the ribbons in a bow under her chin. They were lilac, to match her lilac "nightgown," a loose dress without any stays or hoops, for she was not yet "dressed," and her hair was still unpowdered.

She went out through the window, across the lawn to the terrace, and down the steps between stone Cupids bearing bowls of growing tulips and narcissus. The scent of these latter was almost too sweet in the hot air. It was like midsummer, not spring.

Juliana did not pause in the drive but went straight to her seat by the lake. There she lay sideways, her elbow on a cushion from the summer-house, and her journal lay closed beside her. There were already dragon-flies on the lake ; they darted over the white and gold buds of the water-lilies that had just begun to show.

She watched the heat dance over the lake in transparent, shimmering waves. Last summer after Fanny's wedding she had lain here hour after hour, looking at the water through half-closed eyes, in a melancholy that was sometimes as exquisite as pleasure, and sometimes so painful that she would weep and wish to die, since death could not be more dull and empty than life.

When she was a child, Nurse had told her two stories over and over again. One was about Jack the Giant-killer, and the other, which she liked best because it always came in the same words, was about a woman who "sat by the fire one night, and still she sat and still she span, and still she wished for company." And "in came a pair of big, big feet," and then shanks and then knees and so on until there was a whole man there on the hearth beside her, and after each portion of anatomy had entered, came the refrain: "And still she sat and still she span, and still she wished for company."

The climax came when the woman asked the strange visitor what he had come for, and Nurse, catching Juliana up in her arms, would shout merrily: "For You!"

The words of the foolish old tale would often drift into her idle mind as she lay by the lake, and sometimes her eyes would close altogether, not because she was asleep, but because she liked to imagine what company she might find when she opened them. A page in scarlet kneeling at her feet? A king, standing on the opposite shore of the lake, looking across the water at her? Or a cavalcade of horses and gallant gentlemen riding down the drive, emerging for one moment from the concealing trees as they crossed the bridge in the sunlight, and then enclosed by the green shade once more—and in their midst a little boy in the dress of a Tudor prince?

Or (and this, of course, was only when she was sleepy and forgetful that she was no longer a child) might she not see water-nymphs rising from the lake, beckoning her to come with them, down, down under the water, to explore the marvels of an unknown world?

But always when she opened her eyes, she saw only the lake and the lilies on its surface, and the slow swans passing to and fro; and on the opposite shore the tall twisted chimneys and turrets and irregular red roofs of Chidleigh House rising from the trees. And there was no clatter of harness from the drive and the bridge was bare in the sunlight.

"It is always the same," she would say to herself, "it will always be precisely the same."

But the disappointment never lost its sting, for she never ceased to hope that one day when she opened her eyes she might find it not precisely the same.

CHAPTER II

JULIANA closed her eyes, then opened them, slowly, expectantly. For a single flicker of an eyelash, she thought that one of her dreams had come true and that a gorgeous stranger stood on the opposite shore and looked across the lake at her. But when her eyes were fully open she saw that it was the peacock that had come down to the water's edge and spread his dazzling tail in the sun.

Yet the scene was not quite the same, for a cloud had partly obscured the sun so that the trees higher up the slope in front of her looked cold and blue, and the house had turned dark. In another instant the shadow of the cloud had raced down the hill, covering the peacock, and then the lake, and then Juliana. She shivered, and the peacock lowered his tail with a dismal discordant shriek.

The cloud passed and Juliana opened her journal, determined not to be so idle. She turned the pages to find what she had last written before this morning. There was no entry until almost a fortnight ago, when Mamma had had to go to Reading for a night to inspect some property there, and Charlotte and Sophia again came to spend the night with their cousins. Next day Juliana had written :

" We did not go to bed till this Morning, for after we had play'd as many Games as we could think of

in the Drawing-room, we went into my Closet where
Fanny play'd the Harpsickord, and my cousins and
I danced about the Room like Mad Things till 3 o' the
Clock.''

It set too high a standard. Nothing she could write
now could equal that. Juliana shut the journal and
fastened the clasps. Another cloud had come over
the sun, and then another. There was a whole bank
of them behind her, piled up dark against the sky.
George had said quite early this morning that he believed there would be a storm. He had said it when
he suggested riding with Vesey to Windsor to accom-
pany their sister, Fanny, thus far on her way back to
the town.

It was certainly much colder ; a slight wind ruffled
the surface of the lake into steely-grey ripples. She
would go and fetch Watts's Historical Catechysm and
get by heart those two-and-a-half pages where it treats
of the garments of the High Priests, until she could
say it to Mamma without any mistake. She rose
and went indoors up to her room, through the hall,
up the wide stairs and along the corridor.

It had grown very dark. Juliana stood at one of
the corridor windows and looked up at the black and
ragged clouds. The trees in the garden below and the
park beyond, and the two straight lines of trees in
the drive, bent suddenly all one way, and she could
hear the moan in their branches through the closed
window. Their brilliant green had a peculiar, almost
an unnatural appearance against the black and livid
sky. Two or three large drops were trickling down
the pane.

Juliana thought that she saw something stirring
between the trees of the drive. Her thought soon
became a certainty. A company of horsemen were

riding towards the house. It might be that tomboy Charlotte, with a hunting party, come to pay them a surprise visit, or perhaps the whole family, nine in number, of the Hilburys. But her heart was beating as if in terror, and she found that she was saying to herself again and again : " At last something is about to happen," not in pleasure but in apprehension that seemed almost to stifle her.

She did not wait to see the riders emerge from the drive, but turned away to her own room and looked everywhere for Watts's Historical Catechysm, as though it were necessary, even urgent, that she should continue to do some ordinary, everyday thing. Far away, she heard a confused uproar in the courtyard, the champing and clatter of harness, voices shouting, dogs barking, steps running within the house, up and down stairs, and again the voices of servants calling and laughing. But she continued to look hurriedly, almost feverishly, for Watts's Historical Catechysm, turning over papers, rummaging in drawers, passing her finger along the line of books in the book-case, and all the time repeating to herself : " The garments of the High Priests—two-and-a-half pages—I must learn them by heart to say to Mamma without any mistake."

She heard steps come running towards her room, the door was knocked and flung open on the same instant, and Molly stood before her, flushed and wide-eyed, a new cherry-coloured ribbon having miraculously appeared in her cap.

" Miss, miss, why miss, you here, and everybody else in the house down below in the hall, even my lady stepping down the stairs quicker than she'd care to show, and everybody running this way and that way and calling to everybody else——"

Juliana stood up from where she had been kneeling by a low shelf, the long-sought Historical Catechysm found at last and clasped tightly in her hands as if for support.

"Who is it, Molly? Who has come?"

"Who? Why, who but your own eldest brother, miss, his lordship himself, at last."

CHAPTER III

JULIANA could not understand afterwards why she had
felt such absurd reluctance to go down and find out who
were the newcomers, nor why, when she knew that it
was her brother, Lucian, she still hesitated and loitered
and found so many reasons why Molly should be detained
to adjust her sash, to arrange the loose curls on her
shoulders, to tie up her shoe-strings anew. And Fanny
had left only this morning—it was a thousand pities
that Fanny had left. She told herself so again and
again, in foolish, hurried agitation, without knowing
why it was that she so particularly desired Fanny to
be here.

But, indeed, it was very odd and agitating that
Lucian should have come home at last, suddenly and
unannounced like this. It was nine years since he
had been at Chidleigh, though he had come into the
title two years ago at their father's death, and had
been expected home ever since. But he had not even
attended the funeral. True, he had been abroad then,
and it would not have been possible for him to have
returned in time. But it had always been very odd
about Lucian, no one could say exactly what it was,
but the house was certainly far more peaceful after
he had left it. Yet he himself had been the quietest
person in it.

Juliana's childish recollections were of a dull, quiet
schoolboy, sallow, lank-haired, and unlike a boy, and

then a magnificent but equally quiet young man, setting off for the grand tour with an equipage of servants and horses, and a smirking, submissive tutor.

Yet, though he was so dull and quiet, there was that quick way he sometimes had when he cocked his head and looked at one, like a robin she had thought ; and, very occasionally, the smile that came unexpectedly as though he were smiling at something that only he knew of. It was that smile that once caused all the trouble. How Papa, stout, red-faced and terrible, had roared at him for it, and even thrown a chair at him with all his force, merely because poor Lucian had smiled !

Papa had never liked Lucian, though, of course, one must not say that. Yet it was not surprising as Lucian was so different, and George and Vesey did not like him either. They did not show it like Papa who was always storming at him, but were only quieter and rather sullen and constrained when Lucian was there. And even that was rather odd, as in general George and Vesey were hot and quick in temper, and it was Lucian who seemed the sullen one.

Then there was that dreadful scene just before poor Papa died of an apoplexy, when he told them all that he had written and forbidden Lucian to come home or communicate with any of the family. It could hardly be described as a " scene," as no one, not even Lady Chidleigh, had ventured any response, nor asked for any reason, but to Juliana, at least, it was the most frightening moment of her life.

Even now, she could feel her knees tremble as she saw again Lord Chidleigh in his brocaded coat, standing at the foot of the table, the purple veins swollen on his forehead, the hard, blood-shot eyes roving the table for any that might dare meet them in question or remonstrance. There had been the marks of death on that enormous, tottering figure, though no one then had known it. And when, with a mighty effort, he steadied himself, putting out his hand to the back of his chair, and stood there silent after his angry roar had ceased, it seemed that the vengeance of the Lord had become personified in that huge and dreadful being.

There had been a reason for that awful anger, she knew. Her Cousin Charlotte, who swore like a stable boy and rode to hounds so constantly that her skin was nearly as rough as her speech, had once rapped out to Juliana that it was no wonder " the old cock " (as she irreverently referred to her Uncle Chidleigh) " had crowed the young cockerel off the dunghill, seeing that Lucian was known to be chief and head of the Hellfire Club." Even Juliana had heard of the Hellfire Club, that yet more famous, or infamous, successor of the Mohock Club, so delicately but gravely reproved of Addison. She knew that their headquarters were at Medmenham Abbey, that they were supposed to worship Satan in place of Christ and Venus in place of the Virgin Mary ; and of their excesses she had once heard it whispered that at their banquets they were waited on by naked women.

It may be regrettable, it is not perhaps surprising, that Juliana thought much more frequently of her eldest brother since the imprudent Charlotte had dropped that surprising information.

It seemed incredible that anyone so impious, so strange, so wicked, should have been born into their family. She herself was sadly idle and had a secret aversion to church and sermons, when Dr. Eden preached, though he never preached his own. But, apart from this, none of them seemed to have any faults. Hard drinking and violent temper in the men of the family did not appear to her as faults but merely the necessary masculine attributes. Her father and two brothers had always spoken with reverence of God and the King, and slept very comfortably through the two long services on Sunday, whenever, that is, Papa's gout permitted him to attend Divine Service.

And Mamma, of course, was faultless.

Anyone who has seen the youthful portrait, as Diana, of Harriett Clavering, afterwards Lady Chidleigh (a remarkably fine specimen of Hudson's work), will agree with Juliana that she must have been faultless. No shadow of reproach from without, no twinge of conscience from within, can ever have come to trouble that clear and open brow, that indifferent stare, that general air of rectitude, too secure to require the approval of others. She looks surprised, it is true— perhaps it is only because the eyebrows are so highly arched, but I incline to think that it is a genuine surprise that all would not walk in the paths of virtue and prosperity as firmly and confidently, as proudly, gracefully and faultlessly as she.

But Juliana could linger and dawdle no longer, thinking of all these things while Molly besought her to hurry. Lady Chidleigh had actually had to send up a message for her to come down to the drawing-room.

All the family were there assembled, even Grandmamma Chidleigh, who usually never appeared till dinner, yet was now at this early hour rigidly stayed and dressed, with two bright spots of rouge on her gaunt cheeks. Juliana had a momentary wonder lest the grim, upright figure on the high-backed chair sat like that always in the seclusion of her rooms, fully arrayed night and day for the hour when she should descend.

Her unyielding old eyes looked at the newcomer as though she did not see him, and turned from him to her younger grandsons who were leaning their broad shoulders against the mantelpiece. They looked awkward and out of place, but they were fine young men, they were true Clares—either of them would have made the better inheritor to her husband's and her son's name and estate.

Always a silent woman, she had grown to be almost speechless. The wives of the Clares were apt to develop a strong family likeness. A tradition of firmness, of upright security in themselves and their surroundings, was imparted by each dowager or reigning Lady Chidleigh to her daughter-in-law. Lady Chidleigh's opinions, even her manner of declaring them, were a repetition of that rigour, yet more uncompromising though so seldom expressed, of the Dowager Lady Chidleigh.

The Dowager's daughter, eager, fluttering, always propitiatory Aunt Emily, hovered behind her chair. Her big, thin nose, half-open mouth and restless movements gave her the appearance of some anxious bird. She had been the youngest of her generation and had never married. Her whole life appeared to be led in perpetual apology for this omission.

Near them, hunched on a low seat, sat Cousin Francis, a poor relation. He was widowed, childless, and impoverished through law suits, and had drifted long ago to the centre of the family. This sudden home-coming of its head was of no interest to him. He had had sons of his own who had died when they were stout, hearty lads, better grown, better mannered, better educated than any young men to-day. Whoever sat at the foot of the table, he would always have his place half-way down it ; also, there would always be his seat in the walk by the south wall where the nectarines ripened earliest, and an old copy of Horace in his dressing-gown pocket which he was too blind to read now. But it opened of itself at the passages that he knew by heart, and he could still imagine that they were legible to his eyes.

Lady Chidleigh sat in remarkable resemblance to her portrait as Diana, and conversed between many pauses with her eldest son. He had risen as Juliana entered and made her curtsy to the head of the house. He kissed her and handed her to a chair, where she sat looking at Grandmamma Chidleigh, at Aunt Emily, at Cousin Francis, at George who was scowling at Vesey, at Vesey, the taller, handsomer and lazier, who kicked George when Lucian used a French phrase.

At Lucian she did not look, for she was prevented by her uneasy consciousness that so many pairs of staring eyes were fixed on him. She listened to his low, quick tones as he talked to his mother, apparently never at a loss for things to say, but she heard nothing that was said. It was Lucian who filled up the pauses. He was talking a great deal more than he used to do.

But at dinner, Juliana now stole glances from time to time at her brother, who sat at the foot of the table where her father used to sit. And the last time her father had sat there had been that time when he had insisted on coming in to dinner, ill as he was, to tell them all that he had disowned Lucian. It seemed incredible, almost impious, that that vast red form, bull-necked, with eyes glazed and staring, should not come forward and eject the slight dark figure sitting in his place.

Lucian was not big like his brothers, and beside their fresh-coloured faces, particularly Vesey's round and ruddy countenance, he looked as sallow as a foreigner. His eyebrows were peaked just at the corners, which gave his face a slightly crooked look, rather like the stone satyr on the terrace, Juliana had long since decided. His mouth, too, curled up at the corners even when he was not smiling. His head was generally bent a little, slightly on one side, which gave

54

him the appearance of one who was watching, or was it listening ?

In answer to his mother's questions he talked fluently of foreign courts and English people abroad of the notorious Lady Di who still had the impudence to show her face at the French Court, albeit it was much the worse for wear—of the elderly, witty Mr. Walpole who was making himself ridiculous in Paris by his fear of ridicule, on account of a friendship with an old blind French lady old enough to be his mother.

" Every time she mentions ' amour ' he corrects it to ' amitié.' He is in bashful terror lest he should be suspected of any warmth of feeling, and his friends find it useless to assure him that there is no danger of such an accusation."

There was, occasionally, a good deal of laughter, but not from George, who scowled worse than ever.

" Can you drink port ? " he asked roughly of Lucian, and his lips curled back from his long white teeth as he said it, so that he looked like a handsome, grinning collie. " We have none of your light French wines here."

" I will do my best, brother," said Lucian, eyeing him gravely, " but my head has grown unaccustomed to anything heavier than claret."

George was visibly delighted. He nudged Vesey, who was more stupid or less ill-humoured. He had not his brother's grudge against Lucian, since, as the youngest, Lucian was not his only bar to the estate. Therefore, he only murmured, half shutting his large sleepy brown eyes under their long lashes : " What does it matter ? Let every man drink what he likes, I say."

Such dangerous tolerance could not commend itself to George, who plied his elder brother continuously with port. This kept the wine in more constant circulation than usual, and had its effect on the younger brothers. But that on Lucian was strangely disappointing, since he continued to talk exactly as before, without any sign of intoxication.

"Gad, it's unnatural," muttered George to Vesey, as he watched his elder brother's unflushed face and cool demeanour, qualities that in another would have commanded his deep respect. "He must be one of those inhuman, unsociable devils whom wine cannot affect. 'I hate him as an unfilled can.'"

Vesey, recognizing their father's favourite quotation and a vague need for protest, roused himself sufficiently to laugh, stared at Lucian, and said in a muddled way :

"Brother, you're welcome. But if you can't drink like a good fellow, damn you, why then what's the use o' drinking at all ? "

"Vesey," said his mother severely, "we have not yet left the table."

Lucian, unruffled, continued to talk.

Juliana heard that the daughters of the French King were dowdies, and that there was a very poor show of gold plate at Fontainebleau—"Oh, shocking, Madam, so short of covers that some dishes had to be used to cover others," and Lady Chidleigh looked highly complacent at the superiority of her own dinner service to that of the King of France.

Juliana thought him very merry, very different from the quiet, sullen boy she remembered. Once, while he was speaking to George (for he had been most polite and grateful for George's attentions, and had frequently reminded his brother when his own glass was empty), his small, bright eyes shot down the table and caught one of her timid glances. He seemed to be laughing ; she wondered if it were at her.

CHAPTER IV

THE Clares were, for the most part, a family of bucolic tastes, sluggish wits, but sturdy good sense, and an inclination to stoutness in middle age. These commonplace characteristics were in general enlivened only by furious tempers that had been pampered by long indulgence and lack of opposition, also by a certain pride that people of a former time seemed to have felt in their rages as though they were a testimony to their force and originality of mind.

There had only been two outstanding exceptions to this character of the Clares since they had acquired Chidleigh.

Chidleigh had ceased to be a royal residence after the death of Edward VI. It passed into private hands and was finally purchased by a certain Thomas Clare, one of the new gentry who had risen in Henry VIII's time by dint of a judicious understanding of the flexibilities of religion.

It was believed that his name was merely that of his birthplace, the village Clare in Suffolk, and that he had in early youth been gardener's boy at the Priory. It was certain that he was afterwards the means of wrecking that institution and evicting the monks—a service to his sovereign which brought him great wealth and enabled him to buy the place of Chidleigh, in Berkshire, at a comfortable distance from his birthplace.

This ignominious beginning of the prosperity of the Clares was soon forgotten. Thomas Clare's sons served with distinction with Elizabeth's armies in Flanders, his grand-daughter, Lucy Clare, became a most notable beauty at the Court of James I. Later on, she became rather too notable, for she was accused of sorcery against the King himself, but conducted her defence in court with such eloquence and majesty and, above all, with such a potent enchantment of beauty, that none of her judges would declare her guilty, despite the witch-hunting fury of King James. So that her life was spared, but she was disgraced and ruined, and, it was believed, left England disguised as a page in the service of the Duke of Buckingham, and disappeared.

In the village of Clare in Suffolk, there were many who shook their heads over this downfall of the upstart family's most brilliant member. They saw in it retribution for the fate of the Priory, and remembered how they had heard tell of old Goody Crickle, Thomas Clare's grandmother, who had been ducked for a witch by all the villagers when Thomas was a young boy.

But there were no other serious aberrations to mar the peaceful and fortunate course of the Clares.

As a family that owed much to royalty they fought on the side of King Charles in the Civil Wars, but contrived very early to come to an understanding with Cromwell after the Protectorate. They were equally prompt to understand the wishes of the country with regard to the Restoration.

Under Charles II the head of the Clares cut something of a figure at Court through his extraordinary capacity for carrying liquor. This honourable distinction to his family was, however, tarnished by a miserable younger brother, a starveling, a "filthy toad," who had become a religious enthusiast and wrote verses about visions, which some took to be allegorical, but others considered treasonable. He was put in prison where he made the acquaintance of a low fellow called Bunyan and became confirmed in his tedious notions.

After his release he went abroad, no one knew where, and was believed to have become a kind of hermit, living in solitude and shunning all women. His family collected all the copies of his verses with laborious care and burnt them, and the matter was gradually allowed to pass into oblivion.

His was the only example of eccentricity for more than a century. No other Clares wrote verses, even of the most light and worldly nature, nor plays, nor anything at all. Nor were they ever " enthusiastic " either in religion or in politics.

Lucian Clare, the head of the family in Queen Anne's reign showed at a suitable moment an intelligent interest in the Hanoverian succession and was created First Baron Chidleigh.

From that time on they remained staunchly and safely Whig in principle and Tory in spirit, lived on their estates, supported the Church and the local sports, hunted and drank a great deal, planted trees in the park, and occasionally had a hobby for gardening.

Robert Clare, the late Lord Chidleigh, deviated slightly in his youth from the regular course by setting up for himself in a town house in the fashionable quarter of Soho. He did this primarily as the result of a quarrel with his mother, whose ferocious silence in anger had procured her the nickname of the Basilisk.

Robert's rages knew no such chilling restraints. He was a big, cheerful, floridly handsome man, popular enough in the town, where he was nick-named Robin Goodfellow and known as a roaring blade, a good boy, a lad of mettle, and, with the ladies, by such endearing terms as filthy creature or agreeable toad. For, in this urban retreat from his mother, he proceeded, as he announced, to " harry the old b——" by his extensive dissipations.

His mother's counter-stroke was to prepare and educate a wife for him. She chose a healthy, high-coloured girl, with some spirit, but more sense, one Harriet Clavering, whose family was older and more distinguished than the Clares, though not so prosperous, and instructed Robert that if he did not marry her he should forfeit his mother's fortune ; no inconsiderable sum.

Robert, like most of his family, had a sound instinct for the winning side. He capitulated to his mother and married Harriet, who thus enjoyed the distinc-tion, envied by all her friends, of marrying a fashionable rake in order to reform him. A year after the event, Robert's father broke his neck in the hunting field, a circumstance that annoyed his son, as he would not have surrendered to the women had he dreamed he would so soon inherit his father's estates. He continued to live in the town and quarrel with his mother.

The Dowager, however, was well pleased with her policy. She decided that she could not have made a better choice for her son. The new Lady Chidleigh modelled herself on her mother-in-law in all matters of careful housewifely management, in her sedate imperturbability when any of the males saw fit to lose their tempers and their senses, above all, in her superb air of indifference to all that she felt it better not to notice. She had need of this last quality in the early years of their married life.

But Robert's bitter disappointment in his first child, Lucian, brought him to his senses. His own sturdy health seemed to be no whit impaired by the life he was leading, but the baby was miserably weak and puny, a lifeless little object—" just like a little old man."

That was what his plain, silly, unmarried younger sister, Emily, kept saying in her high chirruping voice and laughing as though it were a piece of wit. " Oh, la ! such an odd child, so shrivelled and fatigued, and won't look at a rattle—*just* like a little old man."

" Emily, you are a fool," said the Dowager, and Emily would offer up an assenting silence for five minutes and then say it again, or make some observation equally exasperating to those concerned for the heir of Chidleigh. Robert's chief hope for his heir was that it would die, but this it obstinately refused to do. In spite of doctors' and nurses' predictions, in spite of the medical treatment of the time, the baby went on living, though it cannot be said to have thrived.

Robert let the house in Soho, where he had lived chiefly since his marriage, retired to Chidleigh, and reformed in good and almost sober earnest.

He was rewarded by the birth of a fairly robust daughter. But what is a daughter ? She was christened Frances and called Fanny at once by her mother, who made up her mind in the first week of Fanny's life exactly what her future should be. Fanny would be her help and companion, Fanny would run by her side, hanging on to her skirts as she inspected the stillroom and the linen room and went about her household duties, Fanny would prattle to her as she stitched at her first sampler, and repeat Watts's hymns at her knee, and later on Fanny would make a good, comfortable match with a very worthy man who had not been a rake, and come and stay at Chidleigh with all her children.

Fanny, an obedient girl, did all these things.

Meanwhile, after two more years, George was born, and, a year later, Vesey—two fine boys, true Clares, fine healthy children who roared in their cots, and broke their toys and, later, each other's heads. Vesey was a particular favourite. He was such a beautiful child, as large as George who was a year older, and with a sweeter nature. He was spoilt by everybody, but kept his pleasant sleepy smile and let George take and smash his things, with only rare outbursts of fury. "What a pity he is not the eldest," everybody said, and Vesey thought it too, though not as much as George thought it for himself.

Lucian called them "the little boys" and refused to play with them. Nor would he play with his sister, Fanny, though he once or twice frightened her into fits by telling her ghost stories. He was an odd, sneering, unchildlike being, secretly nervous of horses though no one ever knew it, and he overcame this before he was twelve years old.

He had outgrown his early delicacy, and was never ill after the age of three. But his father had not outgrown his dislike of the boy as his heir. Lucian was not "a true Clare." He remained slight and colourless, his hair of that dull hue which is called black because it is no other colour, but is really almost green, the greyish green of dead leaves. His eyes were of the same nondescript no-colour, and though often bright enough, they were small and slantingly set, unlike the large, clear-coloured, finely set eyes of the Clares. People called him ugly and "twisted-looking," though his bright glance and quick, graceful movements often struck his mother as charming. But she did not say this to her lord, whom it would have certainly displeased.

Juliana was not born until four years after Vesey. A good deal of attention was paid to her as the youngest and almost unexpected arrival; and later, because she showed greater promise of beauty than Fanny. Her father, whenever he happened to notice her, called her his poppet, his sweet angel, his pretty rogue.

She was not as strong as her sister—a tiny, fragile creature, crying very easily, and as easily made to laugh through her tears, starting at noises, caressing and liking to be caressed, running about the great rooms and gardens, with her head thrown back, and her eyes gazing upwards at all the marvels above her head with an air of delight that was almost ecstasy.

It was not an age of child-worship, but there were several who felt an involuntary catch in their breath when they saw that strangely rapt smile, as though it were enchanted by some secret vision of loveliness. Aunt Emily explained it by saying she was not long for this world.

Young Mr. Daintree, of Crox Hall, was one of these admirers. He called Juliana his fairy, and did his best to spoil her with presents of sugar plums and little books with pictures, in which all the good children died early but peacefully and all the bad ones died later but miserably. He gave her these long before she could read, so as to coax her into a glance at him. But she was very shy of visitors and would hide her face behind Mamma's skirts or Sister Fanny's shoulder, and only peep at him when she thought he was not looking.

Before she was four years old, Mr. Daintree brought home a beautiful young wife to Crox Hall and ceased to pay his former sweetheart so much attention. Aunt Emily said a dozen times a day how much devoted he was to his wife. It was very sad that she died after two years, and now Aunt Emily said twenty times a day that poor Mr. Daintree was inconsolable.

Grandmamma Chidleigh said he had seemed inconsolable for some time before his wife's death, but that no doubt was merely the result of exasperation with her daughter's repetitions. In any case, he did not marry again, which proved to everyone his devotion and inconsolability.

Vesey's nose was put out of joint to some extent by Juliana, but he never appeared to notice it, and his good humour continued unabated. He frequently enjoyed having a little sister to patronize, and protect from George's bullying inclinations. And Fanny adopted her as her especial charge from the very first. The equilibrium of Fanny's nose was not disturbed by this new star. She had come already to fill her own place in the household at Chidleigh, a very necessary and ease-giving place.

"Dear Fanny is so dependable," her mother would say when Fanny had staved off bloodshed between her brothers, or rescued Juliana from the staircase, or heard the younger boys their lessons, particularly Vesey's which required to be heard very often. Yet she was never fussy nor disagreeably "managing," nor a tell-tale.

Once, indeed, she told, but it was on an extraordinary occasion, so extraordinary that Juliana, though very young at the time, always remembered it. She had been brought down to the drawing-room to play and was enjoying the glorious privilege of riding on papa's foot while papa whooped with delicious, terrifying sounds as though he were calling to the hounds in the hunting field, and mamma chanted the necessary accompaniment :

> " Ride a cock horse
> To Banbury Cross
> To see a fine lady
> Ride on a white horse."

The door was opened quickly, but not flung open and Fanny stood in the doorway, very pale, with a thin trickle of blood on her cheek, and said :

" If you please, papa, George is holding Lucian's
head in the grate and is trying to put it into the fire."

Papa sprang up with a roar like a bull, tossing Juliana
into mamma's lap where she buried her face in a sea of
blue satin and wailed lamentably.

Lucian's head was rescued at a moment when it was
all but touching the burning logs and his face was
scarlet. George's reason for his conduct was that
they had fought because he had told Lucian he ought
to be heir and he was going to be. Fanny's cheek
had been cut by the fender in her efforts to separate
them when they reached the stage of rolling on the
ground near to the fire. Vesey had refused to help
her, because, he said, Lucian began it by teasing George
" very unkindly." Fanny, on appeal, admitted that
Lucian had been extremely tormenting. Lucian said
nothing.

Papa flogged all three boys, giving the lion's share
to George. But it was Lucian who most disgusted
him. Here was the boy, twelve years old, and George,
at nine, had proved himself his superior in strength.
Certainly George was right, and it was he who ought
to be heir.

Lucian, however, grew more tough and wiry as he
grew older, though he never attained to the massive
strength of his brothers. And as they all grew older
the quarrels between him and his brothers became
less and less, though they did not grow to like each
other any better. Lucian would still occasionally
mock and torment them so that they became scarlet
with confused rage, but they now very seldom attacked
him. Also, it now appeared that George and Vesey
avoided him rather than that Lucian avoided them.
They said nothing against him, either behind his back
or to him, but they were shy and sullen when asked
about him and when they were with him.

c   65

As for Juliana, Lucian took no more notice of her than of anyone else. He was a dull boy. He did not care for his brothers' sports, but neither was he studious. His tutors all declared that he had " parts " and all despaired of his " application." It was evident that there was nothing to which he cared to apply himself. He would sit at his lessons, weary and indifferent, paying no attention to his tutor's words nor to his father's rages when his conduct was reported to him, and apparently as indifferent to punishment as to anything else.

During those long hours in the library, while George and Vesey would patiently exert their sluggish brains in a painful effort to master some part of their labours so as to leave them the sooner for the stables or stolen visits to the cock-pit, Lucian would sit motionless, not looking at his book nor at anything else, until his eyes had a fixed and glazed expression that made them appear as dull and blank as pebbles, set in a lifeless image.

It made no difference that he was flogged, that he was made to stay in the library to do his lessons for hours after the younger boys had left. They would rush out through the long French windows on to the lawns and down through the gardens, clearing the terrace steps in great leaps that sent them tumbling over at the bottom, shouting with joy at their release, calling to their dogs, to the grooms, to old Cousin Francis who was an old booby, an old put, but was still useful for making a mayfly or a whip lash, just as he had used to serve them in more childish days by making them boats and catapults. He would come grumbling out from his sheltered seat in the sun to meet their demands, but all the same, he liked these fine young animals who bullied him and ordered him about. He had not yet had his illness which left him

tired and very old, too old to care about any young
people except his own, who had died over thirty years
ago.

One day, when she was about nine years old, Juliana
stood for a little while at a corridor window, watching
the younger boys as they swaggered about in the sunshine and shouted their imperious wishes to the old
man in the snuff-coloured gown and turban, and then
turned away and crept down the stairs at the end of
the corridor, and saw Lucian sitting alone in the library,
which his exhausted tutor had temporarily left, sitting
alone at the table looking at nothing. She had stolen
in with a cake under her apron, having heard that he
was to have no dinner, and seeing him there she had
turned and begun to creep out of the room again, afraid,
she did not know of what. But he turned his head
quickly and called her, in a quick low tone, and she
came up to him and held out the cake.

" For you, brother," she said.

At that, he gave her another swift, bird-like glance,
and smiled, and it was just as though the stone satyr
on the terrace had become alive, for the corners of
his mouth, which always curled upwards a little, went
up in a sharp curve, and his rather crooked eyebrows
slanted quickly upwards, and the eyes beneath them
twinkled so very brightly that it seemed they had only
just come there for the first time in place of two eyes
of stone. Her own eyes remained lowered, but she
felt his upon her and wished he did not look at her
so intently. He teased her to look at him, but she
would not. Lucian had scarcely ever noticed her
sufficiently to tease her. She wished she had not
come.

Then he pulled towards him a book that lay open
on the table and translated a sentence to her. She
was too confused to notice the words, but he read

them again and made her repeat them. Twisting
her flowered silk apron round her fingers, blushing,
miserably, she repeated hesitatingly in a whisper,
that " the passions and affections of the soul may have
a powerful effect through the eyes and glance upon
other persons, that some men hurt little and tender
children by looking at them, that it is even possible
one might injure oneself by reflection of one's gaze."

" Do you, then, agree with Plutarch, and so refuse
to meet my eyes ? " said he. " But according to him
your glass is equally dangerous. Well, Juliana, where
then will you look ? "

She looked into the roses and apples on her apron
and two tears fell down into it. She only knew that
Lucian was being very unkind.

" My sweet fool," he said, and kissed her.

But as soon as she could she ran out of the room.

Not long afterwards, it was decided that Lucian
should travel and see if the grand tour would succeed
in displaying those " parts " which so far he had
managed to conceal. He was taken to the town and
came back a few weeks later with the appearance of
a grown man. His lank, dull hair was curled and
powdered, Lady Chidleigh noticed with pride that his
hands, now they were well-tended, rivalled her own ;
he held his head high with an assured and easy air
of command ; his dress, though sober, was rich and
curious. He had a fondness for dark or neutral colours,
grey or green, or purple that was nearly black, that
contrasted with his father's and brothers' love of bright
colours. Vesey, who had begun to pay attention to
his good looks, was particularly fond of reds and light
blues, showing off his clear, ruddy skin. He was the
handsomest of the family and meant to live up to it.
But when Lucian returned from London everyone,
while still calling him ugly, admitted he was elegant.

"Vastly elegant," twittered Aunt Emily, "more elegant than his brothers," and never noticed Vesey's deep flush of angry jealousy.

It was surprising what a few weeks in the town could do. What would not travel do?

So he departed on his travels, followed by a good many hopes, expectations and fears, by some ill wishes and by the new, submissive tutor, who seemed so singularly inappropriate in his capacity of bear-leader at the heels of this superb youth.

He departed, and a sigh of relief went up after him. The house was much quieter, as even a child like Juliana could observe, after the quietest person in it had left.

Lord Chidleigh still went into rages over people like the traitor and profligate Mr. Wilkes, but that was not nearly so disturbing as his former constant outbursts against his eldest son.

George and Vesey lost the embarrassed, half-worried, half-furtive air they had occasionally had as boys, and grew up into splendidly stupid young men. They still frequently quarrelled and came to blows, but this did not prevent nor embitter their constant companionship.

Fanny and Juliana had lessons with an elderly tutor and a French governess, read and sewed with Mamma, played and drew and rode together and with their cousins, Charlotte and Sophia.

The household was peaceful and happy, not much disturbed by Cousin Francis' long illness, from which he unexpectedly recovered. Everyone was surprised to see him about again; it seemed that death, like everyone else, had overlooked him.

Lord Chidleigh's gout increased so much that he often could not leave his chair for days together and grew exceedingly stout. He became greatly concerned with the immorality and irreligion of the present day and swore blasphemously in his indictments of it.

It was thought that the apoplectic seizure that brought about his death was due to his fury at the reports he had received of Lucian's conduct. These were the cause of that terrible spectacle already mentioned, the spectacle that Juliana would never forget, of her father hobbling into dinner at a time when his gout did not really permit him to walk, in order to denounce his eldest son to all of them, and tell them that he had forbidden him the house for as long as he lived. That proved to be less than a fortnight.

Shortly before that denunciation he had startled his wife by the remark that he was afraid she might sometimes have found him hasty, and he had smiled at her in a tentative fashion as though hoping she would contradict him. She, of course, immediately did so, but with a sense of alarm at so unprecedented a statement or, rather, inquiry. It seemed to her afterwards as a certain warning of his approaching end.

On that event all the rooms were plunged in semi-darkness, the hatchment was put up in front of the house, Fanny and Juliana wore deep bands of *crêpe* on their dresses and mourning rings of black enamel and pearls, enclosing a tiny lock of poor papa's hair.

They escaped as often as they could to Nurse's cottage, as they could pay no other visits for some time. It was very comfortable to find Nurse just the same except for a black dress, baking bread or pies, or brewing delicious sweet concoctions, all precisely the same as usual.

" Well, miss," said Nurse, when Fanny once commented on the fact, " poor folks haven't as much time to attend to death as rich folks. I expect that's it—perhaps it don't mean as much to them either, not when it comes natural."

Juliana was struck by this. It had not occurred to her that death was a natural event. She felt that until that moment—in spite of the many warning Sunday verses on the subject—she had never really understood that all must die. She looked at Nurse bustling about them with her sleeves turned up over her comfortable red arms, she looked round at the neat cottage and the bright garden outside the small square window, and tried to believe that one day, however far hence, Nurse, cottage and garden would be no longer there.

" A cure for gaping ! " cried Fanny suddenly, and popped a cherry into Juliana's mouth, which, it must be confessed, had remained slightly open since Nurse's remarks.

A magnificent monument was erected in the chapel to Robert, Lord Chidleigh ; his portrait-bust, severe, Roman, and unrecognizable, surmounted by a classic urn, looked down in apparent disgust on two very fat weeping cherubs who supported a scroll enumerating his public and private virtues. His first cousin, a bishop, wrote the epitaph and informed the reader that Lord Chidleigh's

" Religion was that which by Law is
      Established,
   And the Conduct of his life shew'd
      The power of it in his Heart,"

a somewhat ambiguous phrase which misses the warmth of the later tributes to his generous condescension, charity and hospitality, although we can hardly be intended to take quite literally the statement that

> " Though naturally enclined to avoid the
>   Hurry of publick Life,
> He was careful to keep up the port of his
>   Quality."

The monument was not yet finished when Fanny married Mr. Daunt. This occurred rather more than a year after Papa's death, and they all went out of mourning.

" It is distressing it should be so soon," said Lady Chidleigh, " but one cannot have mourning at a wedding, and I should be sorry to ask Mr. Daunt to show any further patience."

" Dear Robert always liked bright colours," said Aunt Emily, with her head on one side, murmuring instead of chirruping, since dear Robert was dead. She was wondering if she should wear her crimson paduasoy or the puce-coloured sarcenet. Perhaps the puce colour would be in better taste since they had so recently been in mourning, but there was no doubt that the crimson suited her better—a reflection that had induced her last pensive remark.

" Emily, you are a fool," said her mother. " It can make no difference now what Robert liked, since he is dead." Emily decided it would be wiser to wear the puce-colour.

Fanny's marriage made a much greater break than papa's death.

And now Lucian had returned. Juliana wondered what difference that would make.

CHAPTER V

THE excitement of Lucian's home-coming did not last long. Juliana soon found that she saw as little of him as of her other brothers, and ceased to wonder why he had come and for how long. He appeared to be very busy about his estates; after so long an absence there was no doubt much that claimed his attention. Perhaps he had even decided to settle down at Chidleigh, in any case it did not seem as though it would make much difference to her. Indeed, her life seemed rather emptier than usual just now, for Lucian had expressed a wish not to have any guests and parties until he had settled certain matters on the estate which were occupying all his time. He took no notice of her, nor did she again encounter at table that bright, piercing glance that had so much baffled and surprised her. His return is recorded in her journal, at the end of her entry for the 1st of May, without any trace of the fleeting emotion it had caused.

" This day my Brother Chidleigh arriv'd from France by way of London. His House in Soho was shut up, so he drove to my Sister Fanny's in Hill Street, but finding her and Mr. Daunt away on a visit he lay at the Coch and Horses for that night and so on to Chidleigh."

The weather, after its early promise of summer,

had returned to winter, many days being too cold and gusty for Juliana to venture out of doors at all, so that she had long hours to spend in her closet, and the next letter from dear Fanny seemed the only event left to live for.

Then suddenly it turned quite hot, and one morning she sat again under the great trees at the side of the drive, her journal in her lap and a pencil in her hand. The sunshine made a flickering checkwork on the wide skirts that flowed out in billowing folds of pale lilac on either side of her. Bluebells and ragged robin grew thick round her and stretched away into the open sunshine where they shimmered in a bright haze of colour, and above them the bees hummed noisily.

In the drive itself was a cool green darkness that seemed to remove it from the outer world. No birds sang under those great arches, and no bees hummed.

She heard a step come up the drive behind her, and turned her head to see her eldest brother crossing the bridge over the brook in the full sunlight. He saw her at the same moment and came quickly towards her into the shade of the drive again. He leaned against a tree just by her and looked down on her, scrutinizing her so closely that her head drooped and the white, blue-veined lids nearly shut over her eyes.

" Put back your head," he said, " how can I see you under that Brobdingnagian hat ? "

She obeyed him, but with some annoyance, for she hated to feel she had been put out of countenance ; also she had not read Gulliver and imagined Brobdingnagian to be some strange oath. So she put back her head with just a suggestion of a toss, and looked gravely at him. The smile that she had remembered had come into the corners of his mouth ; it did not appear to be in his eyes.

" Juliana," he said, " why are you afraid of me ? "

" I—I don't—I am not afraid of you, brother."

He laughed very softly.

" Very well," he said, " we will leave it at that and change the subject. You have refused to say what you think of me, so shall I tell what I think of you ? "

" Pray do."

" I think you are a rebel and an adventuress. Has anyone told you so ? "

She was staring now in her astonishment.

" None, brother. I did not know it myself."

" That is not necessary. And I think something else of you."

" What is that ? "

" That you have a pair of delicate eyes. And how many have told you *that* ? "

" No one," she said in a very small voice, for she had turned extremely shy, and he would now have had no opportunity to consider her eyes.

" What ! Am I so happy as to be the first ? But not the last I'll wager."

She had flushed with pleasure at his compliments, which had been uttered gravely, unlike the careless badinage which George and Vesey occasionally vouchsafed her when in a specially good humour.

" Have you come to live at Chidleigh ? " she asked. " I hope you have."

" Why do you hope so ? "

She knew it was because he had admired her eyes, and called her a rebel and an adventuress, and was ashamed to give these as reasons, so she hung her head.

" What is that book on your lap ? " he asked suddenly.

" My journal."

" Your journal ! What do you write in it ? "

" I don't know. Very little, I fear."

75

" Is there then so little to write ? "

She sighed and smiled at the same time. " I find it so. Mamma says that an industrious and well-filled day gives one more to fill one's journal than a crowd of amusements. But I—yes, I sometimes find it difficult to think of anything to write about."

" That is a serious fault in a journal," said Lucian gravely. " We must see to it that you have something to write about."

A slight tremor that might have been pleasure or excitement, or even fear, ran through her at this very ordinary remark. She looked up at him again and wondered if he had ever really worshipped Satan and Venus. The sunshine through the branches danced up and down on his face ; his eyes, fixed on hers, looked very bright and merry. This time she did not look away but continued to meet his gaze, so long that she forgot what she had been saying or thinking of, forgot even what she was looking at, for the eyes she had thought so bright just now, seemed to have become two motionless points, devoid of light or colour. She said at last :

" I was walking down the drive once when I saw a little boy sitting on the stone bridge there in the sunshine. He wore odd clothes, a plumed cap fastened with jewels, and a jewelled dagger. He was looking down at the fishes and didn't see me. I didn't like to speak to him, but I was not afraid."

" Who was he ? " asked her brother.

" King Edward VI. As you know, this house was rebuilt for him to come and stay here."

" Two hundred years ago," said Lucian softly. " Did you ever see him again ? "

" No."

" Nor anyone else ? "

" No one like that."

He must have moved his eyes from hers, for she saw the green of the trees again, and through them, hot and dazzling in the sunshine, the old bridge where she had seen the boy sitting on the low parapet. A hot rush of amazement fell on her that she should have told such a thing to Lucian. She had never told it to anyone.

Once she had asked Fanny if she believed in apparitions, and dear Fanny had been certain that God would not permit a departed spirit to return to this world. She, therefore, could not have seen an apparition, which was consoling, for the fair, delicate-looking little boy, sitting astride on the bridge, his scarlet silk knees shining in the sun, and his head bent in absorbed attention to the fishes below, had not seemed in the least like an apparition.

She had long ceased to wonder about it, even to think about it, supposing vaguely that she might have dreamed it. And now she had told Lucian, the most critical and sceptical audience that she could have chosen, and told it as though she believed it, whereas, of course, she did not believe she could really have seen it—well, it was certainly impossible that she should have done so. Her face was burning, and she looked steadfastly at the grass beside her. She heard at last his voice above her, as cool and quick as usual and not at all amused.

" Thank you," he said. " I was hoping you would have something of interest to tell me. I asked you at dinner, the day of my arrival, you may remember, but you did not take my message."

" I—I don't remember your asking me anything, brother."

" No ? Think again."

She did, and said : " You looked at me once, but you were talking to George."

" Yes. Well, remember in future that when I look at you, it is to you I am talking. This is a tedious hole, but the description would do for most places. I am here, as you may imagine, from necessity rather than choice, and the same reason I fancy applies to your sojourn here. Shall we enter into compact, my pretty sister, to make it as little tedious as we can ? "

" *We*, brother !——"

Juliana was looking full at him now in flushed and perplexed astonishment. He flung back his head and laughed, a funny, cracking laugh that disconcerted her.

" Yes, *we*, sister. Is this modesty or scorn ? Do you reject me as an ally, or do you think I would rather join with George or Vesey in such a compact ? Is there anything I can do with them that I have not done a thousand times before ? To hunt, fish, drink and make love to village girls who giggle like peahens—are you shocked that I should occasionally tire of such distractions ? "

" No. But I cannot see what distractions I can offer."

" No ? Perhaps you think that noisy young hoyden Charlotte could offer better ? And do you also see no possibility of my power to afford you any distraction ? "

" Oh, as to that," said Juliana, smiling, " I am aware I do not know all your capabilities."

" Then you do not despair of my capability to amuse you ? Come, shall it be a bargain ? You have shown me what I had suspected, that you have certain qualities and powers which might be of considerable use to us both in helping to pass the time here. Let us see what we can do together."

He held out his hand to her to help her rise. They walked across the bridge and down the drive in silence.

Lucian left her in the gardens to turn towards the stables, and Juliana went up alone into the house. As she passed through the hall, still too much surprised to think clearly, she noticed the ugly old portrait of her ancestress, Lucy Clare, stiff and wooden as a dummy in the uncompromising dress of a Court lady at the time of James I, and wondered, as she had done a thousand times, how that could have been the portrait of a beauty.

Juliana was fascinated by all she had heard of that amazing lady, who had been accused of sorcery by the fanatical witch-hunter, King James, and had had such strange adventures. She had always felt an envious thrill when she thought of this ancestress, which shows, perhaps, that Lucian may not have been entirely wide of the mark when he called his sister a rebel and an adventuress.

But the portrait was like an ugly Dutch doll Juliana had had in her childhood; Lucy Clare could not have been like that. She looked at it longer than usual this time, for she thought that the narrow eyes were like those of her Brother Lucian. But the eyes in the portrait (whether through the fault of the old painter or of faded paint) were dull, a rather muddy brown, whereas Lucian's were particularly bright.

Then she remembered that when she had looked so long at Lucian's eyes, while telling her story of the boy she had seen on the bridge, they had no longer looked bright, but had been dull and opaque like pebbles.

CHAPTER VI

SOPHIA CLARE had been paying a visit of some weeks to her cousin, Fanny Daunt, Juliana's married sister, at her town house in Hill Street. Now, on her return home, she rode over to pay her respects to Lady Chidleigh and give her news of her daughter, and, incidentally, to gossip with Juliana. She had brought one of the Hilbury girls with her, a plain but graceful little creature of twelve or thirteen, and the three girls withdrew as soon as they conveniently could to Juliana's closet, Sophia very eager to tell of all her gaieties in the town.

This she did with much laughter and self-interruptions such as—" Oh, my love, but I must first tell you"—and "Oh, but you haven't yet heard how I met the dear toad"—and "such an agreeable rattle—why are there no agreeable rattles in the country ? Nothing but dull, good, worthy men like Mr. Daintree."

Yet as she proceeded she felt vaguely disappointed and perplexed. She thought Juliana did not attend quite as closely as usual to all she said ; she seemed a little fatigued, but when asked she declared herself quite well. Juliana herself could not understand why she was not more excited by her cousin's account of her doings with dear Fanny. She supposed it was because she had been spending the morning with Lucian in the library, and anything seemed dull after that.

She spent a good many spare hours with him there now, always undisturbed, for no one came to the library except Dr. Eden on Saturday afternoons to hunt in the old volumes of sermons for two that he might preach next day. So that Lucian and Juliana had the great musty room to themselves. Sometimes he read to her, sitting on the top of the ladder, from a book he had pulled out of an upper shelf, while she lounged in delightful abandon in an armchair of carved wood and leather, contentedly aware how shocked her upright mamma would have been ; half listening, half dreaming, her eyes following the peacock as he strutted on the lawn outside the long windows. Sometimes he told her strange and rather alarming stories of other times and nations (" *any* time must be less dull than the present," Juliana would say), but not of himself nor his own adventures. She had not yet discovered whether he had really worshipped Satan and Venus, and she did not think she would ever dare to ask.

And sometimes he would do what he called his experiments, which Juliana could never remember clearly afterwards. They would begin by his burning something in a little dish that gave out a heavy, sweet scent, making her fall into a drowsy state in which she seemed to be neither asleep nor awake. Then he would give her a china bowl of water to hold, or a sheet of clear glass, or the great library inkpot with the top screwed off, showing the ink in a round black pool, surrounded by four silver sirens whose outstretched hands just touched each other round the bowl. And Juliana would look into the water, glass or ink, at her own shadow or reflection, until she began to dream that she saw other faces in it looking back at her, and that she heard Lucian's voice speaking to her, though she never remembered if she had known what he had said or if she had answered.

She could remember, however, that when first she began to see a vague shadow in the substance that she held, saw it beginning to take form and colour a thrill of excitement and triumph that was almost ecstasy ran through her. It was as though she and Lucian had just begun to find something they had long desired and sought—no, it was more than that.

It was as though, if they were Pagans, she had discovered themselves to be equal to the gods. " How very silly ! " she would comment at the wildness of her own suggestion, and as she was not used to speculation she would decide that it was all very odd and surprising but that Lucian did not appear to find it so.

One dream, or fancy, she had, that she could remember distinctly afterwards, though she wished that she could not.

She thought that she had seen herself quite clearly, sitting in the library armchair, as though she were someone else who was standing at a little distance. She could see herself leaning forward, holding the silver inkpot in her hands, her head bent, looking down at it, and a long curl at the back of her head dropping forward on to her neck.

She recounted this to Lucian with distaste and even fear. " It was like the nightmare," she said. " I wanted to return—to be inside myself again—and could not."

" The nightmare—to see yourself ! " exclaimed Lucian. " My pretty one, you should be delighted with your good fortune. For once in your life you have been enabled to see what is the most charming sight in it."

But she could not be teased nor complimented out of her aversion to that particular dream she had had of seeing herself, and ever after she was inclined to shrink a little from the sight of her own reflection and even of her shadow.

Lucian once observed her start back at the edge of the lake, and he, taking her hand in a manner half formal and half caressing, led her to the brink of the water and bade her look at herself among the water-lilies.

"It was an ancient belief," he said, "that the reflection or the shadow was the soul, and that one should not look at one's reflection in the water, for by so doing one projected the soul out of the body. That enlightened race, the Greeks, considered it as an omen of death if a man dreamed of seeing himself so reflected. They feared that the water-spirits would drag the person's reflection or soul under water, leaving him soulless to perish. Is that your fear, Juliana, when you see your pretty soul before you?"

She thought of her fancies by that lake, of water-nymphs drawing her down, down under the water to explore the marvels of an unknown world.

Her narrow shoulders and tiny, tight-bodiced waist emerging from a balloon of petticoats, her small intent face beneath a tower of powdered hair, all lay at her feet, quivering a little as if about to take flight. Beside it, and a little behind it, was another image, a mockingly smiling image, confident and secure, whose hand held hers. She gravely regarded that other laughing, glittering face in the sunlit water.

"I should not fear it, brother," she said, "if your soul came too," and then she also laughed at the nonsense they were talking.

She had been with Lucian in the library on the morning of Sophia's visit, but he had been reading and had not done anything to interest her as yet. At the sound of her cousin's arrival, she had run out, eager to meet her, yet annoyed and dissatisfied at the interruption. If she had not come so early, Lucian, perhaps, would have found time to continue his tale about the German doctor who called up Helen of Troy from the dead to be his paramour. She had heard of it vaguely as an old child's story and puppet play like Punchinello, but Lucian made it seem quite different—like a possible, almost a true, story.

She was dreaming of it half the time that Sophia was talking.

"I declare," cried Sophia, in the middle of a full account of her meeting at a ball with "the most agreeable, witty, severe creature in the world—but 'tis true he's monstrous severe—Oh, la! the things he said to me about the other women and all the old beaux, but I assure you I put him down a peg—but I vow and declare, Juliana, you have never observed that I am wearing the new riding hat I bought in London. Has it not a strange, mannish air?—come, say!"

Juliana, blushing guiltily, hastened to assure her cousin that she had just been considering how well it became her, and that long green plume went amazingly with her riding dress. Sophia's pertly pretty face, its pointed, inquiring nose, thin, mobile lips and cocked chin, did indeed look charming in her cavalier hat. Juliana was smitten with a pang of real self-reproach, for never before had Sophia thus enhanced her charms by any new article of dress without her "dearest coz" at once observing it.

But Sophia, more readily appeased than Juliana's tender conscience, rattled on. "And how do you like your eldest brother? I heard it said in the town that he is only at home to see what rents he can get out of the estate. They tell the oddest tales of him there. It is certain he is a sad rake, is he not?"

"He has not told me so," said Juliana.

" Oh, la ! what an answer ! As if he should tell you so ! "

But seeing her cousin did not like the subject, she asked what drawings and flower-paintings she had done since that day when Fanny and they had had such a merry time, using little William as a model.

" He had come up from Nurse's cottage with a message," she explained to Miss Hilbury, " and sat quite still for us with an apple in his hand, looking a very Cupid."

" We told him stories to make him smile," chimed in Juliana, " and he knew he should have the apple to eat when the drawings were finished."

She searched among the loose drawings and sketches that lay scattered all over the oval table in the middle of the room, to find those of little William, and then held them up, delicate pencil drawings in the rounded manner of the elegant eighteenth-century amateur that Bartolozzi so often etched. Fanny and Sophia had drawn him as the glorified idea of the little peasant, pretty and appealing in his humility and innocence ; Juliana, still more romantic, had transformed him to " a very Cupid "—plump, winged and naked, playing with the apple that Venus had won from Paris. Venus was lightly sketched in the background, her draperies very like the loose white dress that Juliana was herself wearing at this moment, with cherry-coloured ribbons round the waist and tying back her light brown curls, not yet powdered and dressed for the day.

There were very few other drawings to show, and Sophia rallied her cousin on her idleness. Miss Hilbury said that she had never seen anything so sweet in her life as Miss Clare's sketches, they were a vast deal finer than anything in the town, she was sure. Juliana repaid the compliment by saying that Miss Hilbury must sing to them—would she not give them that pretty air, " Chloe's Lament " ?

She rose to open the clavecin, and saw a figure in brown cross the lawn outside the French window, and a girl's face looked into the room. The girl stopped, and for an instant she and Juliana looked at each other. Juliana saw her clear, open eyes, wide open in surprise, it seemed, her lips just parted in a kind of pleased wonder. She turned to her companions and said low and hurriedly: "Who is it? Shall I ask——"

But Miss Hilbury was turning over the music and had not noticed the passer-by. Sophia was idly flicking at her dress with her riding whip, gazing out of the window, but she did not seem in the least surprised, and now looked up, evidently puzzled by Juliana's question.

" Who is what, my dear creature ? "

Juliana looked back at the garden and saw that the girl in brown had gone. She looked again at Sophia and saw that she had not seen anything. But she must have seen, she was looking straight out of the window.

" What is it ? " repeated Sophia, with some impatience.

" Nothing. I think I am very absent this morning."

" It is the fashion to be absent in the town," said Sophia. " If you wish to be in the mode you declare you are the most absent creature alive."

She said it with an air and the girls all laughed. Miss Hilbury sat at the clavecin and sang " Chloe's Lament." Juliana, her hands in her lap, wondered who the passer-by could have been. She had known it was a girl by her face, pretty, though sunburnt, framed in loose brown hair, not curls, but looped in

86

some curious way beneath a sort of cap that came down low on the head. But her dress was so extraordinary that she might well have wondered if it were a girl at all. Now that she was thinking it over, she could not remember ever having seen any dress like it, not even in pictures of outlandish or old-fashioned costume. It was such a loose, straight, boy-like figure—she supposed there had been skirts, but if so they had been most inadequate.

CHAPTER VII

THE visitors stayed to dinner. Miss Hilbury, a little
crushed, as were most people, by the presence of Lady
Chidleigh, sat next to Vesey and answered by subdued
titters whenever he spoke.

He spoke seldom, for he was in no humour to try
and entertain a bread-and-butter miss, with a snub
nose—thank God, no Clare had a nose like that !—when
his cousin, Sophia, the finest girl in the family, no, by
gad, in the whole county, was sitting next to Lucian
at the foot of the table, watching him make a fool
of himself positively as though she liked and admired
it. And what in the world were they talking about ?
Nothing but absurdities—sheer crinkum crankum—
and not at all suitable at that for a young girl like
Sophia.

" What ! Paris gay, Paris modern, Paris worldly ! "
Lucian was exclaiming. " But I assure you, dear
cousin, they have changed all that. Paris is monstrous
serious, credulous, speculative. It is full of magnetic
healers and alchemists who talk of the life of the spirit.
Oh, yes, the spirit is everything now—and *l'esprit*
is nowhere.

" The most popular person in Paris is the Comte
de Saint-Germain, whom nobody sees. He claims
to have lived five hundred years and to have sum-
moned the loveliest women of antiquity from the dead
for his mistresses—Aspasia, Sappho, Faustine, Semira-

mis. Such, cousin, is the life of the spirit. It cannot be denied that it has compensations—for those who have not had the good fortune to meet the loveliest woman of the present time."

He dropped his voice at this conclusion, and Sophia, shy at first and then flattered by his treatment of her as a companion habitué of the great world she had so lately visited, was excited by this compliment into blushes and laughter.

" Such impostors ought to be whipped and branded," observed Grandmamma Chidleigh, as unexpectedly as if the bust of William III had suddenly addressed them from the corner where he gazed in cold severity upon the company, " unless, indeed, the man is really the Comte de Saint-Germain and of noble birth."

" Unfortunately, madam, it appears to be the only reality about him. These things, undoubtedly, should be better arranged."

" Pray, my lord, continue," said Sophia. " Have you met these alchemists ? Is there not a report that Signor Cagliostro invokes shades from the dead to sup with his guests ? I have heard of him in London, but all his alchemy could not prevent him from getting into debt there and ruining poor Lord Bareacres."

" But London," said Lucian, " is a sad, irreligious place, where there is no longer any true respect for the Infernal Majesty. And that is an important power to conciliate in invoking shades of the dead, since the only shades one would ever desire in company must necessarily come from below. You should visit Paris, cousin—with your understanding of history you would find it entertaining, as many a French Court lady has done, to dine with the shade of Lucretius or Petronius at Count Cagliostro's house in the Rue St. Claude. Only the week before I left, the shade of Voltaire attended a midnight supper party in, I fear, an almost indecent haste to return to the earth he has so lately rendered null and void by his absence. He declared that he had conversed with half a dozen Popes since his death, and found them good to listen to. After that, one can believe anything that happens at the house of Count Cagliostro."

Sophia laughed extremely, and Miss Hilbury, whose eyes and mouth had opened very wide, supposed she had better laugh, too. Aunt Emily gave a nervous titter and declared it was all vastly droll.

"How exceedingly absurd, Lucian," said Lady Chidleigh. "Have you nothing better to tell us of your travels than of a flock of quacks and charlatans?"

But Sophia no longer minded her severe Aunt Chidleigh. How easy and affable her cousin was! No doubt he was wearied to death at home and thankful to have someone fresh to talk to. It was evident that his attention was entirely engrossed by her.

Juliana, far down the table, wondered why Lucian was talking of such nonsense. It was strange that he should speak, though, in that careless, scoffing way, of shades rising from the past. It was almost as though he had known what she had seen that morning, and had thought—what *had* he thought? At that instant, Lucian, still chattering with his fair companion, looked down the table and met her eyes.

It was no more than an interchange of the briefest glance, but Juliana knew that he had asked her what she had to tell him and that she in her turn had asked him to explain it. He had told her to remember that when he had looked at her it was to her he was talking, and she had learnt her lesson well.

She was distraite and ill at ease after that, unable to think of anything but her wish that their guests would go so that she should be able to talk with Lucian. She had never wanted Sophia to go before and it made her feel uncomfortably guilty, especially when they were strolling together in the garden after dinner. But, oh dear, how Sophia rattled ! It was so difficult to attend, to show interest in the right places. How was it she had never before perceived that " her dearest Sophy," her own particular friend, chattered about so many things that did not interest her ? She supposed she had never thought before what had interested her and what had not—never before Lucian's coming, Lucian, whose life, unknown as it was to her, made her own pastimes and occupations appear so empty of all but tedium.

At last the two girls rode off, their groom in attendance behind them, and she was alone with Lucian on the terrace, telling him of the figure she had seen on the lawn.

As she had half expected, he showed no surprise.

She described the strange dress as far as she could, she even made a rough drawing of it in her journal as she sat on the little wall that ran along the terrace. But he could think of no country nor even any period in which anyone was dressed like that.

" You are certain it was a girl ? " he asked.

" I *think* I am certain. But—could it perhaps have been a girl dressed as a boy ? "

A thrill of terror, as exquisite as joy ran through her, and she clapsed her hands together. " *Lucian !* Lucy Clare fled England disguised as a page ! Could it have been her ghost ? "

She fully expected him to laugh at her. But he replied quite gravely that a page's dress in James I's time included the full trunk hose and wide-sleeved doublet, whereas the figure in Juliana's sketch apparently wore a long, loose-skirted coat to below the knees, not unlike those their father had worn as a boy, about forty years or so before.

"But I know it was a girl," said Juliana, "though indeed she had an odd, boyish air. She looked so— so free, I think it was. Her eyes——" She stopped in the difficulty of telling clearly her brief impressions, but Lucian, leaning forward on the wall, was looking at her with a new and extraordinary interest.

"Yes?" he said, "tell me, quickly. Her eyes, what were they like?"

"Wide-open," said Juliana. "She looked as though she were surprised to see me. But I was going to say when I began, that they looked so—I don't mean so 'brave'—no, fearless, that was it."

"Ah," said Lucian, "Light or dark?"

"Neither, I think. They were very clear."

"That clear golden-brown," he said softly.

"Yes," said Juliana, "a peculiar colour." She turned suddenly on him. "But you, brother, how did you know their colour? I did not say it."

"No?" he said. "Perhaps I guessed. Shall I guess a little further? Were the lips just parted, not in vacancy, but a kind of eagerness, a half-childish yet intelligent curiosity?"

"Yes, oh, yes! Oh, Lucian, how do you know?"

"And the skin pale, a little sunburnt, yet clear too? And a few golden brown freckles on the tip of a straight nose, and of a small, firm, tilted chin?"

"Lucian—Who—Where, where have you seen her face?"

"Juliana, my dear, kind, useful little helpmate, I would give the world to know."

"What! You know her face, but don't know where you have seen her?"

"Precisely."

She stared at him, for he appeared to be repressing with difficulty a burst of laughter. His sallow, colourless face had flushed slightly, and his eyes were

unusually, even unnaturally bright. As he met her
surprised gaze he seemed to make one more effort to
contain himself, and then flung back his head with that
loud cracking laugh that had so startled her once or
twice before. He laughed as though he could not
stop, and he looked extremely ugly, his skin a dull
purple, his eyes screwed up, and the upturned corners
of his mouth stretching almost to his ears, revealing
white, sharp-pointed teeth that made her think of
some wild animal. For one shocked and self-
reproachful instant, she could not but remember Lord
Chesterfield's admirable advice to his son in those
letters not yet published but widely quoted among
his circle of acquaintance, to be careful always to avoid
the ill-bred and illiberal facial distortion of a laugh.
And *what* could Lucian be laughing at ?

" A thousand pardons," he began at last, suddenly
grave, " but do not you yourself find it exhilarating ?
I spoke by chance of the Comte de Saint-Germain—
of Cagliostro—of the strange company they entertained.
It seems I was extremely *à propos*. Yet what have
these modern charlatans in comparison with your
powers ? Is it then possible, just possible, that you,
Juliana, you, the most gentle and docile of daughters
to the most correct of mothers, should, like Dr. Faustus,
mightiest of magicians, have the power of calling up
the spirits of the past ? A power not entirely unassisted,
perhaps, by the preparations of your humble and willing
servitor."

He rose and bowed low, his hat before his eyes, as
if to veil their intolerable brilliance—so it seemed to
Juliana at that moment.

" Of the past," she echoed, dazed. " But you have
seen her."

But he paid no attention to her.

" For all your meek airs you are an arrant rebel,''

he continued, still with that strange air of triumph and elation which he positively seemed to find it necessary to curb, talking fast and in a manner that suggested the need for speech as a concealment rather than as an expression of his thoughts. " Juliana, I fear you have not given sufficient attention to the philosophy of the learned and venerable Bishop Berkeley. No? I feared so. It might enlighten you on this affair. But though all the theologians in the universe inquire ' What is matter ? ' you will reply ' Never mind.' And should they further desire to ask ' What is mind ? ' you answer, ' No matter.'

" Yet you rise superior to matter and the accidents of time, where I am but able to pave the way for your more puissant spirit. Sister, I compliment your superior wizardry. I can but listen and admire where I would fain follow. I——"

" Brother, brother, pray do not talk so fast. I cannot make out the half of what you say. What is it that you are doing, that you say we are both doing ? What preparations do you speak of ? *We* did not call forth an apparition, if that strange girl were indeed— but no, she was *alive*—all life and spirit."

" Yes, all life and spirit," he repeated as though he were again remembering something, but so softly that she did not notice him.

" She *could* not be an apparition," decided Juliana, and then another thought struck her. " How could it be that in this age of reason, of science, I should see an apparition ? If indeed it could be permitted. Dear Fanny was certain that the Almighty would not permit——"

" So ? And is there nothing in this world but what is permitted by the Almighty, as expounded in the Gospel according to Saint Fanny ? Even, for instance, that rascally politician, Mr. Wilkes ? Consider,

94

Juliana, how heavy a responsibility you lay upon the Almighty. Would our lamented father, a most pious man, have agreed that the presence of Mr. Wilkes in this world could have been permitted by a beneficent God? Was there not even an occasion when our father directly attributed that presence to a powerful though inferior rival of the Almighty?"

Juliana, vividly reminded of a political tirade at dinner many years ago, wherein the late Lord Chidleigh had made the wine glasses spring into the air by the force with which he had struck his clenched fist on the table, was obliged to agree that any dissent from his opinion would indeed have smacked of blasphemy.

"It is all excessively puzzling," she said, with a little sigh of excitement. "Are you indeed at all in earnest? We have been talking like children. It is not possible—Lucian, it is not possible, is it?" A shiver had run through her and she drew closer to him.

He looked down at her, and she felt rather than saw that his eyes were blazing under their half-closed lids.

"What is it? You are not afraid, are you? And, if you are, is it not pleasant to be a little afraid?"

She gasped, and then said: "Yes, I believe it is. But, Lucian, I don't want to be too much afraid."

He caught her up in his arms and kissed her.

"Sweet sister, I will not let you be too much afraid."

He was laughing, not with that disconcerting crack of laughter, but very softly. Juliana, nestling close against him, shivered again.

CHAPTER VIII

JULIANA did not meet Lucian in the library during the following week. She received no message from him either by look or word, and when she peeped in of her own accord she found the great room empty once more wearing its accustomed air of aloof, disdainful desolation.

She began to think that Lucian had been teasing her. He certainly could not have meant a word of all that absurd nonsense when he had talked so wildly. He did not look as though he had ever thought of it again, and she began to feel it was very silly of her to think of it either. There was probably some quite simple explanation of the appearance of that girl in front of the windows; perhaps she was a superior looking gipsy girl in some sort of man's coat; or perhaps she had been half dozing for that moment and dreamed that she had seen her there.

In any case there was something far more important to think about, for her Cousin Charlotte had swaggered over on a new roan mare of Mr. Hilbury's, which proved too unmanageable for her and succeeded in throwing her in the courtyard. Charlotte was more shaken than she would at first admit, and Lady Chidleigh insisted on her staying the night, to her own hardship, for her niece's manners offended her exceedingly. Charlotte had, in particular, a trick of affirming whatever she said by a slap of her thigh and the declaration—

" Wish I may die if it's not true." It was the nearest approach to an oath she dared venture in Lady Chidleigh's presence, and it had failed to be repressed even by her aunt's chilling suggestion : " Do you not fear, my Charlotte, that if you weary us too often with your wish to die should your statement be untrue, *we* may find ourselves wishing for its falsity ? "

George, who usually took no interest in women above the rank of an inn servant, thought her a spirited creature, worth a dozen of that mincing little miss, Sophia. He thought it chiefly to annoy his brother Vesey, who had threatened when they were both at school to fight a duel on the matter. But he was more inclined to think so in earnest on this occasion, as Charlotte was now to be married shortly to one Mr. Ramshall, a wealthy man, but a timid and modest character whom George could have easily ducked with one hand. It was monstrous of her parents to marry a fine girl like that to such a quiz, and he gloomily predicted a disgrace to the family in the shape of Charlotte's elopement with one of the grooms before the year was out.

Charlotte, no whit dashed by her tossing, was as noisy as ever on this visit, and bragged a good deal of the stud she would keep with her husband's money. " Ramshall ! Did you ever hear such a mean-nothing name ? Mrs. Ramshall ! Wish I may die if I don't split with laughing the first time I'm called it ! "

Her thin, handsome, high-coloured face did indeed look as though it might split when she laughed, her mouth formed such a wide gap between her prominent nose and chin. One could see then what a nutcracker face she would have as an old woman.

But, in spite of Charlotte's constant laughter, Juliana did not think her quite the same as usual. It would certainly be very odd to think of Char married to that little nervous man, who cleared his throat like a hen clucking, but it did not incline her to " split with laughing." She felt melancholy and dissatisfied, and wondered whether Char's restlessness did not conceal some misgivings on her own part. But she could not, of course, ask her cousin. It would be a shocking liberty, a disloyalty, in fact, since she was already betrothed. She could not have done it even had it been Sophia, who was of her own age and generally considered to be her particular friend. So she watched rather wistfully Aunt Emily's whole-hearted gushings of delight over Charlotte, and wondered what husband she would have herself.

" If he is a hump-backed toad, Aunt Emily would still be pleased," she decided.

If only she could go and stay with Fanny in London. and meet someone who would be her own, her very own choice—perhaps even a runaway match. And the childish visions she had longed for when she lay on the seat by the lake, rose before her eyes—a page in scarlet, a king. But it was all very silly and romantic, and of course one would be happy whomsoever one married. Fanny was very happy now, but then dear Fanny was gifted in happiness, which was no wonder since she made everyone happy round her.

But she had not particularly wanted to marry Mr. Daunt, so much she had confided one unforgettable night when she had cried and clung to Juliana as though, for once, she were the younger sister and Juliana the elder and stronger ; and had told her that she did not want to leave home, and that she could never care for Mr. Daunt whom she had only met a few times, as she cared for her own sweet precious sister.

Charlotte rode home on one of their own horses,

at Lady Chidleigh's command, and the house seemed the quieter and happier for her departure. Juliana set out with her little dog to see Nurse again, and as she had missed her visit for three days she stayed a particularly long time, gossiping about the wedding, and what they should all wear, and what chance there was that " Miss Fanny " would come home for it. Then she would be sure to stay at least three weeks after the journey.

When she left Nurse, she continued her walk for some way beyond the cottage before she turned back to the house. She was sauntering back, thinking idly of Fanny's possible visit and feeling that there was much to be glad of in Charlotte's wedding after all, when suddenly she stood still and exclaimed aloud : " What can the gardeners be about ! "

She had that moment been struck with the fact that the drive had become surprisingly untidy and overgrown with weeds. She wondered how she could have failed to notice it before, even she, who was so sadly lacking in observation. She must find one of the gardeners at once and point it out to him. She hastened her steps ; Bruno, thinking it was to please him, ran barking at her side. She threw a stick for him and broke into a run. A rabbit ran across the drive, Bruno became frantic and disappeared after it into the undergrowth. She ran on, laughing and panting a little, for the drive went uphill just there.

On the top of the incline, she stopped and caught her hands together. Some way down the drive in front of her was a straight, brown figure walking towards the house. She knew at once that it was the girl she had seen crossing the lawn outside her windows just a week ago. She was walking fast, and in another minute was lost to sight under the overhanging green branches.

Juliana walked on, slowly now, but breathless, as when she had been running. She had forgotten the gardeners and the bad condition of the drive. She wished Lucian were there. She wondered if she should go and find him, and then, suddenly, she decided to follow quickly and see if there were any chance of catching sight of that figure again. Yes, she would speak to her, ask her who and what she was, and why she was there. She could not hurt her. She was sure there was nothing supernatural about her, she was a girl like herself, with a frank, pleasant look. There was nothing to fear. In the courage of this resolution she hurried again, but soon realized that the girl in brown would have left the drive long before she could reach the end of it.

And now another thought struck her—very curious, almost disconcerting. She had returned down the drive just as she had come, yet she could not remember that she had re-passed Nurse's cottage. She must have done so, of course ; she must have been too much hurried and occupied with the glimpse she had again had of that strange figure to notice the cottage. Yet it was odd, even extraordinary, to find herself wondering so persistently whether she had indeed passed it—that bright coloured patch of garden, the only clearing and break in the whole of the long drive.

But now she was coming out of the drive, and the girl was nowhere in sight. Juliana ran through the gardens and up and down the terraces but could see no one, and then went round to the courtyard. She was coming through the arched gateway when she stopped and stared in amazement at a strange man in still stranger clothes who was standing in the middle of the courtyard, doing something to the gravel with a kind of iron stick. " He *cannot* be another ghost," thought Juliana, as she looked at the substantial calves

100

and red face of the stranger. His odd clothes were very rough. She wondered if, perhaps, he were the new foreign gardener Lucian had said he would get to improve the Italian garden. She hesitated whether she should come forward and ask him, and at that moment two figures came out of the house and down the steps towards him, and one of them was the girl in brown.

The other was a woman in a loose, black dress. She was saying in a loud voice : " Here is my husband, so you can ask him yourself."

The girl went straight up to the man and said : " Good morning. I have a confession to make, and an apology and a request."

" That's a lot of things to make," said the man with a sort of rough cheerfulness.

" Yes, I'm afraid it is. On one or two walks I've trespassed all over your grounds and even the gardens, but I really thought the house was shut up—it does look like it, doesn't it, but I suppose that's only part of it—and the drive doesn't look as though it's used now."

" Oh, the old drive ? No, we don't use that now," said the man, who was staring at her in a very rude and open manner. " We've cut a new one that goes straight to the station. Yes, most of the house *is* shut up. Can't fill a house this size now, you know. Families don't run to it."

" And that is the confession and I am really very sorry," she said rapidly in her low clear tones, as though she were anxious to finish all she had to say at once. She was apparently not at all put out by his stare, which made Juliana tingle with annoyance and the longing that she would cease speaking to him. But the girl continued to speak : " I want to ask if I may go on doing it, and that's why I came to the house

101

and asked to see Mrs. Harris"—she turned to the woman in black—" I don't mean I'm asking to go into the gardens again, of course, but in the drive and the park ? There used to be a right of way through it, wasn't there ? I'm only staying here for a few weeks—would you mind ? "

" *Not* a bit," said the man patronizingly. " You won't hurt the place strolling about it. Nice old place, ain't it ? "

Juliana had been too much confused and astonished to grasp at first what was happening, or to feel uncomfortable at hearing all that was being said—though as they must see how near she was, the rudeness was theirs in ignoring her presence. For it was manifestly absurd to try and imagine these people could be apparitions. Apparitions do not talk, some of them in loud cheerful voices, and grin, and hack the gravel with their boots. No, they were plainly real people though of the most amazing kind.

But she now saw that this uncouth stranger was actually granting permission to the girl to walk in their grounds (where of course there was a right of way in any case) and was behaving generally as though he were master of the place. It was so odd and his tone of complacent ownership so ridiculous that she broke into a peal of laughter.

The same instant she was shocked at the sound of her own merriment. However rudely and astonishingly these people were behaving, it was unpardonable to laugh aloud at them, and she came forward a step or two from the archway wondering what she could possibly say in apology and beginning hesitatingly to speak. But her words faltered and died away, for none of the group turned to her, none looked at her, they did not appear to have heard either her laughter or her speech. She stopped, a cold terror

n her that turned her numb. What was it? What
vere they? Why could they not hear her? Why
id they not look at her?

They had not stopped talking. They were talking
bout the house. The man had turned to his wife
nd was asking: " Who was the Tudor gentleman
hat built the house, Milly?" and then to the girl:
Yes, we keep up all the old feudal customs, you know.
Regular old castle it is. Costs something to keep up
oo, I can tell you. And so you're staying here? In
he village? Whereabouts? What's your name?"

" Miss Challard," said the girl. " Thank you very
much for giving me leave." She bowed and left them,
alking quickly away through the arch. She passed
o near to Juliana that she could have touched her,
ut she never turned to look at her. Juliana stood
ooking after her, and her hands were pressed together,
s cold as ice.

" Nice little girl," said the man. " Milly, this weed
uncher's no good."

Juliana turned and saw that he, too, was looking
fter the girl in brown, so that he was looking straight
t herself. But he, too, did not see her. With a
idden, panic-stricken movement she ran through
he arch and out into the park, ran blindly until,
xhausted and panting, she fell under one of the oak
ees, and lay there clutching at the grass.

" They weren't living people," she kept saying to
erself. " How could any real, living people have
oked at me and not seen me?"

She lay there for a long time, her breath gradually
oming more easily and her hands ceasing their con-
ulsive movements. She sat up and looked round
er. Everything appeared the same. She heard the
eacock scream from the garden.

She started as she saw something small and white

move close by her, but it was only a large piece of paper fluttering in the grass. It blew a little way towards her and she saw that there were two pieces, with writing all over them. She went and picked them up.

The writing was not hers; indeed, compared with Juliana's beautiful calligraphy, it looked the most slovenly, ill-formed hand, and both paper and ink extremely thin and poor. Juliana turned the pages over. They were written on both sides and appeared to have no beginning and no end. As far as she could make out it began in the middle of a sentence:

—" but won't I be a fool to go and ask permission even if I do get it? To see the Harrises in the flesh and know they're really there, having their beds turned down in the evening and hot water put in their rooms. Barney, I can hear you laugh at me, but why should they be *here*—and not even enjoy it? They don't even fill the house with a cheerful jolly vulgarity of house-parties and week-ends. The place crushes them; it's not surprising. And now if I go to them, will the place ever be the same after that, however much I'm allowed to prowl about it? Perhaps I'm just throwing away the shadow for the substance, and the shadow is the only thing that matters here.

" It's not a real house at all. It's a city in a fairy tale or in one of Dürer's pictures, and when I first saw it I expected to see a hunting party in silks and velvets ride out from under that great archway.

" When I first saw it, I turned away, but when I looked back it was still there.

" I found it at the end of a beech drive, the straightest and longest drive I've ever seen. I was already late for lunch when I hit on this drive, coming out of a little wood, but I had to go on and see where it led to.

was tired too, and I thought I might as well come back to-morrow, but no, I had to go on. And it led to tall red chimneys rising above the trees of the drive and then iron gates three times my height, and behind them lawns, terraces, a flight of steps, and then that vast house. As far as I could see at that distance the windows were all closed, with blinds partly down, and they looked like brooding half-shut eyes that were all looking at me.

" I felt quite glad to turn away, round by an enormously high red wall, and then I saw those twisted Tudor chimneys again, over the wall, and then old red roofs and a little tower and the tops of the tallest cypresses. It was then it looked most like a city and there was no sight nor sound of life.

" I came then on the archway into the courtyard, and so on round till I was nearly at the front of the house again. This part looked more gentle and homely, and had lawns and little gardens in front of it. I thought by now that the house must be empty, and I boldly trespassed across a lawn, in bright sunshine, close up to the house. There was one room with long French windows that were open on to the lawn, and I heard girls' voices and laughter coming from it.

" As I went past the window I saw three girls gathered round a table looking at something on it. Two of them wore a sort of long riding dress of green velvet, and the third, who was just coming across the room, was in a loose, flowing robe, all white, with a red ribbon, like Sir Joshua Reynolds' ladies when they're not in full dress. It was this one in particular that I looked at, for she was just in front of the window, and she looked up and saw me.

" She was as shy and exquisite as a fawn ; yet not wild. A tame fawn that would eat out of your hand if you did not startle her. I did startle her, for her great shining eyes opened wide and she turned quickly back to the others.

"Then it struck me how dreadful it was of me to be trespassing right under their windows, and I fled. For at the time I thought they must be the daughters of the house, dressing up or something. It was only afterwards when I heard that the whole of that side of the house is shut up, and that the Harrises are a childless couple and haven't anyone staying with them, that I began to think that I must have seen the ghosts of girls who used to live there.

"What do you think, Barney? Were they ghosts?

"It is strange to think of happy ghosts, isn't it, ghosts laughing and chattering? They looked so gay and so pretty and I thought I heard one singing as I went away, to a tinkly old instrument like a tiny piano. They were too pretty to be dead. Though— there's de la Mare :

> ' But beauty vanishes, beauty passes,
>   However rare—rare it be.'

"And, Barney, she saw me. That is so queer. You never hear what ghosts think of the changes in the place they visit, or the people they appear to, yet we must look just as strange to them, I suppose. Was it she, or I, who was the ghost!

"The Vicar's nice. He's told me what he can about the place and lent me a funny old book that comes from it—he bought it for 6d. in the sale—but I haven't——"

There the writing came to an end.

CHAPTER IX

JULIANA did not know how long she had been sitting under the oak tree. It did not seem so very long, yet she noticed when she got up that the shadows in the park had lengthened, and she was as stiff as if she had sat on the ground for some hours. It must be nearly dinner time and she was not yet " dressed." She rose, and moved slowly towards the house.

The arched gateway into the courtyard soon appeared, huge and grey, through the trees. It was the oldest part of the house, a relic from the days when it was a mediæval castle. The wall that surrounded the house came up to the side of the gateway, and above it rose the irregular line of red brick roofs, straggling chimneys and a little white stone peppercaster of a turret, put up in Charles II's time.

Juliana stood still and looked at the gateway. The sunshine came from under it in a wide semi-circle. It all looked very still and peaceful, very familiar. But what might she not see if she went through the arch ? Would she meet with the people she knew ? The thought of encountering those unnatural strangers again was so terrible to her that she drew back and thought she would go round by the terrace and enter the house from that side. But if the strangers were still about the place it was as likely by this time that they should be on the other side of the house as this. It was, in fact, most improbable that they should have remained so long in the courtyard. Not a sound came from it. Juliana plucked up courage and stole up to the arch.

There was no one in the courtyard. The sun beat down on the white gravel. The massive stone trough, overgrown with ferns, made a bright green patch against the wall, just by the arch. Juliana looked at it with a sudden fresh apprehension. She had never noticed nor thought of it at the time, but she now could not be sure if there had been ferns in that trough when she was in the courtyard a short time ago. She had been standing just by it ; it would have been strange if she had not seen the ferns in the otherwise bare courtyard.

But, then, she was very unobservant, and there had been so much to agitate her at the time. She touched the ferns gently. " You were here before, were you not ? " she whispered, and the rough surface of their fronds seemed to answer her smooth fingers, solidly reassuring her of their reality.

She went into the house, not through the hall but up a side passage that led to a little stair, hesitating and listening whenever she heard a sound. She ran as though she were pursued down the corridor to her room, then stopped at the door and listened, her heart beating in great thumps, for she heard someone moving about inside. " It is only Molly. Is it one of *Them* ? " came tumbling over and over in her mind. She could not open the door and find out. Suddenly she hit her hands together in anger at her own cowardice. What would Lucian think of her ? What did she think of herself ? She went in.

Molly was arranging the folds of a silk paduasoy on the back of a chair.

" Molly ! " gasped Juliana, and the next moment had flung her arms round the neck of her maid.

" Why, miss ! What's the matter, miss ? My own precious lamb, what is it ? "

" Nothing. I am only so glad to see you again, Molly."

Juliana felt much ashamed of having exposed her emotion, but it was better to have done so to her dear Molly than anyone else.

Whatever Molly may have thought of Juliana's remarkable display of pleasure at seeing her again after the not very lengthy interval that had elapsed since she had bathed and dressed her young mistress that morning, she asked no more questions but set to work at once on the elaborate business of the toilet, with many exclamations at the impossibility of finishing it in time. Only half an hour to dinner ! What *had* her young mistress been about ? Her tortuous operations on Juliana's hair had to be sadly curtailed. There would have been no time to learn her Geography Cards during their operation, even if she had been so disposed. The task of squeezing her tiny waist into yet tinier stays was performed with unusual speed, the voluminous folds of the paduasoy were rapidly arranged over the hooped satin petticoat, and the charming result of these hasty labours was arrived at within five minutes of the booming of the dinner bell.

It was while she was thus engaged that Juliana made a discovery, she did not know if it were disquieting or not. She was sure that after she had read those papers over several times, she had folded and put them in the bodice of her dress. But when she was undressed they were not there. They had been perfectly secure, they could not have dropped out. Yet they *had* dropped out. For the moment, however, she felt positively glad of the disappearance of such a substantial proof of her strange terrors.

She walked downstairs composed and easy. There is something in a hooped paduasoy that must inspire confidence in the breast of its wearer even as it imparts dignity to her appearance. Juliana might not be able to breathe quite as freely as she could have done an hour ago, but she certainly felt more capable of sustaining her part in whatever might befall her.

Even Lady Chidleigh's brief reproof of her unpunctuality did not cast her down. There was something positively reassuring in being scolded by Mamma again. She even pictured to herself what it would be like if Mamma could encounter the creature called Mr. Harris, and the shudder caused by the thought was not solely one of terror.

It revived her spirits infinitely to look down the long table, weighted by heavy dishes, to hear Aunt Emily offering every dish to everybody and raising her voice to a very good imitation of the peacock as she addressed Cousin Francis, who was nearly stone deaf; to see George, in the abundance of his manly appetite, sending Zachary for more sauce and Daniel for another bottle, the while he carved himself something like two pounds of beef. Vesey had ridden over to Barton to see a cock fight, and Lucian was also absent, but George could not say where he was when his mother inquired.

It was a hot evening and they all, except old Cousin Francis, went after dinner to sit on the wide flight of steps in front of the house, above the terraced garden. The elders sat on chairs at the top of the flight, Juliana perched herself on one of the steps. Last summer it had been very hot and they had done this almost every evening. Often, some of the Hilburys and their schoolboy brothers, or her cousins, Charlotte and Sophia, had ridden over and sat with them on the steps until it was too chilly to sit there any longer, even with shawls, and they had gone in to dance or play blind-man's buff indoors.

It had been a merry summer. Juliana wondered if this one would be as merry. She hoped things would not change. She had been foolish, always wishing for change, for life to be different. Could it be pleasanter than this?

They had sat there some time and the sun was setting at the end of the long drive. It looked black in the twilight, and the tree-tops were not stirring in the still air. She wondered whether she had not always been a little afraid of the drive, even in the sunlight.

Vesey came home, demanding supper, and giving George elaborate accounts of the cock fight and his bets on it. Grandmamma had gone to bed, Aunt Emily shivered and fussed for shawls, and the party went in. Juliana lingered in the doorway to watch the new moon rising over the trees of the drive, and heard the thud of hoofs coming down it. "That is Lucian," she thought, and went to the top of the steps. He might see her as he came out of the drive and then he would leave his horse at the gates and come straight up to her through the gardens instead of going round by the courtyard.

Would he see in this dim light at such a distance? She waved her scarf, but was sure it was of no use, for her pale-coloured dress did not show on the white stone. But she heard the horse stop, and for a minute there was nothing to break the exquisite stillness of the evening. Then there came the sound of a man's steps on the gravel, a dark figure showed against the dim grey of the lawn and came up the steps to her.

"I did not think you could see me," said Juliana.

"I can see in the dark," said Lucian. "Did you not know I was a feline animal?"

His voice was light and pleasant, but she knew that

something had made him very angry, and she felt more afraid than she had done at any time that day.

" Well," he said, " you waved to me to come. Now tell me quickly."

The imperious form of the request suddenly roused her. He may have had reason to be angry, but not with her. In any case she did not choose to be so commanded.

" It cannot be told quickly," she said in her quiet voice, and began to move towards the house. He laid a hand on her arm.

" Sweet sister, have I displeased you ? " he asked, half mocking, half coaxing. " Was I abrupt, discourteous ? If so, see how humbly I pray for a return of your favour."

He knelt with deliberate grace and raised the hem of her satin petticoat to his lips.

" Lucian ! " she faltered, embarrassed though she laughed, " how ridiculous ! And what am I to do, pray ? Make my best curtsy ? But, indeed, there is a great deal to tell—if—I am not sure that I want to tell it—not just now, perhaps."

She had drawn her scarf a little closer, glancing round her. That old familiar terrace, faintly seen— it had always been the same. Would it always be just the same ?

" No ? " said Lucian, who had risen and was looking down on her with very quick, bright eyes. " Then I will tell you what I have been doing instead. Is that someone calling you ? Come, we'll take a turn on the terrace."

" But it is Mamma," said Juliana.

" So ? But if you were farther down the terrace you could not hear her."

He drew her arm into his and led her farther down the terrace. The white roses shone dimly in the summer dusk; the moonlight had begun to make faint shadows of a hooped skirt and a sword as they walked up and down the terrace. Juliana felt as though they were walking in a dream. Was it a true belief held by the ancients, and were their shadows that they saw before them in reality their souls? She did not fear to think so now.

"Sweet," said Lucian, "you have gone far away."

"No," she answered, "I am here and with you." Indeed, it was as though she had never been, would never be, anywhere else.

They walked past the tall box hedge again. Shadows stole out on the milky ground, of a bent head, ribbon at neck, of a head, upturned to meet it, under a high-piled tower of hair.

"We have never walked here at this hour before," said Juliana. "Yet it seems as though we had done so for a hundred years."

"Or will do so for a hundred years more," he answered, and then both fell into silence again. Even their steps made no sound on the grass walk of the terrace.

Now, or a hundred years ago or a hundred years hence, it was all one. Wherever they were, whatever they would become, something of them both would always walk together at this summer hour on the terrace. So Juliana felt, though she could not have put her feeling into words, nor even thoughts, and she knew that Lucian felt it too.

"I have been seeing Mr. Daintree," he said, "on the subject of the offer of marriage he has made you."

A hundred years ago or a hundred years hence fled away in a flash. Juliana was in the present moment again, in the summer of 1779, and rapidly

surveying what might happen by the autumn. Mr.
Daintree, so kind, but grave—and old, oh, monstrously
old! He had given her a doll on her sixth birthday,
so kind of him—a beautiful wax doll that had come
from Paris—but he had been quite old even then.
She remembered his maroon satin knee breeches and
the jewelled fob on his waistcoat, as she had held the
beautiful new doll in her arms, too shy to look any
higher than the fob while she thanked him as mamma
bade her.

"Mr. Daintree make an offer of marriage!" she
exclaimed. "Mamma never told me and I do not
wonder. How preposterous! The man must be at
least forty."

"Thirty-eight," said Lucian judicially.

"That is twenty-one years older than I. And a
widower!"

"He has been one for twelve years."

"Exactly," cried Juliana, as though that made it
worse. "To think of marrying an inconsolable
widower!"

"Then the prospect of the match does not please
you?"

"Please me! How could it? An old man—well,
middle-aged—and a widower—and someone I have
known all my life!"

He chuckled at this last, but Juliana did not notice
it, for his reticence had begun to alarm her.

"Surely," she said, catching closer at his velvet
sleeve, "Mamma does not approve it?"

"She most surely does," said Lucian.

She gasped and would have dropped her hand, but
his arm held it tight against his side.

"You seem to forget," he said, "who is the head
of the house."

"Lucian! you would oppose Mamma?"

" I did not say so. I said that my consent would be necessary."

" And you will withhold it ? "

" I have withheld it."

The muscles of his arm tightened again as he said it. Juliana wondered if this had been the reason of his anger when he had first met her. Had there been a quarrel ? And why had he ridden over to give Mr. Daintree his answer first and not told her about it until afterwards ? If he were acting only in accordance with her wishes, he might have found out more certainly beforehand what those wishes were.

For undoubtedly in every other way it was a most suitable match. Mr. Daintree was of very good family, and wealthy ; the estates joined, the families had always known each other, and there was no one else at all eligible for miles round. And then he had always been very kind—a good man, oh, yes, only dull ; but a nice way of looking at one.

" I hope his feelings were not hurt," she said.

Lucian suddenly laughed. " You would have liked the opportunity of refusing him yourself, would you not ? "

Indeed she would not. It would have been most painful. And she could not see why Lucian was laughing at her. She asked a trifle coldly :

" What reason, brother, did you give for your refusal, as you had not then inquired into my wishes ? "

" My own wishes," said he. " I have other plans for your future."

She naturally longed to ask what they were. But he had become remote, forbidding. And an unmistakable call in Molly's tones rang out suddenly from the steps of the house : " Miss, miss, are you still in the garden ? You will be catching cold. Come, miss."

"I must go," whispered Juliana. "The others all went in long ago. I expect she is waiting to put me to bed. Goodnight, brother."

"Goodnight, little sister."

Juliana ran towards the house. Lucian turned on his heel and walked away from it.

CHAPTER X

Lucian did not ask Juliana again what it was she had to tell him. She did not know if this were out of consideration for the reluctance she had shown to speak of it. But certainly, as the days went past and he did not press her confidence in any way, not even by seeming to wait for it, she thought more frequently of the loose pages of writing she had found in the park, and wondered the more what he would say if she told him of them and the events of that strange morning.

But there was something else she wished, and that was to ask him what were those " other plans " for her " future " that he had made. It seemed that she could not do one without the other, and fear of the latter held her back. She could not have said why, for surely she had every reason to be curious as to her own future.

But there was singularly little opportunity for a talk with Lucian these last few days. He was never in the library when she looked in now in the mornings, and when she saw him he appeared busy and pre-occupied. Mamma, too, was frequently distraite, and a most unwonted cloud sat on that usually unruffled brow.

Vesey, in a moment of expansion, remarked to her that Mamma and Lucian had been at it hammer and tongs, and he supposed *she* knew what all the to-do

was about; for his part he thought Richard Daintree
as good a match as any in the county, but no doubt
Lucian had a mighty fine alliance up his sleeve for
her—they would see her an archduchess or a princess
one of these days.

With this he gave her an affectionate pinch on the
ear that caused it to glow as deeply as the ruby ear-ring
that dangled from it. He was interested in marriage
just now, even to the extent of feeling a trifle sentimental at the thought of his little sister's match. If
only those two old bachelors, his elder brothers, would
marry, it could be decided how much money he would
have for that purpose and which of the dower houses
to live in. Or—better still—Lucian would have to
marry, of course, but what did a low old brute like
George, with his perpetual taste for village girls, want
with a wife? Himself, he was as fond of a wench
as anyone, but, damme, he was capable of knowing
what a sweet girl was like. The "sweet girl" of his
imagination was, in fact, remarkably like his cousin
Sophia.

Juliana's entries in her journal were sadly meagre
at this time.

"I attempted a Study of Cottagers before their
Door at evening, but found the subject too difficult."

"I tried unsuccessfully to make a Pail Work-bag,
for the Cardboard was too small."

The drawings of ancient and gnarled oaks in the
park that *would* appear like bunches of wool on her
paper seemed a dull and trivial occupation; she even
began to wonder what was the purpose of it. But
that was an absurd thought and must be on account
of her bad performance.

Of the adventures that she found so disturbing, yet so interesting, there is not a word in her journal. She found them too strange to write of, even in a book that was never to be seen by a soul beside herself. She wrote instead of Madame de Sévigné's letters, and an account of the reign of King John, summarizing a chapter of Goldsmith's history.

Among these sparsely covered pages is a loose sheet of paper inscribed with some verses in a small, neat, firm handwriting—not her own.

Juliana found them late one morning when she had returned, after receiving a brief morning call, to the seat by the lake, where she had been studying Goldsmith. She had left the book open on the seat, and on her return found it closed but with a paper protruding from its pages to mark the place. She quickly opened it, to find, in the middle of the reign of King John, a copy of verses in Mr. Daintree's writing. He must have placed it there in her absence, only a few minutes before.

She leaned in her accustomed lazy posture along the seat, and, as so often before, the sunlit lake danced lazily in front of her half-closed eyes. She had not yet read the verses; she was prolonging the delectable sensation of her discovery that Mr. Daintree—dull, quiet, elderly Mr. Daintree, that inconsolable widower—had become a poet for her sake and written verses to her. That anyone should write verses to her was bewildering, dazzling; but that Mr. Daintree should do so seemed in the nature of a miracle and to invest her indeed with the powers of a goddess.

Her eyes closed altogether as she played again the old game of imagining what she might see when she opened them again. But this time she did not imagine a page in scarlet, nor a king, nor a cavalcade of horses and gallant gentlemen with a Tudor prince in their midst. Instead, she pictured to herself a familiar figure in a brown suit coming over the grass towards her and looking at her with the intent and kindly gaze she knew so well.

But when she opened her eyes she saw only the lake and the lilies on its surface, and the slow swans passing to and fro ; and on the opposite shore, the tall twisted chimneys and turrets and irregular red roofs of Chidleigh House rising from the trees.

" It is always the same," she said to herself, " it will always be precisely the same."

She was not thinking the words, they were mechanical, the effect of that habitual reverie. Her eyes fell again on the paper in her hands, and she began to read the verses.

> Ah, Chloris that I now could sit
>   As unconcern'd as when
> Your infant Beauty could beget
>   No pleasure nor no Pain.

> When I the Dawn used to admire,
>   And praised the coming Day,
> I little thought the growing Fire
>   Must take my Rest away.

> Your Charms in harmless childhood lay,
>   Like Metals in the Mine :
> Age from no Face took more away,
>   Than Youth conceal'd in thine.

> But as your Charms insensibly
>   To their Perfection press'd,
> Fond Love as unperceiv'd did fly,
>   And in my Bosom rest.

She stopped at this point, just half way through

the poem. She was lost in an admiration that was more than half at her own " Charms." How little she had dreamed they possessed such power ! She went back to the second verse and read it again, twice over.

" And praised the coming Day."

She remembered how she had once heard Mr. Daintree observe to Mamma that her youngest daughter would be a notable addition to the phalanx of rising belles, and had wondered what it meant. Since she had known she had thought it merely one of those necessary compliments, like the " elegant little creature " that the lady visitors had all bestowed on her.

Was it indeed possible that her " growing Fire " should have taken Mr. Daintree's rest away ? Enchanting possibility ! Her hands trembled slightly as she held the paper before her eyes again and finished reading the verses in a delicious agitation that left her little room for understanding. Something about Cupid and " his Mother," " flaming Dart," and " Chains." The ardent passion of such words overcame her ; they danced over the sunlit page in front of her like actual tiny flames.

And now she heard a familiar step on the grass, and knew that for once in her life she would see what she had imagined she would see when she looked up. But she did not look up. She looked more and more closely at the page before her and saw nothing.

The steps ceased close beside her and still she did not look up. She could not, dared not look up.

" I beg your pardon," said Mr. Daintree's low voice above her, " for thus intruding on you."

It was not the remark of a poet. For that reason, probably, it recalled her to herself. She rose and curtsied and saw that it was the Mr. Daintree she had always known, who stood before her and bowed. He had a grave air, but then he was always rather grave. No, he was not altogether grave ; his eyes looked as though he were smiling, in spite of those deep lines in his broad sunburnt forehead and round his mouth, which shut closely with a stern expression. If it were not for those lines he would not look so old, she decided, for his eyes were clear and his figure was well-knit— not, indeed, as massive as Vesey's.

And there was certainly a smile in them as he regarded her now, a smile that made her lower her own eyes after that hurried glance, for it seemed to her to reflect that fire that had taken his rest away, and the thought of Mr. Daintree's wakeful passion for her was something too unfamiliar, too—almost—indelicate to be easily confronted. How could she have looked at him so uncomprehendingly all these years and not known him for a poet ?

" May I dare hope," he said, " that Sedley has met with any small success as my ambassador ? "

" Sedley—? " she faltered stupidly.

" You have read the verses ? I took the liberty of leaving them in your book, as I knew you must soon return for it, and so waited and watched until you did."

" Sedley ! " said she again. " Sir Charles Sedley— the poet ! "

" Did you not know them to be his verses ? "

" No—I do not remember to have read them before— I had thought——"

Her disappointment was too acute for her to proceed further.

His eyes twinkled again, but this time she perceived no reflection in them of " growing fire "

" Those verses," he said, " have expressed my feelings

122

for you so exactly these two years now—I have read them so often, and thought of you as I read—almost I could have made your mistake and fancied that I had written them myself. But even you, Juliana, could not make me a poet."

" I had thought——" began Juliana again, and again was unable to go further. In fact she was very near tears. Not *her* charms had inspired those ardent words, but Sir Charles Sedley's Chloris, dead these fifty years. And she had believed herself capable of creating a poet out of " dull, good, worthy men like Mr. Daintree." Viciously she recalled Sophia's slighting words which, at the time, had given her a faint prick of pain.

And with them, she recalled much else that she had forgotten or ignored until she had heard of Sedley's authorship. Mr. Daintree had no right to present himself to her since Lucian had refused her hand. Was it possible that in spite of that refusal Mamma had sent him to her ? What an intolerable situation !

She waited, not choosing to do or say anything to put him at his ease. Her silence did not seem to embarrass him. He appeared to be considering her under a very close scrutiny. At last he said simply and without apparently any sense of its obviousness, " I wished to see you."

Politeness decreed that she should speak by now.

" No doubt my mamma——" she began.

But he, with very little politeness, broke in upon her.

" No, Lady Chidleigh has not sent me to you. Is that what you imagined ? You thought I would use her consent to force my suit on you ? "

" I did not see how else you came to be here."

She became troubled by the silence that followed, looked up and was the more troubled by his face. He had never looked at her like that before. But then

123

she had never spoken to him like that before. Oh dear, oh dear, what in the world was about to happen now, and what was she to do ?

It was all the fault of those tiresome verses and that great bloated creature who wrote them—she remembered Sedley's portrait now in a book in the library—if only she had not known the verses to be his.

" I am very sorry," she said, " but I do not know precisely—Mamma has not spoken to me——"

He suddenly smiled at her, not merely with his eyes, but a frank wide smile of tender amusement that lit up his whole face. She remembered his smiling at her like that when she was a child ; perhaps he had done so when she was thanking him for that doll, and she need not have been afraid to look higher than the watch-fob on his waistcoat.

" Then," he said, " let us for a moment not speak of Lady Chidleigh. I want to speak of you and of myself. Dare I do so, though I am not a poet, nor romantic ? "

" Oh, sir," she cried, convicted of her own ungraciousness, " indeed your compliment of the verses pleased me infinitely—I was put about only because you discovered such ignorance in me."

He did not attend to her and seemed to be thinking what he should say. When he spoke it was not quite as calmly as before, and his agitation increased as he proceeded.

" I have no right, I know, to ask you to speak with me in this irregular fashion. I have asked for the honour of your hand, and your mother and brother have answered—their answers do not agree. I wish to know what you—no, pray do not speak yet. I do not think you can know my reasons for wishing, as I do, to marry you. You will, I beg, pardon me if I speak much of myself."

He paused, and then said slowly: " You know that I was married—a long time ago." Here he stopped completely. Juliana was much distressed.

" I know, I know," she said as he still kept silence. " Indeed you need not try to tell me. You must have been very happy to remain so long unmarried since."

" No," he said at last, " I was not happy, nor was my wife."

He was speaking now as though the very words caused him difficulty, and his voice was gruff, even harsh.

" I found soon after my marriage that she did not love me. I soon ceased to love her. The two years we were together were years of utter wretchedness for both of us. That was—for a long time—why I could not bear to marry again. I wished never to do so. I was still fond of children, I wished for heirs, but I decided that I would rather leave my inheritance to my cousins than incur a risk of the repetition of that misery."

He stopped again, but this time he seemed to be remembering something, and with pleasure, rather than considering painfully what he should say.

" You were almost an infant then, and I had never seen a child such as you. When you smiled—It was wrong to say:

' Your infant Beauty could beget
No pleasure nor no Pain,'

or that strange, dazzling smile of yours gave pleasure so exquisite, it was almost pain. I used to think it the smile of one who saw a vision."

The effect of this was almost as great as if it had been in verse. So, then his compliment to Mamma

125

on the notable addition of her youngest daughter to
the phalanx of rising belles had *not* been just the same
as the stale and perfunctory " elegant little creature "
of the lady visitors. She would have given the world
to receive such a compliment gracefully, but though
she could have taken or ignored one with the greatest
ease from gallant Mr. Chalmers or facetious Mr. Bolsover,
yet now she could not think what to say.

Mr. Daintree, however, did not seem to expect her
to say anything, and was speaking again himself.

" I am thirty-eight and you are seventeen. You
could have been my daughter. In those days you stood
to me for that—for what I had missed in children.
But not that chiefly, not chiefly. I loved you for
yourself, the loveliest of children. I have always
loved you. But now it has changed. For some time
I have felt——" He broke off, and when he spoke
again, his voice was gentle and pleading. " Juliana,
I want you to be my wife. I want to make you happy
I would like to give you everything you could desire
to shield you from every trouble. I am much older
than you, I am not gay, nor young, nor handsome—
do you feel it is impossible that I should ever do it ? "

Juliana had sat down again on her seat some time
ago. Daintree was standing beside it, looking down
on her, but she kept her head downcast and the broad
brimmed hat did not permit him a view of her face.

A host of bewildered feelings struggled togethe
in her mind, and amongst them was a slight sense o
indignation. So Mr. Daintree was *not*—had *neve*
been—the inconsolable widower she had always sup
posed him. It made him much more interesting
she felt she had been to some extent cheated.

Sometimes he had looked at her in a way that ha
struck her at the time—he had very steady grey eye
though not as bright as Lucian's—and she had though

126

e was thinking of the beautiful wife who had died
o young, long ago. And he was not thinking of her
t all, at least not like that. She wished she had
nown that before, though, of course, it did not make
ny difference. She was very, very sorry he had been
nhappy. His wife must have been odious to make
im unhappy when he was so kind. But it was dread-
ıl that he should want to marry her so much when
. was impossible.

"I am very sorry," she said at last, "but you know
 is impossible."

He made a sharp movement which suddenly recalled
o her what his last words had been and how she had
eemed to answer them.

"No, no," she said, "I did not mean that. Indeed,
. think you could make me or any woman happy.
ray do not think me so insensible to the honour—oh,
ear!" she broke off suddenly, for she felt that every-
ing she was saying was wrong. But then it was
rong that she should have to say it. Why should
ie have to answer his proposal herself? It was
nheard of.

"I think my brother gave you his answer," she said.
That is why I said the marriage was impossible."

"To your brother and Lady Chidleigh," he replied,
my requests and my offers were different from what
. have just made to you. Lady Chidleigh approves
ie match, but I am glad she has not spoken of this
o you. It was my urgent request to her that she
iould not, especially when I found that Lord Chidleigh
pposed it. But *your* wishes——"

"But my brother has told you of them," she said
s he paused.

He bent low over her and, to see her face, deliberately
ıshed back the broad-brimmed hat.

"And you have nothing further to tell me?"

127

Oh, but this was monstrous! Whatever she sa
she would hurt him, alienate him, and she had know
him all her life. What an intolerable, painful situa
tion! It was most unfair, too, to put it on her whe
the matter should, of course, have nothing to do wit
her, at least comparatively little. Certainly, nothin
to do with her decision. She was glad that it ha
not, for she had never felt less capable of decidir
anything. But Lucian had decided and that wa
enough, should have been enough, at least.

If only Mr. Daintree had not such very steady eye
They would not waver nor look away from hers.
had really behaved in an excessively odd manner—
not to take Lucian's answer, and to come into tl
Park on purpose to speak to her, and alone like th
She ought to be very chilling and indignant, why cou
she not think of something Mamma might say? B
she found to her consternation that her hands we
trembling and she had to bite her lip to keep it fro
doing so too.

A large firm hand came down on the top of her
What, oh, what was going to happen? Sudden
she felt the air ringing with the sound of her nam
not loud, but low and vibrating, and it was not M
Daintree who had called, but Lucian. She becar
intent, rigid.

" Where is he ? ". she half whispered.

Daintree looked utterly bewildered.

" My brother was calling me. Did you not he
him ? "

" No, I did not. He could not have called. It h
been completely silent."

" But I know he called me," said Juliana. " I
is waiting for me. On the terrace."

" If he were on the terrace, you could not possib
have heard him from here."

128

This should have been conclusive. But Juliana
sprang up.

"I must go. He wants me—now. You may not
have heard him but I know he called me."

Daintree caught at her hand. "What if he did?"
he said quickly. "Your brother can wait one moment.
Have you forgotten—one moment ago when you were
on the seat—what were you going to answer me?
You were not going to tell me, were you, that I could
never hope to please you?"

Oh, how could he keep her back when Lucian had
called her so urgently! And one moment ago or a
hundred years, it was all one.

"I am very sorry," she said (she seemed to have
been saying that all the time). "My brother gave
you my answer as well as his."

His face did not change. It did not seem that he
now expected another answer. He continued to look
at her, but still more gravely, more piercingly she
thought, than before. There was an acute anxiety
in his gaze, and she felt that it was, for some obscure
reason, on her account. She was embarrassed, but
she did not try to withdraw her hand. She even held
it up a little, for him to salute at parting. He kissed
it slowly, then raised the long ruffle that fell from her
elbow and kissed that also.

"I would give my life to serve you," he said.

The words were a courtesy, almost a formula. But
to Juliana they seemed to touch a terrible significance.

CHAPTER XI

LUCIAN was on the terrace. As she came up the steps
Juliana saw him to her right, the sunshine gleaming
on the pale grey satin of his coat. He was sitting on
the very low red wall that ran along the second terrace,
and as he sat there, hunched forward a little, the blue
lupins on either side of him nearly reached his shoulders.
His head was bent in her direction, his lips were pursed
as though he were whistling, his hair was already
powdered for the day, and she noticed, as she had so
often done, how much darker and sallower it made
his complexion appear. She had always thought
that only fresh-coloured men, like her other brothers
or Mr. Daintree, should wear their hair powdered.

And yet how graceful he was even in that careless
position, and how exquisite were the lace ruffles at
his wrists! She admired the crescent-shaped patch
on his cheek that accentuated in mocking mimicry
the upcurled corners of his mouth. Nobody she had
seen dressed as well as Lucian nor had such an air
not merely when he chose, like George or Vesey, but
always, however haphazard or careless or even absurd
he permitted himself to be. As for Mr. Daintree, he
had a grave air, and a dignified air, and a polite air,
but that was quite a different thing from having an air.

"That's my dear charmer," said Lucian. "I knew
I should not be disappointed."

"I heard you call," said Juliana, a trifle proudly,

although I was far away down in the park. But you did not actually call, did you, any more than you are now actually whistling ? "

"Well, no, I did not put my hands to my mouth and shout. But I was here where we walked a hundred years ago, where we shall walk a hundred years hence, and I was wanting you to come to me, here, now this minute. I certainly called."

"And why did you want me, brother ? "

"Why ? I hardly know. Perhaps you can tell me. You were gliding away from me when I called, were you not ? "

The quick and burning blush that surged up to her face and neck took her by surprise. She had not expected this, that she should feel guilty when she next met Lucian, guilty of disobedience to his commands, and guilty of something else—was it of disloyalty ?

And had he really guessed what had happened ? How could he have guessed ?

He took her hands in one of his and drew her closer to him where he sat on the wall.

"It occurs to me," he said very lightly, very gently, "that you have a good deal by now to tell me."

"Oh ! "—it came out in a rush and all sense of guilt to Lucian for the moment dispersed—" Oh, I have been so odious. I have hurt him and I am sure he must think me a toad—so prim and mincing and pert and, and—*missish !* "

She ended by dropping her head on to his embroidered waistcoat, and the long-suffering hat, its ribbons finally unfastened, fell off altogether. Lucian put his arm round her in the kindest, most brotherly and protecting way. But his face looked over the top of her head with a curious expression, difficult to describe. It was amazed at first, but that passed quickly. It was not angry, but neither was it kind, brotherly and protecting. He did not speak for a minute and then he whistled " actually."

" So you have been giving Daintree a stolen meeting down in the park ? "

Juliana raised her head quickly. " Why, you knew— did you not ? "

" How should I know ? Do you take me for a wizard ? " He flung back his head and laughed.

Juliana grew pale.

" I thought—you said you called because you felt I was gliding away from you—and you said I had a good deal by now to tell you."

" Any fool could have said that who had seen your face then," said Lucian. " You should not blush so easily, my dear, if you intend to carry on many secret interviews. As to my reasons for calling you I was here on the terrace, where, the other night, I flatter myself, we both felt a peculiar sympathy. I thought of you—I found you were not there—I cannot explain it more than that. I suppose I had a fear an old-womanish fancy. It seems it was well justified. For the rest, it is as easy to draw secrets from you as favours from an elderly beauty. I cannot congratulate you on your diplomacy, my pretty one, nor myself on my fraternal care. It seems I should keep better watch."

He began to sing very low a verse of Lord Rochester's—

" My dear Mistress has a Heart,
Soft as those Kind Looks she gave me."

But there was no mistaking his sincerity. He had spoken with a bitterness which completely overshadowed the light and easy measure of his tones. Juliana looked at him in wonder.

This was a new Lucian, a Lucian who could feel hurt

and angry and even afraid. Afraid of what?—of her disobeying, forsaking, perhaps deceiving him? Oh, he could not!

"Lucian, Lucian!" she cried in an agony. "It was *not* a stolen interview—how could you think I would think of such a thing?"

"Think of it, sister? Lud, no, 'twere impossible!

'But her Constancy's so weak,
   She's so wild and apt to wander,
That my jealous Heart would break,
   Should we live one day asunder.'"

She clasped her hands across his arm. "Brother, I beg you to listen. I have no secrets from you—I never wish to have. He came on me as I sat there, drawing, in the park—I was surprised——"

"Oh, were you much surprised?" he said under his breath, but she went on without appearing to mark him:

"He wished to hear my answer from myself. And I gave it to him—indeed, brother, I did—as firmly as you yourself could have wished."

"And since then," said Lucian, with his head slightly bent to one side, "you have much regretted your firmness, your prim, mincing, pert, *missish* firmness."

It was too much. Two large tears glistened on her eyelashes, welled slowly over and rolled down her cheeks.

"You are my dear, sweet, pretty little sister," he exclaimed, and caught her to him and spoke all in a rush, only pausing occasionally (generally in the very middle of a word) to kiss her, each time in a different part of her face. "You are not to call yourself ugly names. I won't have it, even from you. How pretty you are when you cry! No other woman can do it as

well. No, no, I didn't mean you did it on purpose;
I am only your great, rough, awkward brother and
you must put up with my teasing. And do you think
I'd let a great, rough, awkward lout of a country squire,
a widower, a grandfather, or if he isn't one, he ought
to be, carry off my dear, sweet, pretty little sister and
shut her up in his great country house where she'd
never go to the town and have balls and parties and
see the gay world, when I have a beautiful French
duke all in readiness for her as a surprise that not even
Mamma knows anything about—an accomplished
courtier, a favourite with the King—no, with the French
king, simpleton—can you imagine I would mean our
heavy Hanoverian?—who owns châteaux out of fairy
land, and lakes, and great forests where he hunts the
wild boar with cavalcades of gallant gentlemen, a
prince so absolute that in his own country the law
permits him to disembowel any of his peasants if, on
his return from the chase, he should wish to warm
his feet by placing them in the belly of a freshly-killed
man. Juliana, what great, round eyes you have!
Have you never read in your French history of the
droits des seigneurs? No, of course they don't
carry them out. No, never; and would you like to look
at his portrait?"

He drew out a snuffbox of blue Sèvres enamel and
gold and opened it. Juliana, leaning against his
shoulder, looked, and saw inside the lid a miniature
of a young man's face. His powdered hair curled
back from a high, white forehead, his eyelids, drooping
over clear blue eyes, showed delicate veins on the white
skin, a veritable triumph of the miniaturist's art, as
was the painting of his lace cravat. His high-bridged
nose was aquiline, haughty, contradicting the expression
of his indolent eyes. The chin was long and pointed,
the mouth too perfect for a man—but then miniatures

are apt to err on the side of perfection. His complexion also erred in this respect, but it was of the pale and not the wild-rose variety of " miniature " complexions.

" Do you like him ? " asked Lucian.

" He is beautiful," breathed Juliana. " Brother—do you—mean it ? "

" We are great friends," said Lucian, as though he had not heard her. " It chanced that I was able to render him a service when he was in some danger, and he wished to exchange snuffboxes in recognition of it and of our friendship."

" And did yours have your portrait inside too ? "

" No, it had a very pretty picture of Antiope surprised by Jupiter."

" Oh, and was she much surprised ? " murmured Juliana, repeating his former tone.

" You rogue ! "

They laughed together. She was deliciously happy, not so much because of the French duke whose name she had forgotten to ask, as because Lucian had never been quite so charmingly easy and friendly with her.

" There is Mamma come out on to the lawn," said Lucian. " Shall we show the portrait to her ? "

" Oh, no—not now." She had flushed deeply. " You said it was a secret even Mamma did not know."

" So we'll keep it a secret at present just for our two selves, shall we ? "

" Yes, yes."

Mamma had begun to approach them, her wine-coloured, hooped skirts filling the path below them like a vast inverted tulip. Juliana sighed.

" And I had so much to tell you."

For she was wishing now to tell him of that day when she had seen the strangers in the courtyard. Lucian would tell her if it could really have happened so.

" Come to the library to-night after you have gone to

bed," said Lucian. " Be there at quarter to twelve—and be punctual."

" But why ? I can tell you at any time."

" It is not for that, child. I had meant to speak of it before—it was, at first, why I wished to see you. There is no time to tell you now. But be there."

" Lucian "—Mamma was advancing up the steps at the end of their terrace, her skirts heaved and billowed in the rhythm of her stately progress—" it is not for further experiments ? "

" Certainly. The mornings are liable to be interrupted—besides, it is not such a good time."

" But why do you want me ? "

" You, my angel ? You are a most important part in them. Have you not always wanted to be there ? "

" Yes, but——" She had felt a sudden and unaccountable aversion to the experiments. Was it because Lucian had said she was an important part in them, and she had never before known this ? But very likely he was only laughing at her when he said that. She could not think why Mr. Daintree's eyes came before her at that moment, his look when he had kissed her hand and said he would give his life to serve her.

" I think I will not come," she said in a little gasp.

Mamma was now quite near them.

" What are you both about ? " she inquired benignantly.

" I have been discussing possible matches for my sister, Madam," said Lucian gaily, as he stepped out into the path to meet her. " She has, I find, a catholic taste."

Lady Chidleigh did not approve of this light tone on a subject that had caused her so much displeasure. But she did not address her son.

" Juliana," she said, " you are treading on a lupin. And your backbone—pray remember your backbone."

CHAPTER XII

ULIANA sat at the top of the staircase and peered
through the banisters down into the hall below. She
had gone up to her room more than an hour ago and had
dismissed Molly, after her hair had been taken down and
her stiff dress exchanged for a loose wrap. She had not
altered her refusal to go down to the library that night,
but she thought it would be as well to be ready in case
she should alter it.

Lucian had said nothing more to her about it. He
had never reproached her nor even laughed at her for
her sudden decision, nor had he urged her to revoke it,
though he had had plenty of opportunity to do so, for
they had ridden some way together that afternoon. He
had suggested they should all ride over to the Hilburys'
for dinner, and Vesey, who knew that his Cousin Sophia
was quite as likely to be at the Hilburys' as at her own
home, was nothing loath. George, too, wished to ask
Mr. Hilbury about the new roan he had bought as a
brood mare, and Aunt Emily was always glad of " a little
excursion."

It was on the ride that Juliana, finding herself some
way ahead with Lucian, had told him about the extraordinary events of that day on which she had found the
papers under the trees in the park. She also told him,
as nearly word for word as she could, what she had read
in those papers so unfortunately lost.

He did not seem much disappointed at the loss of the

paper—in fact he remarked that it was probabl
inevitable, though she could not make him say what h
meant by this. He made little further comment an
was peculiarly thoughtful. She missed the eager intere
he had shown before, an interest that had seemed to giv
him the satisfaction of a personal triumph, and asked
he found the recital tedious. He replied gravely that h
could never find tedium in a recital that paid so high
tribute to her parts and to his industry—an answer sh
found as incomprehensible as the glance that accom
panied it.

When they arrived at the Hilburys, however, he wa
at his gayest and most delightful. Vesey told Georg
that the fellow behaved like a mountebank, but tha
may have been because Sophia laughed at h
conversation rather too often.

" Oh, my love ! " she exclaimed to Juliana, " I decla
Lord Chidleigh is the most infinitely agreeable, divertin
man I have ever met ! What a world of difference
makes—a little travel, and *le bel air*, and a *je ne sa
quoi!* I vow I cannot look at a man who has nev
travelled."

Juliana regarded her cousin anxiously. It would h
dreadful if Sophia really liked Lucian better than Vese
particularly as there was no chance that Lucian wou
ever care seriously for her—a gushing, affected chi
always so ready with the last new words. Then it struc
her that she was thinking very unkindly of her cousin
she supposed it was only on poor Vesey's account. N
Sophia was not, could never be, beautiful and brillia
and bewitching enough for Lucian.

George called at the Parsonage on the way back an
brought Dr. Eden back to a light supper at about nin
followed by heavy drinking. Dr. Eden had be
appointed to this parish by his late patron on accou
of excellent and diverse talents. He could train a sette

make an angling rod, play an admirable hand at whist, and carry an extra bottle or two with a dignity and discretion suitable to a bishop on some great occasion.

It is true he could not put two words together of his own accord in the pulpit, and very few out of it, but one does not want a man to talk in the hunting field or at cards, and in church—well, what were all the volumes of sermons in the library for ? Juliana hated him, his large face and little tight eyes, his tight black clothes over his portly figure, his tight pursed button of a mouth that could open wide enough on Sundays in the pulpit when he bellowed forth the sermon he had borrowed from their library the afternoon before.

As she sat now, with her forehead pressed against the banisters, she could see the four men playing whist in the hall, George plying Dr. Eden with port, for it amused him to witness the parson's portentous solemnity, which was almost the only sign he gave of drunkenness.

She wondered whether Lucian had given up his intention of being in the library at a quarter to twelve. It would surely be difficult for him to leave the cards and the wine till the others were ready to go. What a noisy game of whist they were having ! It was her brothers who were making all the noise, especially Lucian. He kept filling up everybody's glasses as often as George filled up the doctor's.

It was evident that Vesey, at least, was getting too drunk to play. His cards kept slipping out of his hands, and he mixed up hearts with diamonds and clubs with spades.

" Damned rid—iculous," he announced gravely, " to have only rid—no, red and black. Ought to have *four* colours—red, black, blue, and—and red."

Lucian, who was fumbling with his cards, suddenly threw them down.

" Curse 'em, slippery rascals. Who cares for cards

when there's wine ? Doctor, your glass is empty.
George, you're sober. I say you are. Sober as a
Quaker. Where's your ' light French wines,' my boy ?
Let's have a toast instead of the game. I'll give you
a toast. I'll give——"

" A toast ! " mumbled Vesey. " To the finest girl
in the county—my pretty cousin."

" A toast ! " exclaimed George in a sudden roar. " I'll
give you a toast. Here's to the finest girl in the country
—Black Bess, my mare ! and damn all women, say I."

He fixed Vesey with a challenging eye, but Vesey,
after this last drink, had sunk down too far in his chair
to notice it. George's eyes, glazed and staring like those
of a bull, removed slowly to his elder brother.

" A damn good toast, Chidleigh," he said thickly.

" And I'll give you a better," shouted Lucian.
' Here's to the finest girl in the world, the girl I've never
seen." He ended this declaration with a flourish that
lost him his glass just as the others drained theirs.

Dr. Eden pursed up his mouth so tight that it seemed
impossible another drop of wine should enter it, but the
impossible was repeatedly performed. He highly dis-
approved of the untimely end to the rubber, which only
he was sober enough to win. Sitting exceedingly upright and resembling a tightly upholstered black bolster
he made a curious contrast to the splendid and disorderly
figures round him.

Vesey had slipped down so far in his chair by now that
only a pair of broad white satin shoulders remained
visible above the table ; George, on the contrary (whose
worst enemy could not now have accused him of
sobriety), had gradually slid forward as his chair slid
back so that his head and arms rested on the table.
As the line of his crimson coat became more and more
horizontal it seemed a miracle it should still remain
suspended between table and chair. Lucian, his grey

suit turned to pearl-colour by the candlelight, staggered restlessly from the table to the side-table where most of the bottles were put.

He could not be going to the library—it was already half-past eleven by the great clock in the hall, and in any case he was far too drunk now to conduct the smallest " experiment." Juliana heaved a sigh of relief that was not unmixed with disappointment. She was startled by the sudden booming of Dr. Eden's voice, as loud as when he was in the pulpit.

" I deplore," he announced, " the weak and tremulous spirit of this age."

Lucian appeared much offended by this reflection. He was leaning against the wall with his hands outstretched on either side as if to balance himself the better, and it struck Juliana that he looked like a great grey and silver moth confronting a fat, black slug. He suddenly began to talk very fast in defence of the spirit of the age, so fast that one could not well distinguish what he said. Dr. Eden, evidently somewhat confused, declared that he had meant no offence to his lordship, he had on the contrary been about to point out that his lordship and his noble brothers were the only firm and steadfast exceptions in a weak and tremulous age. Here the horizontal line of George's back startlingly collapsed.

But this only seemed to annoy Lucian the more. He declared that nobody and nothing was weakanjemulous but the doctor himself, though the accusing finger he tried to point at the doctor with this proved a staggering denial of his statement.

Juliana wished she had not stayed to see Lucian get so drunk. George's and Vesey's monumental oblivion did not seem so shocking nor so absurd as this foolish quarrelsomeness. It was certainly quite unnecessary now to stay any longer, and she rose and turned away just as Lucian was shouting : " You're an infidel, sir, a damned infidel. I'll not stay in the same room with an infidel," and reeled off. But it suddenly struck her that she did not hear him coming towards the staircase. She turned quickly back and looked over the banisters. Lucian was going down the passage that led to the library.

She stood still a moment in astonishment. What could Lucian be going to do in that condition ? Experiments in chemistry, she knew, could be dangerous. She *must* go, if only to see that he would do nothing dangerous. But curiosity, wonder, and a sudden strange doubt also urged her to go. She ran along the corridor to the narrow side staircase that led direct into the library by a door of its own. She had no candle and had to feel her way very cautiously. At the door she listened for a moment but could hear no sound but her own heart, which was thumping in an odd, irregular fashion. She opened the door and stood still in amazement on the threshold.

Lucian sat at the table, on which was a single lighted candle in a tall silver candlestick. He was doing nothing, his fine hands lay on the table, the finger-tips just touching, in steady immobility.

In the huge darkness of the room, he seemed so singularly isolated, motionless, that Juliana could scarcely believe it was her brother who sat there, or that it was indeed a living man.

The candlelight gleamed on his silken shoulders, and seemed to make a faint powdery halo round the dead whiteness of his hair. A silvery reflection of him shone on the polished table, and behind him an enormous shadow was heavily spread, as still as if it had been painted on the wall and ceiling.

But now he looked up and nodded as in welcome. His eyes were brilliant, and an amused smile twinkled into them as he saw her half-fearful astonishment.

"Wh-what!" gasped Juliana, "you are not drunk at all?"

He flung back his head in a sudden cracking roar of laughter.

"Oh, don't, brother!" she whispered, glancing in alarm at the other door of the library.

"Why, who do you think can hear us? Our worthy relatives above us in their bedrooms, safe and snug on their feather mattresses, with the bed curtains drawn tight round them? Or the servants above them in their attics? Or our brothers in the hall at the end of this long passage, lying drunk asleep, the one on the top of the table and the other underneath it? Or Dr. Eden who still sits between them, bolt upright, and fixes the wall with a glassy stare, but knows no more than they what he's about? Oh, no, we're safe, very safe—safer than we have ever been."

He laughed again with an extraordinary exhilaration and freshness that struck Juliana as unnatural to him.

He motioned her to one of the large armchairs that had been placed by the table on the side nearest the windows. There she sat and faced her brother, whose eyes never left hers.

"Very safe," he repeated. "And now that we are safe here together, what company would you like to amuse you?"

"What company?" she repeated dully.

She saw herself, a tiny white figure, in the pupils of Lucian's eyes, and as she looked, the white figure seemed to grow in size and to approach her. She was afraid, as once when she had dreamed that she had seen herself, sitting, as now, in the library armchair.

The figure receded until it was no more than a white dot again in the pupils of Lucian's eyes. When it had done so, she shook herself, shut her eyes, then opened them, staring, and said suddenly, " I do not wish for company."

She remembered Mr. Daintree's face when he had bidden farewell to her that morning in the park. She had told Lucian that she would not come to the library to-night. Why, then, was she here, sitting by him at the table ? She half rose, confusedly, clumsily.

He laid a hand on her arm.

" Stay," he said quietly. " You do not wish for company, you do not wish for experiments, is it so ? But are you certain there is no way in which I can entertain you ? Not by tales of my travels, of the odd characters I have encountered on them ? Yet you have often expressed a wish to hear."

Juliana felt most stupidly confused. It was certainly absurd and unnecessary to come down to the library after she had gone to bed, in order to hear Lucian tell tales of his travels. But she found it difficult to say so to him in words that should not sound pert. He was already speaking again, and she now for the first time noticed that a peculiar perfume had stolen upon her senses. It proceeded from a minute spiral of blue vapour which was rising from a small dish placed on the floor. As before, the incense was making her feel drowsy and it was not until she looked away from it, and looked again at her brother's oddly bright eyes, that she noticed what he was saying. He was speaking low and persuasively. He was not telling her of his travels, he was telling her to do something—what was it ?

" You will find her for me," he said. " Juliana, you will find her for me. Whoever she may be, wherever she may be, you will be able to find her. If she has ceased to exist, if she has not yet existed, she exists for me. She exists somewhere beyond my dreams. Go and find her."

He rose, and with his eyes still fixed on her, he moved

her chair round so that it faced the windows, which were unshuttered and uncurtained, open to the summer night. She saw the stars, and the trees on the lawn.

She watched the windows so intently that the grey and silver darkness of the sky seemed to enter the room and press upon her eyeballs. The stars and trees became hidden and there was the sudden sound of violent rain, like the rattle of kettledrums. This at first alarmed her, for she remembered something that Lucian had once read to her about " an exceeding great rain " and " the beating of drums " before the appearance of spirits of the past and future. But nothing appeared, and presently it diminished and then ceased altogether. She then wondered what Lucian was doing behind her and why he kept so very still, not speaking any more.

But now she began to dream in earnest, so that she no longer knew that she was sitting in the library arm-chair. She dreamed that she was walking down the drive to take some flowers to Nurse's cottage. The drive was untidy and overgrown and did not appear to have been used by carriages or horses for a very long time. She dreamed that as she passed she touched the beech trees one by one, and whispered, " You were here before, were you not ? "

She walked on, but she did not come to Nurse's cottage. She reached the end of the drive and thought she must have passed it without noticing. She turned to walk back, touching the beech trees one by one so that she should not fail to notice when she came to it. But Nurse's cottage was not in the drive.

At last she felt so terrified and so much alone that she tried to cry out, but no sound would come from her. And then she noticed that her steps made no sound as she walked over the dry twigs and withered leaves and beech nuts that strewed the drive.

CHAPTER XIII

JULIANA looked up from the armchair to see a cold light in the windows in front of her. Lucian knelt beside her, rubbing her hands. His face looked drawn and grey in the raw early morning, and his eyes were as dull as pebbles. There was a little sharp frown between them that she had never seen there before. But it disappeared as she looked at him, and he gave a deep sigh as if in relief.

" My sweet," he said, " your hands are so cold. You have been asleep a long time."

" Yes," said Juliana.

It was odd how tired she felt in spite of having slept ; she supposed it was because she had been sitting upright in a chair. After a time she said, " I have been dreaming." She passed her hand over her forehead with a perplexed gesture. " I cannot remember, but it was something very disturbing."

" Then do not try to remember," said Lucian. " In any case it was only a dream."

" Was it all a dream ? I remember that someone said ' Time is. Time was. Time will be.' That was what Roger Bacon said, in my old copy book Then someone else, or the same, said ' There is no Time.' " As she looked at him she added sharply, " You heard that too."

" Yes," he said quietly.

" Then—*was* it a dream ? "

" Perhaps."

" But which of us dreamt it—you or I ? "

" Perhaps both. If it were you, my sister, may I not be permitted to enter your dreams ? And, if it were I, I assure you I should have made you welcome. In any case it appears to have been a highly obvious statement contradicted by a remarkably untruthful one."

" It did not seem so at the time," sighed Juliana, " it seemed—oh, the most important thing in the world." Suddenly she opened her eyes on him, wide in horror— " Lucian, I remember now—I dreamed that Nurse's cottage was not in the drive."

" And does that frighten you ? But it is not strange that you should dream it. You must have remembered the story I had told you of Charnacé and his obstinate tailor. Do you not remember ? Charnacé was a whimsical fellow. He had a long and beautiful avenue which was spoilt by a peasant's cottage plump in the middle of it. Charnacé offered the peasant enormous bribes if he would allow a cottage and garden to be built for him in another part of the grounds, but the man refused, and such is the position of the down-trodden peasant in France (as you will hear all the philosophers call it) that Charnacé was unable to enforce his commands.

" He tried guile. He told the man, who was a tailor, that he required a new Court suit in a few weeks, that he was to come to the Castle to make it and have his meals and sleep there so as to finish his work the quicker. And while he was at the Castle, Charnacé had his house and garden exactly copied, and even the position of every piece of furniture carefully marked, and all was set up in another part of the grounds, and the old cottage pulled down.

" Then when all was done and the tailor had finished embroidering the fine new suit at the Castle, he was sent off at dusk to go home to his cottage. He went down the drive, and it was not there ; he went back up the drive, and it was not there ; he wandered up and down all night and could not find it. When the morning came he saw his cottage in a field behind the drive, not half a mile from its original place. He ran up to it, he found all exactly as he had left it, the vegetables in the garden, the pots and pans on his hearth, the tiny windows winking at him under the low roof as he ran outside to stare at it again.

" He rushed and called all his neighbours to come and look at it, he called 'Sorcery ! Sorcery ! Some powerful magician has picked up my cottage and garden and popped them down here instead.'

" And they all laughed at him, Pierre, and Jacques, and Susanne, and old Mère Madeleine, running up with their sabots going click, clack on his cobble-stoned path—all held their sides and roared with laughter as they told him how finely he had been tricked while he was working at the Castle at the grand new suit for his master to wear at Court ! "

" Oh," cried Juliana, " and what then ? I hope he did not mind, as he found it all just the same ? "

" Mind ? He was mad with fury at having been fooled. He tramped all the way to Paris to demand justice, he went to all the chief judges, he even gained admittance to the King. But they all laughed too, when they heard the story, and he was advised to swallow the affront.

" The late Duc de Saint Simon tells it in those memoirs that have been published privately in Paris—you would find them entertaining. And now you will go to bed and get some proper sleep and dream no more of Charnacé's tailor and his lost cottage.

" Remember also what the wisest of physicians has told us concerning visions—that ' Pythagoras might have had calmer sleeps, if he had totally abstained from beans.' ''

He gave her hands a final rub, then kissed them. But she was sure she had never heard the story before.

Juliana breakfasted in bed that morning, as was by no means infrequent with the ladies of the household. But Molly insisted that as she was so obviously sleepy she should stay in bed till three o'clock, when it was time to dress for dinner. Juliana accordingly slept soundly till one, when she woke much refreshed, and, ringing her bell, announced that she intended to get up.

" You can't do that, miss," said Molly, who looked red and perturbed. " Her ladyship is just coming up to speak to you."

" To speak to *me* ? But Molly, I must be up and dressed when she comes. Quick, quick."

" It's no use, miss. Her ladyship is on the stairs this very minute."

" Oh, Molly ! Could you not have told me before ? "

To be spoken to when in bed by Lady Chidleigh was to be taken at such a serious disadvantage ! She entered on the moment and Juliana, observing her mamma to be already stayed and dressed, sighed " I knew it," within herself. When Mamma had anything important (which generally meant something unpleasant) to say to one she never did it until she was fully dressed for the day.

" I am sorry to hear you are indisposed," said Lady Chidleigh.

" Oh no, madam," protested Juliana, feeling that she was committing an unpardonable error in her inability to rise as her mamma entered. " I am not indeed indisposed, only a little tired."

She stammered something about the heat on the ride to the Hilburys' yesterday. There was something peculiarly formidable about Mamma this morning.

What could be coming? Was it Mr. Daintree again?

"Your brother, Chidleigh," said her mother at last, "has spoken to me this morning on a subject that I admit has startled me. It appears that he has for some time entertained the prospect of a match between you and one of his foreign friends—Monsieur le Duc de Saint-Aumerle. Yet he has not consulted with me on this subject until this morning, and I fancy has only done so now, because he has just had an express messenger from the duke to say that he is now in England and intends shortly paying us a visit. Has Lucian mentioned this matter to you?"

Juliana wished she could lie. But she knew how little her face could do it.

"Yes, madam," she said hesitatingly. "I believe he did just mention it."

"You *believe!*" exclaimed Lady Chidleigh. "Is it possible you were not paying any attention to such a subject?" She added after a pause, "I would not have thought a son of mine could have done anything so indelicate as to speak of such a matter to a young girl without first consulting her mother."

Her colour, always high, actually became a brighter red, and this, for Lady Chidleigh, was to produce much the same effect as if a statue had flushed. Juliana longed to vindicate her unhappy brother.

"Oh, madam," she exclaimed, "I am sure Lucian could not have intended an indelicacy. Indeed, he did not even mention his name," she added, as though that proved it. He spoke of it more in jest."

"Marriage is no subject for a jest," said Lady Chidleigh, "especially between you and your brother Lucian. His way of life is not such as to render him fit either as companion or adviser to you."

Juliana's cheeks flamed scarlet. She thought she

knew better than to say a word. Nevertheless an instant later she found herself speaking.

"I know nothing against his way of life, madam, since nothing in him, either as companion or adviser has ever led me to suspect it. And I naturally have heard no criticism from others."

She kept her hands under the coverlet as she finished speaking, to hide their trembling. It was a beautiful speech, it was a speech Mamma herself might have made, but how had she ever come to make such a speech to Mamma! The silence was so dreadful that she looked up, though she knew well how that haughty stare of surprise would be fixed upon her. But, to her amazement, Mamma was smiling—a smile in which there was certainly surprise, but also some pride and a little tenderness.

"That was well said, Juliana. If I have seemed to criticize your brother to you, it is in my concern for you. Any intercourse, you may have together must be, I think, to his benefit. But you are at a period of your life when a delicate and important decision must be made, and I am naturally anxious when it can, legally, be finally determined by a young man who—but I will spare your loyalty. ' A young man ' by itself should be sufficient to justify my anxiety." And she again smiled.

Such kindness naturally overwhelmed Juliana. It was very difficult after it to follow really closely all that Mamma was saying about the proposed match with Monsieur le Duc de Saint-Aumerle. She heard that it might be considered a very grand match by some, but that in Lady Chidleigh's opinion a good old English family was more than equal to any foreign dukedom, that she could not say she cared for foreigners and, from Lucian's own account, the French king kept up a very poor sort of state at Fontainebleau. A hunting lodge ? Yes, but even a hunting lodge should be an indication of one's standards. To have so poor a show of gold plate that some dishes were actually used to cover others !

Lucian had made a great point of the families having known each other so well during the time when Juliana's grandfather had been ambassador in Paris, but she herself had never met Madame de Saint-Aumerle, the young man's mother. She greatly disliked the idea of any daughter of hers going so far from her supervision ; it was bad enough that James Daunt's post at Court kept him and his wife so much in London, and that his country seat should be on the outskirts of the next county.

She then spoke of Mr. Daintree.

" You are my dear, sweet, pretty little sister," hummed in Juliana's head. And Mr. Daintree would shut her up in his great country house where she would never go to the town and have balls and parties and see the gay world. She did not want to hear of Mr. Daintree. But why had he looked at her like that when she had left him ? So grave and anxious, so terribly anxious. But then he had always a grave air.

" I assure you, madam," she said in the pause that called for it, " that my only wish is to please you. "

CHAPTER XIV

Monsieur le Duc de Saint-Aumerle arrived two days later. He arrived in a coach drawn by six cream-coloured horses, with pictures of the Graces painted on the doors. The coach was lined with blue silk, stamped with golden fishes, for there was a fish in Monsieur le Duc's coat of arms. Four servants in the ducal livery of blue and gold preceded him on horseback, two rode behind him, then came a wagon to contain all the clothes. The cavalcade drew up in the courtyard, a footman sprang down and flung open the coach door, a hand in a cascade of ruffles appeared on a carved ebony cane, and Monsieur le Duc stepped out with deliberate cat-like steps.

Lucian and his brothers were waiting in the courtyard to receive him, the sun shining on their bare unpowdered heads. Vesey's hair was positively ruddy in the sun, as he noticed with affectionate pride. The guest embraced Lucian warmly on both cheeks, then turned to be presented to the brothers, to whom he bowed beautifully; low to George, a shade less low to Vesey. Juliana could not hear what they were saying (need it be said that she was watching from an upper window?). She could hear Lucian's voice, quick, low and merry, and once or twice the deeper and slower tone of Vesey, the harsher one of George, and, interspersed among them, a thin rivulet of sound, persistent, monotonous, from Monsieur le Duc de Saint-Aumerle.

An hour later she met him in the drawing-room whe
he was presented to Lady Chidleigh and the rest of th
family. He was as bland, as smooth as his miniatur
not quite as beautiful. He sat with elegance and eas
in one of the high-backed armchairs, his fingers playin
perpetually with the knob of his cane, which was carve
in the semblance of a negress's head, grinning to sho
two rows of seed pearls for teeth. It was an inventic
of his own of which he spoke with simple pride. No,
had not yet become the fashion, even in the Frenc
Court. It was too new, too daring. He ventured t
prophesy that it would not be for twenty, thirty, perhaj
even fifty years, that the world would be ready for suc
an innovation. Then all mankind would carry Ethi
pian canes, and he, the inventor, who had been the fir
to see how its proper carriage set off the length an
whiteness of the fingers, the turn of the wrist, would b
forgotten. It was the way of the world. Yes, he wa
something of a philosopher, but all the world now wa
philosophic. In France, now, they talked of nothin
else—philosophy and the return to nature. For his pa
he thought nature very pretty in her proper place. Th
maternal instinct was quite charming, but it was a pit
to encourage it too much. Half the young mothers
the French nobility now were nursing their own babie
In consequence, half the babies were dying of insufficie
nourishment. A pity, a great pity.

Lady Chidleigh thought it a pity for a young man t
talk of such matters at all within half an hour of h
presentation to the ladies of the household. No dou
it was the result of a different standard of delicacy, b
that in itself was another example of the inferiority
the nobility of France.

Lucian joined in the conversation and was askin
questions of his guest, who answered readily and crispl
They were talking of events and people that Juliana d

ot know. She ceased to listen, and she discovered
that the longer she watched the Duke's face the less it
appeared like a face and the more like a large, white egg.
She could not tell if he had ever looked at her or not.

The big enamelled and ormolu clock ticked and ticked.
Monsieur le Duc and his host talked and talked. Lady
Chidleigh bowed, occasionally smiled, occasionally made
an observation. George and Vesey concealed their
yawns, but not their glances of contempt and aversion.
Cousin Francis nodded sideways over his stick ; he often
fell asleep now in company. Aunt Emily fidgeted
nervously, not knowing whether to wake him or not.
Grandmamma Chidleigh stared before her, remote,
forbidding.

How long had they all sat like this ? Not very long.
An hour, perhaps an hour and a half. Why did it seem
so inexpressibly tedious ? It occurred to her that all
the figures in the great white and gold room were like
dolls in some mechanical contrivance that spoke and
looked and bowed when moved by wires—all except
Lucian, and he was not there, but behind them, laughing
at them. What an absurd fancy ! She shivered and
looked again at Monsieur le Duc. Had he looked at her
or not ?

She knew she should not look at him so much, but he
did not appear to notice her, so it could not matter.
She looked at the clock and this time noticed the hour.
It wanted nearly two hours to dinner. And then there
would be conversation again after dinner, all the evening.
She looked again at Monsieur le Duc and wondered if she
liked him better than Mr. Daintree. She did not know.
She did not know what she thought of him. She did not
know what they were saying. Was she always as vacant
as this ? How long his face was, and how white. No,
of course she meant how red. And how round—as round
as the clock. He must have dropped his cane—what

was that short black stumpy thing he held in his hand
"Look here, Milly," Monsieur le Duc was saying in
loud rasping voice, "when I say I'm going to smoke i
the drawing-room, I'm going to, do you hear?"

It was *not* Monsieur le Duc. Who was it? Wha
was this crammed, pink place? There was the cloc
surrounded by Cupids just the same on the mantelpiece
tick, tick, tick, tick—but oh! what were those tw
monstrous pink and white vases on either side of it
And where were all the family? She saw vaguely
woman's figure seated by the fireplace; but looked, no
at her, but at the man who sat in Monsieur le Duc'
chair. Yes, it was the same chair, and the room was th
same though so different. And the man—there was n
longer any doubt about it—he was the stranger whom
she had once before encountered in the courtyard.

As before, he was looking in her direction but did no
appear to see her.

"It's all nonsense," he was saying, louder and louder
"All damned nonsense. We're exclusive enough, aren'
we, feudal, old world? Shutting the gates at nin
o'clock and all the old feudal customs. And don't se
a soul——"

"I'm sure I wish we could, Oswald," interposed th
other figure, "but there's not a soul to see. Not a sou
that *is* a soul, as you might say."

"Well, there you are. What do I say? Exclusiv
enough, you bet, even if it isn't only us that does th
excluding—and yet there you go on and on——"

He had stopped and his face changed; it turned from
ruddy to purple, and the eyes became glazed. The
knuckles grasping the arms of his chair had turned to
round white knobs, and the fingers swelled below them.

"Oh, *Oswald*," said that thin, weary voice again
"you've gone and dropped your pipe. On your chair
And it's one of the things that went with the house—a

real antique. Whatever's the matter, Oswald? You look as though you'd seen a ghost."

Juliana felt herself quail before the abject terror in the man's face. An agony of fear beset her, unreasoning, unknowing fear. She put her hands before her eyes, rose slowly and tremblingly, and walked out of the open French window on to the lawn outside. She heard a strange harsh whisper behind her.

" Milly," said the man who sat in Monsieur le Duc's chair, " did you see anyone go out, Milly ? "

She walked across the lawn, not looking back at the house. When she had entered one of the paths at the side of the lawn, she began to run. She ran till she had left the gardens and was in the drive, and then she walked slowly again, holding her hands against her side and looking from right to left. There was no doubt about it, the drive was different.

And now she was sure that there had been differences in the gardens as she came through them. Surely there had been a strange flower-bed, scarlet and blue, under the great cedar ; and the fountain that her father had brought from Italy, had she passed it at the end of the cypress walk ? There had been a grey and crumbling stone that she had hardly noticed among the dark trees ; *that* could not have been the Italian fountain she knew, whose delicate shape shone so white in the sun. But she could not go back and make sure ; no, she could not.

She went over the little stone bridge ; that at least was the same, the same as when she had seen the small fair boy in Tudor dress, sitting astride the parapet, looking at the fishes in the stream below.

That had not frightened her, but she did not want to think of it now. She entered the drive again ; it was her own dear drive, it could not be different ; the gardeners had neglected it of late, that was all. Yes, they had neglected it shamefully, the branches needed cutting, but she had noticed that before. She remembered noticing that before. And the ragged-robin had been allowed to grow all over the edge of the drive. How pretty it was, even though it was a weed. She stooped to pick one or two of the longer stems, saying to herself: " Yes, it is all the same, it is precisely the same."

She walked on and on, not conscious of any weariness, though now she had come nearly to the end of the drive. There were the lodge gates in front of her. Yet it was odd that she should have come to the end of the drive. Had she missed Nurse's cottage while she was picking flowers ? Yes, it must have been so. She stood still, deciding that she would go straight back and find it. At that moment, she saw a figure reclining under one of the trees at a little distance, a slight brown figure, the back turned towards her.

Juliana clutched the ragged-robin, twisting the stems between her fingers. She knew at once that it was the girl whom she had seen before, from the windows of her closet, then in this drive, and then in the courtyard talking to the man whom she had seen but just now in Monsieur le Duc's chair.

She would speak to her, she would ask her who she was, what it all meant. She would be brave. Even if she were an apparition, she could not hurt her. And then she had liked her in that first glimpse of her on the lawn before she had had time to notice how strange was her appearance—yes, she had liked her and wanted to know her. She remembered now how that had been her first thought before even she had observed her clothes. She had seen the clear, frank gaze, the eager mouth, the delicate eyebrows. She had seen these things first.

But Sophia and Miss Hilbury had not seen her, and Sophia had looked straight at her. She must be an apparition, then. " Oh, I must speak, I must, I cannot

ear it," thought Juliana, rolling up the stems of the
ragged-robin between her fingers.

She approached the figure very softly. She did not
ant her to look round and see her coming, she did not
now why. But the girl in brown never looked round,
though Juliana now stood close behind her. She lay at
full length on her side, reading, her bare head propped
n her shapely though sunburnt hand. Juliana looked
own on the brown hair drawn loosely back from the face,
lowed to flop a little over forehead and cheek, and rolled
at the back of the head. She lay in that loose, shape-
ss brown coat, or whatever it was, as freely and as
arelessly as a boy, and, lying thus, it reached only a
ttle way below the knee. Juliana was so close to her
hat she could have touched her shoulder; she leaned
rward, meaning to speak, now, at once, but unable to
hink what she should say. As she did so, she saw over
he girl's shoulder, and saw what she was reading.

Juliana stood there, poised, her hand a little
utstretched, her head bent down over the recumbent
gure. Her breath had stopped, a black mist swam
efore her eyes, she wondered if she were fainting—if she
ad fainted some time ago and were only dreaming all
his that had happened since. The black mist swam
way, and with it the sensation of sickness that was
aking her eyes water and smart. Yes, she was coming
o herself, she would find that she had only fainted, and
reamed the rest.

But she found that she was still standing there, poised,
ver the recumbent figure, her hand still a little out-
retched, her head bent down, still gazing at the
andwriting, though brown and faded, of her own
ournal.

159

CHAPTER XV

JULIANA stirred and put her hand up to her forehea[d]
which felt cold and wet. It was a great effort to do s[o]
and before it had reached her forehead it was seized fro[m]
behind and covered with kisses—eager, hasty, breathle[ss]
kisses. She tried to move her head and found it w[as]
resting on somebody's knee, and a wet handkerchief [on]
her forehead.

" Thank God," said Mr. Daintree's voice.

" What has happened ? " she contrived to ask.

" You had fainted."

" Fainted ? I do not remember that. I have be[en]
asleep for a long time." She added drowsily, " Over [a]
hundred years."

" I was passing the lodge gates and saw you at the si[de]
of the drive. You lay so still, I could not wake you [at]
first. You must have fainted. Juliana, what h[as]
happened ? For God's sake tell me what has happened[."]

There was an agony of distress and anxiety in his voi[ce.]
She tried to raise herself, but with a firm though gen[tle]
movement he pressed down her shoulder on to his kn[ee]
again. Well, perhaps she was not yet quite stro[ng]
enough, and it was certainly very comfortable. S[he]
wondered what had happened.

" You were riding by, on the high road ? " she bega[n,]
and then something swam back into her brain. " T[he]
high road ? What was it like ? Was it differen[t ?]
Was it black and shining and a little curved ? "

160

" No, it was not different. What is it, child ? "

" I want to see it. I want to see the drive. Is it all precisely the same ? "

She felt herself shaking. His arm came round her shoulders, lifting her a little higher, and his voice sounded very calm and reassuring.

" It is all precisely the same. And now will you not tell me what it is all about ? "

But that was just what she could not do. Besides, for some reason or other, in this position she found it very difficult to remember. That was odd, for as soon as she was with Lucian she knew she would remember it all clearly and want to tell him.

" Can you not tell me ? Why can you not ? " he was urging.

" I think," she said, pursuing her own thoughts, " it is because you are not Lucian."

He started back from her.

" Ah, it is *he*, then——" he began in a voice that was unrecognizable. He stopped quickly, however, and was very still.

Juliana felt miserable and uncomfortable. She again tried to raise herself, and this time he did not prevent her. She sat up, looked round, and at the sight of her bewildered face his own softened a little.

" I am sorry if I startled you," he said. " I think you know that Lord Chidleigh and I are not friends."

" I regret it," said Juliana.

Mr. Daintree did not look as though he regretted it. He had sucked in his under lip in a way she had not seen him do before, so that his mouth made a thin, tight line across his face. His eyes were half shut and gave a quick, she thought an angry, glance at her as she spoke. She did not think just now that he had a nice way of looking at one. But the next moment he stretched out his hand and said : " I beg you, do not let me offend you.

F

Tell me, you love your brother Lucian very much, d
you not ? You would do anything that he wishes ? "

" It is my duty to obey his wishes."

" In some things, not in all. You also owe obedienc
to a higher authority."

" Do you mean to my mamma or to the Almighty ?

" I mean to God," he said simply, which seemed t
dispose of her reference to the Almighty as prim an
unreal. " Are you sure that Lord Chidleigh alway
wishes you to do what is right ? "

Was he thinking of the marriage to Monsieur le Duc
she wondered. Monsieur le Duc—what a long tim
ago—whose face was so round and red—no, of cours
she meant so white. And long, as long as an egg. C
was he thinking—but how could he know—
the experiments ? Were they not right ? She ha
wondered ; they were so very strange. And why did sh
now continue to see such unaccountable things ?

What had those experiments in the library to do wit
them, those bewildering, enthralling experiments
She remembered Lucian's strange excitement when sh
had told him of her first glimpse, from the windows
her closet, of the girl in brown. She could glow no
herself at the thought of his triumph. He had not see
her, yet he knew what she looked like, and he seemed t
claim a share in that vision, he had spoken of " prepara
tions "—later, he had spoken of his " industry " and he
" parts." What did it, what could it all mean ?

She felt the blood flow to her face and leave it in th
quick alternations of excitement and fear. She ha
gone far away indeed from Mr. Daintree, and now as sh
raised her eyes she found that his were fixed upon he
with disconcerting intensity. They seemed to see righ
through her. What did they see to make him look s
grave and so severe ; and so anxious, so terribly anxious
She did not want him to look at her like that. It mad

162

her feel ashamed, she did not know why, and frightened, she did not know of what. It was not of Mr. Daintree. Could it be of Lucian ?

" For God's sake, speak ! " he broke out suddenly. " What is it you think of as you sit there, what is it you are afraid of ? What is this power he has over you ? How can he call to you from the terrace and you know it far down in the park ? Your face—yes, by Heaven it was that !—how was it your face grew like his for a moment—just now—but just now——"

He had sprung to his feet and catching her by the arms he dragged her up till she was standing facing him, white and amazed at this new creature that confronted her. He stood there, holding her by the shoulders, that ight line across his face again that changed it from its pleasantly familiar aspect to something alien and terrible. He was speaking agitated, incoherent words. He spoke like a man in mortal fear, and again and again he asked her : " What is it you are afraid of ? "

Suddenly he caught her to him and kissed her. She tried to break from him, but he held her and was speaking again, though very differently now, in a low voice that he recognized, though immeasurably more tender than he had ever heard it. " Juliana, I cannot let you go. My love, I want to keep you always. I would keep you safe. Juliana, sweetest, dearest, forget that I frightened you, that I asked you more than you can answer. Forget it all—yes, all—all that you fear, all that you hate, et love. Come with me. Come now—on my horse. will take you to Crox Hall and we will start at once for Scotland. It is the only possible way. Juliana, you know I would never urge such a course on you if—if it ere not—Oh, God, do not cry like that ! "

But Juliana could not at once stop crying. She was red, so tired, she would like to sleep for over a hundred ars—no, not for that, not for a hundred years. And

here was Mr. Daintree of all people urging an elopement
on her ! Mr. Daintree, so grave, so quiet, so elderly, a
widower whom she had known all her life. She tried
hard to think of him as she had known him all her life.
But it was impossible since he had kissed her. How he
had kissed her ! She would like to do what he told her
and not have to decide nor think about anything. But
an elopement ! Even Mamma, who favoured the match,
would be scandalized. And Lucian—she shivered.

"You are my dear, sweet, pretty little sister," hummed
in her head. But not in the tender, mockingly caressing
tones in which Lucian had said it. No, it was said
slowly, mockingly caressing still, but cruelly so.

"I *cannot* come with you," she said, and sighed.
She had disengaged herself from his arms. She stood
leaning against the trunk of a tree, her face averted.
As soon as she had spoken she forgot what she had said.
An extreme lassitude and vacancy of mind had come
over her ; it was an effort to remember what they were
talking about.

"You did not say that as though you wished it," said
Mr. Daintree.

"I do wish it. I wish to be left in peace. I will do
nothing to cause a breach between my brother and myself. I intend to follow his wishes and abide by his
choice. It is not only my duty but my desire. If you
have any consideration or regard for me, sir, you will best
show it by leaving me."

Juliana was herself amazed at the cold and fixed
determination of her tones. She did not think she had
felt like that a minute or so ago. But now she sounded
as though she actually disliked Mr. Daintree. Well,
no doubt she did, since he persisted in troubling her. He
had no right to try and persuade her to defy Lucian's
wishes. It was odd how vividly Lucian's face had come
before her mind just before she spoke. She had actually

rub her eyes to make sure that he was not there in
ont of her. He had looked straight into her eyes, and
s lips were parted as though to speak. Almost she
d expected to hear him speak instead of herself.

She saw Mr. Daintree's face flush dark red ; he looked
her for one instant, then turned and strode away very
st. She felt no compunction, though there had been
in and bewilderment behind the anger in his eyes.

It had been a dreadful anger. Even her father, whose
ges had been so terrible, had never looked so. Yet
e had felt no fear when he looked at her. She could
el nothing. She wandered away through the trees in
e direction of the house, and entered the gardens. She
oticed that there was no flower-bed under the great
dar on the lawn. The trees, the flowers, the statues,
l were the same as she had always known them. She
ght to feel glad, though she could not remember why,
t she could feel nothing. Nothing but an intense
eariness.

She saw someone in a mulberry-coloured coat come
own the steps of the terrace towards her. It was Vesey.
e called out before he came up to her—" Julie—come,
lie. What's happened to you ? It's almost dinner
ne. Lucky you, to be a girl—pretend to feel faint and
p out through the window. They've been at it ever
nce, chatter, chatter, chatter."

" Is Lucian there still ? " asked Juliana. She knew
at she must see Lucian soon, that she had a great deal
tell him, though at the moment she could hardly
member what it was, and had no wish to make the
fort.

" Lucian ? Yes, of course. You're always with
cian now. There *was* a time——"

He finished by mumbling something under his breath
at she could not catch.

" Vesey ? " She touched his sleeve anxiously.

He looked hard in front of him and spoke the though
that had been too absurd and childish to say before.

" Oh, well, I used to be your favourite brother onc
You liked me a deal better than George, didn't you ? "

" And I do now, dear Vesey "

" Not better than Lucian, though, who's turned
from God knows where after not being seen for year
and upsets all our plans and wants to marry you to
filthy toad of a Frenchman—not better, not as much
Lucian, hey ? "

She had always known Vesey's was a jealous natur
But that he could be jealous of her ! When she ha
been in the nursery George used to try and bully her an
Vesey would prevent him. She had adored the
handsome brother who was kind to her. Also, once,
had floated paper boats with her on the stream. Squa
ting under the little bridge, they had baptized them
the names of kings and queens and started them on the
voyage " to the river and then to the sea." He ha
made her promise that she would never tell anyone
this, for he was ashamed of playing with a sister so mu
his junior.

And for years she had never thought of all this.
might have been because for years Vesey had nev
thought of her, but that did not occur to her. S
tucked her hand under his arm and said ," Dear Vesey.

She could not think of anything more to say. S
was remembering the boats under the bridge and h
the one she had called " King Edward VI " had be
wrecked by a branch in the stream. But Vesey foun
it quite enough and told her she was a good girl.
was surprised to discover how fond he was of her, a
reflected what an excellent husband and parent he wou
make.

They were all in the drawing-room as she had l
them. In answer to Lady Chidleigh's inquiries, s

said she had felt faint and gone out to take the air. She looked at the clock, at its fat gold Cupids, and at all the things on the mantelpiece. She could not remember what she was looking for, but she knew that she was glad it was not there.

Monsieur le Duc de Saint-Aumerle sat in the high-backed armchair and talked and talked. She looked at his face and was glad to see that it was long and white, like an egg. Of course it was so. Why should it be different ? And of course it was a cane that he carried, a long ebony cane with the knob shaped like a negress's head.

" Conversation ? " Monsieur le Duc was saying, " but, my dear madam, there is no conversation nowadays. Not even in France. I assure you, it is a lost art."

She looked from him to Lucian, who had started as their eyes first met, and was now looking intently at her. Suddenly she remembered all that had happened, all that she had to tell him. The inert weight that had hung on her thoughts fell from her. She felt alert, vigorous and eager, tingling with excitement at the thought of sharing with Lucian the extraordinary events of the last—two hours, was it ? There was no fear now, nor dismay, but triumph such as Lucian himself had shown when she had first told him of her adventures. For, with Lucian's eyes upon her, she felt there was little she had to tell. He *knew*. That was the most amazing adventure of all, that they should share this secret with no word passed between them. How could she ever for one moment have wished to marry Mr. Daintree ? To be shut up in his great country house where nothing would ever happen any more than it had ever happened in this house—until Lucian came.

The long hours at her flower-paintings, at her bead embroidery, at her journal (more occupied in wondering what to write than in writing) how could she have endured them all this time and never comprehended their unutterable ennui? Surely bewilderment, even terror, was better than that vacuity. Besides, she was not frightened when Lucian was there, Lucian who shared this secret with no word passed between them, a secret from all the stiff figures who sat round them and talked and talked. She had much ado to keep herself from laughing aloud with this strange new elation, as she looked at Monsieur le Duc in the chair where the creature called Mr. Harris had sat.

CHAPTER XVI

THE Chidleighs' distinguished guest spent the next day in bed. He was not fatigued by the journey, so his valet assured Lady Chidleigh ; it was merely in order to pass the time. No, he required neither books nor company, he was agreeably occupied with his embroidery.

" My master is passionately attached to his embroidery frame," said Chrysole, regarding Lady Chidleigh with his melancholy, anxious eyes.

Sophia, who had ridden over in the hope of seeing the rare foreigner, broke into an ill-suppressed titter.

" Why, what in the world can the man be like ? " she demanded in an undertone of Juliana.

" Oh ! " She drew a deep breath of relief as Lady Chidleigh left the room to interview the cook on the sub-ject of Monsieur le Duc's meals. " Vesey says he is the strangest little creature, and not like a man at all. Is it true that he is but five feet high and looks at Lucian as though he is afraid of him ? "

" It is not in the least true," said Juliana, with some annoyance. " Because Vesey is over six feet himself, he thinks that everybody beneath that height is a dwarf. And, as for looking at Lucian as though he were afraid of him, I have never observed him look at anyone at all, and certainly not with any expression."

" What, not even at you, my love ? "

" No, indeed, not at me. I know because——"

" Because ? Because——? "

" Because *I* looked at *him*, more than Mamma would
have approved."

There was a rush of laughter from them both.

" And tell me, my dear," urged the eager Sophia, " do
you like him, can you fancy him as a lover ?   Oh, yes,
know that he has come here to court you.   Vesey may
look as glum and reserved as he likes, but I know, I know
Poor Mr. Daintree !   A Duchess of France !   It sound
mighty fine, does it not ? "

" Sophy, how you rattle !   Tell me, is there any mor
talk of the water party ? "

Sophia's attention was easily diverted.   There ha
been talk of the water party for over three months, an
it was always certain there would be more talk of th
water party.   It was to be given by one Mr. Bolsove
who was immensely rich—he had had an uncle in th
Indies, and was as yellow as if he had always lived i
them himself.   'Twas true he had visited them, and
so Sophia informed her cousin on this occasion—som
said he had a whole harem of Indian wives there, and a
as yellow as a guinea.   Was it possible, asked Julian
that if you have several wives all like each other yo
would grow like them ?   Sophia thought not.   Nor w
she certain about the Indian wives or, at any rate, tl
exact number.   In any case, Mr. Bolsover gave the mo
delightful parties, and all the young people in tl
countryside would be going to this one.

They would progress down the river in a monstro
barge and stop at Steynes, and at Lord Haversham
place, and have a cold collation there in the evening-
yes, it was to be a " *fête-champêtre*," sitting about on tl
lawns like shepherds and shepherdesses, and they wou
walk about the beautiful grounds and feed Lord Have
sham's famous gazelles, and they would have fiddlers a
dance till quite late, probably till midnight.   Sopl
thought it might be one o'clock before they came hon

he had bought the sweetest puce-coloured ribbons—a
ifle sober, but then her gown was so brilliant they would
e the very thing for it. Did not Juliana think so ? 〈 Or
id she favour the straw-colour ? And what would her
arling Juliana wear for the occasion ? Juliana was
rompt with her decision.

" Dear Fanny has sent me a white China silk from the
〉wn. It is embroidered all over with little silver
〉wers and Lucian says I must wear nothing with it but
 white hat *à la bergère*."

" Lucian ? Does he take an interest in your
othes ? "

" Oh, yes, indeed he does, and his taste is always
〉rrect."

They chattered on in the deep window seat where the
in shone in a bright chequer-work through the branches
 the great elm outside. Above them, in the chief guest
iamber, the sunshine penetrated only in thin golden
ripes between the brocade window curtains.

In the bed, hung with crimson, as large as a small
om and towering almost to the ceiling, sat a slight,
ooping figure in a turban and a blue night-rail, drawing
ie threads of gleaming coloured silk through an em-
·oidery frame. A couple of lap-dogs lay curled on the
·d ; about the room Chrysole, the valet, moved noise-
ssly, anxiously. In the room only one thing could be
·ard—a very low, tuneless humming like the humming
 a gnat. It was Monsieur le Duc singing to himself as
· worked.

The stripes of sunlight moved gradually towards the
all, faded finally from the room. Then, when candles
·re lit in the great rooms below, Monsieur le Duc
·peared like some beautiful bright moth, arrayed in the
·est clothes, his fingers fluttering ceaselessly about the
·rved head of his " Ethiopian inamorata," and played
·rds with the family till far into the night.

171

This was the order of his day during his visit. H
was completely incurious and had no wish to see hi
friend's estate and countryside, nor even the rest of hi
house. Nor did he evince any more interest in th
neighbours that were invited to meet him. Cards wer
his company, he said, and they most certainly were hi
friends. George and Vesey found their contempt fo
" the feather-brained foreigner " rudely shocked by hi
uncanny skill, a skill that had disagreeable consequence
to themselves. As for Lucian, who had been acclaime
on his return as the most brilliant card player in th
countryside, he seemed quite accustomed to lose mone
to Monsieur le Duc, whether at ombre or piquet or a
whist. Juliana, who was not allowed as yet to pla
would sit on her stool and watch and wonder how it wa
that any man could be cleverer with the cards tha
Lucian. The odd thing was that while Lucian wou
laugh and joke about it when he lost, and take it as th
most natural and pleasant thing in the world, Monsie
le Duc seemed positively to dread winning from hir
and would try and avoid playing with him, and when l
won be quite out of countenance.

It was very dull for Juliana. " If it is like this in l
own house, I have no wish to marry him," she said
Lucian, " and he certainly appears to have no wish
marry me. I might have been married to him for t
years already, for all the attention he pays me."

" Admirable. That is a foretaste of how you will
able to speak when you are married. You foolish chil
do you imagine that your life will be to sit in a corn
and watch your husband play ? You will hold a gre
position at the French Court. I know that there is
one there as beautiful as you will be—or as brilliant a
in a little time, you will be. Oh, not with a flashin
obvious brilliance. You will hold your own in your o
way, a way new to them, that will surprise and encha

172

them. In England you might have wealth as great, but not that power and position, the dazzling liberty that you would have in the French Court."

" Liberty," said Juliana thoughtfully.

" Yes, liberty," repeated her brother, whose eyes were twinkling so very brightly that she wondered if he were laughing. " A liberty that I trust you will employ by seeing what you can of an idle, sauntering brother who prefers wasting his time in the French capital to anywhere else. I need hardly remind you that if you had married Mr. Daintree you would have been permitted to see scarcely anything of a relative that he dislikes and distrusts so much."

" Why does he, brother ? "

" Why ? Because he is jealous of me. Oh, no, it is not at all absurd, but quite natural. He fears my influence over you."

" And have you influence over me ? "

" I hope so."

" Why ? Why do you hope it ? What do you wish to do with me ? " She put her fingers over her eyes to shut out his merry, searching glance, as she tried to think of all the questions that she had wanted to ask him at other times and could never remember when she was with him.

" I wish——" She began again, " Can you not tell me ? What use or amusement can I be to you ?"

" And I am to tell you that ! My pretty sister, is it your humility that prompts such questions ? "

" No," said Juliana stoutly, " it is my good sense. I cannot pretend to be an equal companion to you, brother. What is it, then, that we share, and why is it that when you are here I sometimes go—go where I do not know—" She grew confused. It was of no use. She was stupid and blundering, and Lucian understood everything so much more clearly than she could express it. He understood now, for he took her in his arms very kindly and reassuringly.

" Would you be less afraid if I came too ? " he asked. " I tell you I would come if I could."

He spoke these last words with a bitter intensity that astonished her.

" What," he continued, " are you surprised that I should find this life tedious ? Oh, I am not speaking only of life here at Chidleigh. I have travelled since I was fifteen, I have done all that I wished, there is nothing left for me to try or to discover. Paris, London, Rome, Vienna are as dull as Chidleigh, the people there as interminably the same. I am twenty-six, and I am faced with the prospect of finding nothing new to do for the rest of my life. I am not blessed with the resigned spirit of Saint-Aumerle, who, comprehending that there is nothing now left that can divert him, stays in bed and does embroidery in order to pass the time. It is bad enough to be the slave of time, space and circumstance, but added to that we are born in so smug, self-satisfied and prosperous an age that there is not the slightest chance of our living to witness any change in it. When we are old we shall be what our fathers and mothers have been and there's an end."

" Lucian ! Mamma is always telling me that the present age is the most enlightened the world has yet seen."

" Juliana, that is exactly my complaint against it. It is so enlightened that it can wish for nothing better. We are at the pinnacle of civilization and can only hope to remain exactly where we are. Everything is entirely satisfactory, therefore poetry is dead, religion is démodé, enthusiasm is worse than vulgar, it is ridiculous, the supernatural is for children's tales, patriotism for troublesome scoundrels, and the Hanoverians remain heavily planted on the throne."

Juliana looked up, her eyes shining.

" Oh, but," she said, " I know, I have felt so too, indeed I have. I have longed and longed not to have been born in so dull an age, an age when nothing can ever happen and everything is always precisely the same."

" Yet you would marry Mr. Daintree and go on being always precisely the same," he replied quickly.

" I would *not*. But for that matter, if I married Monsieur de Saint-Aumerle——"

" Monsieur de Saint-Aumerle is a cypher," he interposed contemptuously. " If you marry him you will be free to do exactly as you please."

Juliana was silent. She was not certain that she wished to marry a cypher. Presently she said, " It was not so that you spoke of him to me on the terrace."

He shrugged his shoulders. The animation of disgust that had lit up his face when he spoke of his own times had died out, and left his eyes with that dull, opaque look that sometimes seemed to cover them as with a film.

Juliana looked up at him as he lounged against the window-seat where she was sitting. She noticed that there were many lines in his face ; at this moment he had the appearance of a man prematurely old. She put up a hand and timidly touched his arm.

" I should be glad if I could be of use or amusement to you, brother," she said.

That evening when Juliana retired to bed, she found she did not need the glance and pressure of the hand with which Lucian bade her good night to tell her that she should meet him in the library, as before. It had grown unnecessary for him to tell her things. She knew.

As Lucian turned from her she thought that the pale blue eyes of Monsieur le Duc, which never seemed to look at anyone, had been looking at them. She did not see him look, nor look away, so that she had no reason for thinking so. In any case, it was of no importance.

CHAPTER XVII

THE full moon had risen above the trees in front of th
library windows, and in its light the lawn outside looke
a pale and unsubstantial grey as though it were the sky

As before, Juliana sat in one of the armchairs whic
had been drawn up with its back to the table and facin
the closed windows. Lucian had blown out all th
candles but one on the table, and had shaded that, so tha
she could now see the moonlight in the room, three path
of light from the three windows. The path from th
centre window reached just to her feet and shone on he
green and silver shoes, while her white dress was gre
in the shadow beyond the moonlight.

Lucian did not appear to have stirred since he ha
blown out the candles. He was standing a little wa
behind her, as before. She did not know what he wa
doing. The room was very still.

She seemed to be looking into immeasurable gre
space, for the wall and windows in front of her had dis
appeared. Then something small and white passed i
front of her, across the greyness. At first she thought i
was an egg, then she saw that it was the face of Monsie
le Duc, some way off, with the eyes not quite closed, an
a thin red rim showing beneath the lids. It was gon
before she could understand what made it look s
strange, and the space before her was blank again.

Then, suddenly and violently, another face presse
through the obscurity, came nearer, close in front of he

stared and gaped at her. The vague immensity rolled away, she saw the French windows of the library before her again, the branches of trees outside them, sharp and black against the moonlit sky, and, outside the window, that same gaping, staring face, the mouth twisted now as though it were shrieking aloud. Yet no sound could be heard. The stillness was as thick, as impenetrable as before. That strange yet familiar thing outside the window raised hands and seemed to strike against the glass, yet again no thud nor rattle could be heard.

In one movement Lucian flung himself across the room, but before he had reached the window the intruder disappeared as suddenly and, it seemed, as violently as it had come. He tore open the window and rushed outside. Juliana heard his steps running swiftly through the garden, she heard him calling, and then she heard nothing.

She found that she was icy cold and shaking from head to foot. She pressed her hands to her face. " I am afraid—afraid," she said in a low moan. Then she made a discovery that increased her fear. " *She* meant me to be afraid. She was trying to speak to me, to warn me. What did she wish to say ? "

She dared sit still there no longer. She rose and walked about the room, in and out of the three paths of moonlight, her dress now white, now grey, in the shadow, her shoes gleaming on the dark floor.

She was repeating words to herself, as though she were anxious to tell herself clearly what it was she feared. " It was that same girl. She haunts this house. And she comes nearer. She wishes to enter."

She walked more slowly, still repeating the last words. She looked towards the windows, wondering when Lucian would return, then went to the open window and looked out. Would he not come when called, even as she had come to him on the terrace ? She wanted him so much. "Lucian, Lucian," she called at last, aloud.

But the moonlight lay still on the lawn between the black yew trees, and the air was still. There was no shadow of an approaching form, no sound but the churr of a night-jar far away.

It was inconceivable that out of so still a night there should have come that face, distorted in a terrified anxiety that was for her, Juliana, and not herself. She sank again into the armchair and remained there with head averted from the windows.

She heard the door-handle being turned behind her. But Lucian had locked it; no one could get in. She did not raise her head. There came a persistent scratching, clicking noise at the door. She was now too frightened to go and see what it was. She stayed there in her rigid position, her hands over her face.

Suddenly, without her having heard its approach, a quick, light step that she knew came in at the window in front of her, and at the same moment she heard the door flung open behind her. She took her hands from her face and turned her head. Lucian was just behind her and the room was much lighter, but she could not see who had come in, for Lucian was leaning against the back of the chair between her and the door. She knew that he wished her to remain still.

"These are strange manners," he was saying coolly, "to force the lock of a door that you find closed against you. I do not wish to be disturbed."

"A thousand pardons," said the thin, clear voice of Monsieur le Duc.

"Go—and at once," replied his host.

There was silence, so deep that it seemed to have lasted for hours. Then suddenly she heard Monsieur le Duc laugh. It was the first time she had ever heard him laugh. It was a horrible sound, thin and high, and for some unknown reason it made her feel very cold.

" But yes," he said, slowly and distinctly, " I can see very plainly the little green and silver shoes there in the moonlight."

Lucian was quite still. Now that she had been seen, should she rise or keep where she was ? But there was no need to decide, for Monsieur le Duc came forward to the windows so that he looked at her and she at him. He wore his blue night-rail and turban, in one hand he carried a lighted candle and in the other his sword.

" Yes," he said, speaking now very fast. " My friend, Lord Chidleigh, has had uses for us both. I see it well. You go now on his errands as I have done. You go far, very far, farther than I. Your spirit is the better for the purpose—the spirit of a young virgin, a pure child. Mine he has used till it withered. I am not a man—I am a dead instrument. And now I am to be united to you so that your husband may not stand in your way—you shall be free to go where your brother wishes. You may go farther yet, so far that you never return. You may go——"

" Lucian ! " She turned in an entreating question to where he lounged against her chair. " What does he mean ? "

" Nothing, my dear. His spirit, as he is pleased to call it, has never known what it is to be fresh, and there-ore could not be withered by me. For some little time I gave him a new interest by employing him on my own pursuits. He was not much use as he has very correctly informed you. Now that he has wearied of it, as of all else, his spirit is exactly what it was before, that is to say practically nothing. You may now leave us, Juliana, and go to bed."

But Juliana was looking at Monsieur le Duc whose face seemed to have grown smaller and narrower as

179

though it had been screwed up. He said almost in a whisper :

" I serve your purposes no longer, Lord Chidleigh."

Juliana wanted to shriek out, to tell her brother to escape while yet he could, so dreadful was that look on the face of Monsieur le Duc. The next instant she did indeed cry out, for there was a gleaming flash before her eyes as their guest, without warning, lunged at Lucian. There was a sharp sound behind her chair, Monsieur lunged again, but this time the sword clashed on steel. She sprang up.

Monsieur le Duc was leaning against the wall, his hands to his throat. Lucian stood in front of him, his drawn sword in his hand, and the point of it was red. The Frenchman's eyes stared, his mouth gaped. He was breathing with a shrill whistling noise such as Juliana had never heard.

" Lucian," she stammered. " Lucian ! "

" It is done now," said her brother.

He wiped the point of his sword on his lace handker-chief, then rammed it back into its sheath. But Juliana still did not understand. It had all happened so quickly She had thought it was Lucian who was hurt, perhaps killed. The Frenchman could not be badly hurt, there was no wound to be seen, no blood. Yet his face was ghastly and he was staggering ; he could stand no longer Lucian helped him to the chair where Juliana had sat His hands had fallen to his side and revealed a narrow red wound in his throat that bled hardly at all.

" What can we do ? " said Juliana. " The doctor— some cordial—Mamma——"

" They would none of them be of any use," said Lucian " it is done, now."

Monsieur le Duc looked up at him and his lips moved but no sound came. Then in a low, voiceless whisper he succeeded in saying : " I will not forget."

There was a rattle in his throat, his head fell back. Lucian bent over his face, then pressed the eyelids down over the staring eyes. But they were not quite closed, and a thin, red rim showed beneath the lids.

" He is dead," said Lucian.

He remained standing by the chair, looking down at the dead man, and presently he spoke again, the words dropping from him slowly, consideringly, as though he were weighing the matter with himself.

" I once saved his life," he said, " and I saved it in more ways than one. Since then I was his master. He did what I chose. And now he would have done so no longer—he had reached the breaking point—very suddenly. I did not think he would do that so suddenly. It was foolish of me. It is well I killed him for he would not have been safe after that. But I am sorry that you should have been here."

She accepted his statement without wonder or attempt at comprehension. She was too much stunned for that. Monsieur le Duc had seen her shoes in the moonlight and had laughed. He had attacked Lucian and Lucian had killed him.

These events were acted over and over again in her mind without meaning, without sequence or connection. As isolated sounds and pictures they repeated themselves before her until it seemed that she had stood there for some hours looking at the figure in the chair.

She had been taken into the room to see her father when he was dead, but that had been so different.

She heard Lucian's voice speaking to her again, but she did not hear what he said. He stood in front of her and, taking her by the shoulders, thrust her gently into a chair. She shuddered as he touched her, but his eyes were fixed on hers and presently she had to look at them. They were close to her, two hard, dull pebbles. " You will sleep now," he said, " and forget." The eyes receded until they were mere points, motionless, devoid of light and colour. She saw nothing else, and the sights and sounds that had been so vividly imprinted on her mind faded into a blurred and painful impression. Then even that disappeared.

CHAPTER XVIII

JULIANA woke late the next morning. She would have liked to have slept again for she was very tired, and she was sure she had had bad dreams though she was glad she could not remember them. But she wondered that Molly had not brought her chocolate, for it was long past the time for it. She sat up in bed and listened. There was some commotion going on downstairs. People were hurrying, running up and down, calling in an odd, subdued way. She began to tremble violently, and pulled at the bell, tugging it persistently until Molly burst into the room, her eyes very round, her mouth open, her usually red cheeks quite pale.

" Molly, what is it ? " cried Juliana. " I am sure something dreadful has happened."

" Oh, miss, the most dreadful, alarming thing that ever could have happened—and in this house too She had an absurd feeling that she knew what the girl was going to say, that she was only waiting for her to confirm it. But of course she did not ; and how tiresome Molly was, standing there gasping and sobbing and repeating : " In this house—never should have thought it possible—all be murdered in our beds next."

" *Will* you tell me what has happened, girl ? " said Juliana, with more severity than she had ever yet addressed her maid.

" Indeed, miss, nobody knows yet what it is that's happened, but all that's certain is that the Frenchman went to his master's room with his chocolate, all just as usual, this morning and drew the bed curtains and "— she paused with a deep, dramatic breath—" there was no one in the bed."

" No one in the bed ? "

" No, miss. Monsieur the Duke has disappeared."

Juliana lay back on her pillows with an extraordinary sense of relief. Somehow she had expected Molly to say something quite different, she did not know what exactly, but she was glad to hear that all that had happened was that Monsieur le Duc had disappeared.

" He is sure to come back," she said. " Probably he did not go to bed at all last night but set out on some adventure."

" Oh no, miss, he went to bed most certainly, for the Frenchman put him to bed as usual, and such a work as it is too, he tells us, having to rub cream into his face each night with his finger-tips to keep away the wrinkles, and the dressing table a litter of cosmetic jars, for all the world as though he were a lady ; but there it is, he put him to bed and drew the curtains."

" He may have got up and dressed afterwards," said Juliana. " It is what he would have done if he did not wish his movements to be known." She was not shy of discussing this with her maid. Such escapades were recognized to be not infrequent amusements among idle young gentlemen.

" But it's not so," said Molly, " for all his clothes are there in the room where the Frenchman—I never can get my tongue round his name—put them last night, he says, and all that the Monsieur put on, if he did get up and put them on, was his blue night-rail and the turban night-cap that he wears when he sits up in bed to do his embroidery, the nasty, lady-like creature, and his slippers and his sword and the candlestick that stands by his bed, that's gone too, but everything else just as it

ould be. They have searched the house, every room,
very nook and cranny, for there's no knowing but that
e might have come in drunken after a debauch, as you
ery properly suggested, miss, and fallen asleep in any
dd corner, like the gentleman Bessie Pratt of Mud
reen was maid to who would be found sound asleep in
e broom cupboard with his head in the dustpan after
night of it at the ' Saracen's Head ', but then, no gentle-
an, surely, not even a foreigner, could step down in the
iddle of the night to an inn, or anywhere else for that
atter, in his bed-gown and night-cap. No, he's been
arried clean off out of this very house by one as we know
othing of, the Devil himself, maybe, and who's to be the
ext, that's what I want to know. If we can't lie safe
a our beds——"

" Oh, Molly," sighed Juliana in weariness.

" There, my poor lamb, my pretty, I've frightened
ou, and you who are to be betrothed to the French duke,
all they say downstairs is true, but it's good riddance to
ad foreign rubbish, that's what I say, and why shouldn't
 young lady marry a countryman of her own when
ere's many a one that would eat their hearts out for her.
nd to think that you haven't had your chocolate yet ! "

She bustled off to get it, while Juliana, with closed eyes,
ondered what dreams she had had last night that had
eemed so much more important than even the events of
is morning. But she could remember nothing since
e had gone to bed the previous night, after saying good
ight to them all in the drawing-room as usual. She
emembered how she had thought that Monsieur le Duc
ad been looking at her and Lucian as they had said
ood night. So that was the last time she had seen him,
r she did not think he would come back—no, she was
re he would not come back.

There was a tap at the door and Lucian came in with
e chocolate.

185

"I met Molly on the stairs," he said, "and told he I would bring it you and see how you are. She seeme concerned for you. Has this news upset you?"

He leaned against the foot of the bed and looked at he with brilliant, smiling eyes. He was paler than usua yet he seemed positively to exude life and vigour. He had evidently dressed in haste and his unpowdered ha fell loose on his shoulders. Juliana wished he would no look at her so piercingly. She felt even more tired tha she had done before and, just as he had handed her th chocolate, she had shivered unaccountably so that sh was still quite cold.

"I do not feel upset," she said. "It sounds ver mysterious, but no doubt there is some quite simpl explanation."

"No doubt," said Lucian.

"Have they searched the grounds yet?"

"They are now doing so. Two discoveries hav already been made. The candlestick, which was missin from his bed-side this morning, has been found near th garden door by the drawing-room, and the maids say was unfastened this morning, though they declare it wa left locked last night. Also, one of his bedroom slippe has just been discovered in the little summer-house dow in the park. It certainly appears that he left the hous of his own free will some time last night or this mornin I have given orders for the lake to be dragged next. I will be done this morning."

Juliana, who was leaning back with her eyes shu again, had a sudden clear glimpse of the face of Monsieu le Duc, small, as though it were at some distance, wit the eyes not quite closed and a thin, red rim showin beneath the lids. She wondered if that was what peop looked like who were drowned.

"You are not drinking your chocolate," sai Lucian.

She tried to do so but it required a great deal of effort. He sat beside her on the bed and insisted on feeding her with the spoon. Again she felt that strange shrinking as he laid his hand on her shoulder to steady her while she took the chocolate, and she thought he must have felt her shiver. But he did not seem to notice it, and was talking and laughing merrily over his success as a sick nurse. She began to laugh too. Every time that she opened her mouth to speak, he popped the spoon in and she had to close it. It became a contest between them, but Lucian was always too quick for her. That strange, foolish feeling had disappeared. Lucian was just the same as always; how silly it had been of her to fancy there was anything different in him. He did not care at all about the disappearance of one who was supposed to be his friend; but she had not expected him to care. It was she who had not been herself, but she was now, as she listened to Lucian's nonsense.

" It is annoying of Saint-Aumerle to disappear at this moment," he said. " I am in love, and that is no mood to make me relish a search for his insignificant person."

" In love ! Oh, brother, with whom ? "

" Why, with a girl not half as lovely as yourself, and yet she is a little like you too, and yet she is so different it is inconceivable that she should be in the same world— maybe she is not."

" Maybe you talk the strangest stuff, brother. Who is this girl, and are you very much in love ? "

" Oh, so-so. Not enough to keep me awake at nights, yet enough to dream of her when I am asleep. To tell you the truth, that is all I know of her, for she is an odd, capricious hussy who laughs in my face when I am dreaming, and will not favour me with a meeting when I am awake (though by your good offices I had almost secured one). Oh, she is a pert piece, and yet she is a little in love with me too, for she will not let me alone."

" But who is she, Lucian ? Pray tell me more of her."

" Who is she ? I often wonder. Open your mouth again."

" But where did you first meet her ? "

" Sister, you should not speak with a silver spoon in your mouth—it is one of the first principles of etiquette. Well, I began to meet her in my boyhood, and my first clear recollection of doing so was when I happened to be sitting on a throne of carved ivory and gold, watching the tortures of my enemies. At that moment they were that sheep-faced fool we had then as a tutor, Mr. Tebbit, and George, with whom I had just quarrelled, and the tortures had reached a peculiarly satisfactory point when I turned to see that tiresome and ridiculous child beside me. She was crowned also, and on a throne, but knowing that it was in play, and thus turning those elaborate executions to play also, and preventing my belief and pleasure in them."

" Oh, but what was it ? A dream ? "

" What should it be but a dream ? There was little else I cared to do, those long hours in the library, either awake or asleep. Tebbit slept sound enough I can tell you. Oh, my dreams were a sufficient occupation ! I was an Oriental despot, a Roman emperor, a mediæval magician. I indulged in pleasures and powers that raised me above the race of men and made me equal to the gods of the old fables.

" And into these gorgeous and horrible fancies, fancies that would quicken into apparent life and reality in my sleep, there would frequently appear this incongruous and absurd little figure in skimpy skirts up to her knees and untidy hair flying loose—and she would smile at me and all my dream company with an engaging air of friendliness, though I assure you it did not engage me then. Open your mouth."

"But, brother, I cannot understand. Surely you must have met her before you dreamed of her ? "

"Why should I not dream of her first and hope to meet her afterwards ? There is good authority for it in the fables. Your mouth, sister, your mouth ! That is right—a round, red O. Now the chocolate is going down your throat—I can see you swallow it. What a tiny throat it is, and the little hollow at the base—you should keep the chocolate there to fill it out."

"Dear Lucian, tell me some more. Why did she not engage you then ? "

"What—a brat of a girl, an interloper, a nuisance ! Her occasional intrusion into my most unbridled orgies was as disconcerting—to me—as the other untimely entry I told you of.

"But she would not comprehend that though a dream, it was all quite serious ; in fact, she would not comprehend that it was *my* dream and not hers. She treated me as an equal companion in an enchanting game, where I had been accustomed to reign as sole despot of my semi-infernal kingdom.

"Imagine what the hussy once had the impudence to tell me ! 'I make up stories to myself too,' said she, ' but mine are not as good as yours, and there is so little time at school.'

"At school ! At *school !* She compared my voluptuous and terrible imaginings, forsooth, to the stories that a schoolgirl makes up to herself ! "

"Then, brother, when did you begin to like her ? "

"Oh, how can I tell ? She improved, for as I grew older she did too. Besides, she provided a contrast that began to be piquant. She was like a raw and not very ripe apple in the midst of a banquet of cloying delicacies. Why will you not open your mouth ? "

" Indeed, I can take no more."

" So ? It is a pity. I was going to tell you one thing more."

" Oh, tell me, tell me."

" Not till you open your mouth. That is well. It was when I was still a boy. I had fallen sound asleep over my books at the library table and thought that she came softly in and sat down beside me and showed me a silly game on paper that one played by making noughts and crosses, and we laughed over it a great deal, and then she put her arm round my neck and told me to wake up and finish my lessons and run out of doors.

" I awoke with a start after that and could hardly believe I had not just seen a dark blue skirt whisk out through the door. It reminded me of another brat who once crept in with a cake for me under her apron. Do you remember her ? "

" Yes, brother."

" But she," continued Lucian, " had stood at the door, afraid, and had I not turned and called her she would have stolen out again without speaking to me. This other girl was different."

" Did you—prefer her—for being so ? "

Juliana wished she could have prevented those breaks in her voice. It was no wonder that Lucian was smiling so at her. Did he despise her for her former cowardice, her present jealousy ?

" I think I am learning to prefer my sweet sister to any creature in the world," he said, " but you must remember that this other creature has the advantage not to be in the world."

He was holding out the last spoonful of chocolate and now popped it into her mouth. Her lips closed on it, her laughing eyes raised to Lucian, reassured by the tenderness of his tones rather than his words. If Lucian *had* thought her a coward he did not appear to like her the worse for it now.

His fantastic talk of dreams had distracted her mind completely for the moment from the business of Monsieur le Duc. Her glance wandered round the room as her brother stood up with the empty cup in his hand ; it fell on the brocade shoes she had worn last night, now left carelessly on the rose and grey rug by the dressing-table. They arrested her attention and she remained looking fixedly at them. For an instant's flash she thought she had seen them, not dropped there on their sides on the rug, but placed primly together on a dark floor lit up by a patch of moonlight, and she seemed to hear Monsieur le Duc's high, monotonous voice.

" What has frightened you ? " asked Lucian, and then in the same breath, " Oh, you are looking at your little green and silver shoes ! They have a dissipated air, have they not—positively exhausted ? What were they doing last night, do you think, while you were asleep ? Perhaps they were dancing downstairs in the library, all by themselves, in a round, silver pool of moonlight. Or do you think they were even more adventurous and tripped out into the park, down to the summer-house, and saw what it was that happened to my friend Saint-Aumerle ? Or have they been farther yet, over a hundred years away ? "

Juliana could not help laughing, though the reference to the Duke shocked her, since all was still dark and uncertain about him. But it was like Lucian to make fun of everything ; he never minded making himself appear ridiculous and even childish.

" How absurd, brother ! " she said. " You have talked all this morning as though we lived in a fairy tale ! "

" And how do you know we do not ? " he demanded. " Is not life sometimes a fairy tale, a very fantastic fairy tale? I assure you that in my better moments I find it so."

When, by Lord Chidleigh's orders, they dragged the lake that morning, they found the body of the French duke, in his blue night-rail, with a heavy flag-stone tied round his neck. In his throat was a small wound caused by a sword or knife, or other sharp instrument, which the doctor declared to have been the cause of his death. The flag-stone was soon identified as coming from a pile of flags which had been laid together near the summer-house for the purpose of paving the paths in one of the formal gardens.

Lucian had not told Juliana the full extent of the discoveries in the summer-house. A small marble table in it had been overturned, and there were a few blood stains on the bench that went round the walls. It was Lucian who discovered these stains, which had been hidden by a cushion. The grass just outside the door had been pressed and flattened as though some heavy weight had been dragged across it not many hours since.

It seemed certain that Monsieur de Saint-Aumerle had left the house by the garden door near the drawing room, some time after he had retired to bed, and that he had gone down to the summer-house in the park in his bed-gown and slippers, leaving the candle with its tinder box near the door for his return. It was at once assumed that he had had an assignation with some village or gipsy girl, that being the only circumstance that could conceivably take a man out of his bed in the middle of the night to go down to a summer-house in the park. The general opinion was that he had there been stabbed either by some jealous rival or, perhaps, by the lady herself who may have failed to appreciate the quality of his attentions. The murderer must then have conceived the crude idea of concealing the body by throwing it into the lake, and conveyed it there either by carrying it or trundling it in a wheelbarrow. There were certainly marks of a wheelbarrow on the ground between the summer-house and the lake, but this did not help very much as barrows had been wheeled all over the grounds just lately during the reconstruction of the formal garden.

Lord Chidleigh at once instituted the strictest search for the murderer. It was considered significant that a small band of gipsies who had camped for the last week on Tindsley Common, about three miles off, had departed early that morning, none knew where. It was known that one of them was a strikingly beautiful girl. But how had Monsieur met her ? His habits were secluded and Chrysole absolutely foreswore any negotiations on his part of this delicate matter. Further, he refused to believe that his master would have taken the trouble to walk down to the summer-house for any girl on earth. But, in their turn, everybody else refused to believe him.

" We knew he could not really be like that," they said. " It was a mere affectation. No man stays in bed and does embroidery for choice. Depend upon it, it was a cloak to hide his real concerns. Yes. I always thought——"

When Lady Chidleigh told Juliana that the Duke's body had been found in the lake, the girl said stupidly, " No, it is not so. He was not drowned."

Lady Chidleigh agreed that he had probably been killed first, but asked what she had meant by saying that.

Juliana, however, could only say that she did not know, but she was sure it was not so. And she began to cry. Her mother was concerned, and wondered if she could possibly have felt any attachment to her cold and indifferent suitor, or if it were merely her missed opportunities of grandeur that had upset her. But Juliana, with her hands pressed against her tired and smarting eyelids, saw only a pair of green and silver shoes placed close together in a patch of moonlight that shone on the dark floor.

CHAPTER XIX

LUCIAN found it necessary to go to London shortly after this. He departed in excellent spirits, and again thanking Juliana for her " good offices "—in what, she did not know. She felt weary and depressed after he had left. It was not merely because of his absence, but because of an extraordinary difficulty that she found in fixing her interest, and even her attention, on any object. It was difficult to understand, or rather to listen to what was said to her.

Mamma reproved her for so often being " absent " ; it was a word that filled her with unreasoning dismay. Was it Mamma, or was it someone else, who had warned her she might go farther yet, so far she might never come back ?

" Indeed, Mamma," she said, " I do not wish to be absent. I desire above everything to remain where I am."

Mamma smiled indulgently at the odd remark. " Then, my love, surely you must hold your attention."

There was a great deal of talk to attend to, a great deal of talk. Talk about the mysterious death of Monsieur le Duc, talk about Charlotte's wedding, talk about Mr. Bolsover's water-party, which, it was decided, Juliana could still attend with decorum since there had been no public betrothal to the Frenchman.

Juliana thought there had never been so much talk. Charlotte and Sophia rode over, and various selections

of the Hilburys, Miss Hilburys, plain and pretty, wit
their rosy-cheeked schoolboy brothers.

Old Lady Bouverie and Miss Skeerness drove over, an
talked a great deal of scandal—somebody had marrie
her gardener and she was near on seventy—how richl
old Lady Bouverie chuckled, wagging her monstrou
feathers, her several pendulous chins wagging als
beneath her beaky nose ! It was an unfair advantag
to be so fat. Miss Skeerness' thin scream of laughte
could never convey the same enjoyment, though
expressed an appetite as ravenous as that of a starvin
seagull, for any floating scraps of scandal.

General Steynes and Lord Haversham and his ta‖
stooping, sweet-faced daughter, rode over and ha
nothing to say—they never had, but the Haversham
looked so gentle and kindly it was a pleasure to see them

Slovenly Lady Catherine Grey drove over, out c
powder, at four in the afternoon. She was a shockin
example, Mamma said, and so rude too, always gapin
and yawning and declaring she was wearied to deatl
though she had nothing to occupy her, not even a tast
for cards or gossip.

Rich Mr. Bolsover and his friend Mr. Chalmers roc
over—Mr. Bolsover very facetious and waggish ; dapp‹
Mr. Chalmers very gallant, flourishing his snuff-box an
his lace handkerchief, ogling Juliana with his roun‹
rolling blue eyes ; but their company was not so agreeab‖
as to prevent her taking a comfortable stroll by herse
in the park—there is her own word for it in the journa

A host of others rode and drove over ; in fact, now th‹
the long-continued fine weather had made the roads s
good there was a daily stream of visitors at Chidleig‖
who stayed generally for two or three hours or more, an
sat in the drawing-room or on the terrace or on the ste‖
before the house, and talked and talked.

And none of them and none of the family ev‹

appeared to notice the repeated noise of knocking that Juliana heard so often as she sat with them in the drawing-room or on the terrace or on the steps before the house—a noise of knocking, sometimes low, sometimes loud above their talk, and then a noise louder still, a terrible noise of cracking, rending, tearing, and then a crash, as of a great tree falling.

It came always from the direction of the drive. Juliana would turn her head to see what the others thought of it, but Mamma smiled her proudly secure smile, old Lady Bouverie nodded and wagged her chins, or Sophia chattered, or Mr. Chalmers paid a compliment with his triumphant air as who should say : " Now, who can better that ? " and none of them ever turned a head in the direction of the drive.

And they had just ridden up the drive and none of them had said a word to show that they had seen or heard anything unusual.

It was in those moments, when the noise of knocking was very loud, that she found it most difficult, and also most urgently necessary, to " hold her attention." She must hold fast to it with all her might, for in those moments her head swam for an instant as though she were giddy, and her surroundings, even the faces and voices round her, seemed, just for that instant, to alter strangely. Yes, she must try hard to hold fast to something, she was not sure what—something that all the time was trying to escape and elude her.

And Lucian did not come back. If only Lucian would come back.

It was remarkably fine for the day of the water-party ; Charlotte and Sophia, who were to go with them and come back for the night, drove over in the phaeton, with their maids in the vis-à-vis, at least two hours before they were to start, and prinked and preened like peacocks in front of Juliana's mirrors. Sophia's new puce-coloured ribbons were voted charming with her rose du Barri gown, and Charlotte had a most dashing hat with a fall of white and scarlet feathers at the back. After considering them in every posture, as though they had never seen them in the glass before, the cousins had leisure to declare that Juliana's silver-embroidered China silk was sweetly pretty, the most sweet, pretty thing in the world.

They had to go and show their finery to Lady Chidleigh and the Dowager. But Grandmamma, disturbed in her devotions, made no further comment than a verse from the psalm she was reading : " Man is a thing of naught ; his time passeth away like a shadow." It was a discouraging reflection for the beginning of a party.

But Sophia giggled and Charlotte declared, outside the door, that Grandma was an old put, and was rebuked for her coarseness, and certainly the spirits of the party appeared in no whit dashed as they set off, with Aunt Emily as chaperon, in the coach, and George and Vesey on horseback. They reached Mr. Bolsover's house on the river at twelve o'clock. An awe-struck " Oh ! " went up from the girls at the sight of the carved and gilded barge, monstrous, magnificent, under its scarlet awning, on the glittering sunlit river. Many people were already on board, walking slowly to and fro, their satins and jewels glowing with a fiery splendour in the hot red shadow of the awning.

Juliana at once envisaged a hooped and powdered Cleopatra sailing down the Cydnus to meet Antony, hundreds and hundreds of years ago, in just such a barge as this of Mr. Bolsover's.

All the guests had not yet arrived, and when at last they started the number on board was close on sixty. They moved down the river as far as Conway Place belonging to General Steynes, where they landed to explore the grotto and subterraneous passage while

nner was prepared on board. And then after dinner
they progressed as far as Lord Haversham's place on the
ver, where they landed again, " this time," says the
ournal, " in *detached* Partys " and roamed about the
ark, feeding the gazelles, while the sun set slowly in red
ad thunderous clouds, transforming the great, gaudy
arge into something dream-like and unsubstantial
oating on the river.

While the servants were preparing a slight cold colla-
on, the fiddlers struck up on a smooth lawn terrace by
he water's edge, and " the detached Partys " arriving
ere and there from among the trees at once began to
ance country dances and minuets. Juliana danced
ith Mr. Chalmers and Mr. Fokes, and twice with Mr.
olsover, and called with Augustus, the eldest of the
ilbury boys. She danced with the young gentleman
ho had formed a " detached Party " with her to feed
e gazelles in the park, and she danced with him two,
ree, four, yes, five times. He was a charming youth
hose dark, ardent eyes spoke his admiration boldly—
o boldly—but that was tempered by his shy, almost
eprecating smile. He wore the most elegant green and
ver waistcoat and pale green coat, and he danced
acefully. He was a Mr. Pangrie, staying with General
eynes, and Juliana had never met him before. She
ondered if she would ever meet him again.

The cold collation had been spread on the grass in a
ep, cool grove where the tall trees met overhead, and
e green dusk ended suddenly in an open view of the
ver and clear, evening light. Juliana thought it just
ch a grove as must have sheltered the pastoral feasts
Colin and Phyllis, Strephon and Chloe. Others must
ve had the same thought, for everyone began to be
ry merry about silly swains, fair nymphs and faithful
epherds, and tried to talk in character about their
cks and herds and broken hearts. Mr. Pangrie, who

199

was very attentive, addressed her with his modest smile as Daphne or as Amaryllis, and besought her not to transform herself into a tree or fountain, as he handed her the chicken in aspic.

The servants had retired, but the fiddlers continued to play at a little distance among the trees ; tunes from the Italian opera, and old-fashioned airs to which some of the company sang as they felt inclined.

They sat on the grass, the ladies on India shawls and scarves that they had brought to protect them from the damp ; they looked like great bell-shaped flowers dropped here and there under the trees. The colour faded from their bright dresses as the twilight deepened in the grove ; only the cold white statue of the naked Venus still showed sharp and clear above them on her pedestal.

The laughing voices had hushed a little, and those who sang, sang more softly. " Indeed," wrote Juliana afterwards in her journal, striving to fasten on what she could of that strange, happy day, " the whole of this appear'd like the Scene in a Play." It was the nearest way she could find to express her sense of its fugitive and magic charm. She would not have been surprised if, when next she had looked up, those beautiful figures round her had vanished.

Even the figure of Mr. Pangrie in his pale-coloured satins, reclining at her feet, his dark eyes fixed so ardently upon her, his voice dropping lower and lower until he told her, in no more than a whisper, that Venus towering tall and slim and white behind her, was no longer goddess of this grove, now that Juliana sat there enshrined in the rarest beauty that had ever charmed him.

Yes, she would not have been surprised if when she looked up, he had vanished. And words that she never remembered to have heard before stole into her dreaming thoughts :

" But beauty vanishes, beauty passes,
    However rare—rare it be."

And like an echo to it came the memory of
Grandmamma's harsh voice : " his time passeth away
like a shadow."

He may have felt something of her remote mood, for
he put out a hand and touched hers, as though to recall
her, and then, as she did not draw it away, he bent his
head and kissed it, and then the small wrist and elbow,
with shy yet passionate ardour.

But to her, sitting so still in the dim shadow, his kiss
felt as light and cool as the touch of moonlight, and, had
she not looked at him, she would not have known that
he had pressed his lips on her hand and arm. And
because she was no longer looking at him she did not
know that he had ceased and was now looking at her
in a sudden, chilled dismay.

She knew nothing but the dread that had seized her
lest he, and all this gay and gallant company, might
indeed glide away and leave her there, alone and cold in
the darkening grove.

The *fête-champêtre* was over, the company went
on board for their homeward voyage, the fiddles struck
up dance music with renewed gaiety and vigour, and all
danced on deck while they moved slowly, very slowly,
up the river.

That absurd, fanciful dread dropped completely from
Juliana's memories of this part of the expedition, for she
describes in the journal how :

" We danc'd 12 Couple for ten miles with the utmost
Spunk till 12 o'Clock at Night, and for the 2 last Hours
We had no more Light than that of a very little Moon—
so that we could hardly discern One from Another."

She danced and laughed as merrily as the merriest of them, and Mr. Pangrie, recovered from the inexplicable chill that had struck like a sudden, icy fear of death on his glowing fancies in the grove, now thought that his new charmer was the most human as well as the most lovely of nymphs. For he knew, when he spoke with himself and not with her, that she was a nymph and not a goddess.

The barge moved slowly, very slowly, up the river, its awning down, all its gilding pale in the darkness, while the shadowy figures danced on deck by the light of the very little moon.

As they passed Conway Place, Juliana seized Sophia's hand and ran with her to the side of the barge to see the fountain that was still playing on one of the lawns. But it was in the shadow, and only a few flying drops could be discerned where they fell outwards and caught a faint gleam of moonlight. So quiet was the night that, in spite of the hum of voices behind them, they could hear their tiny, tinkling splash as they fell in the stone basin.

" Why do you laugh ? " asked Sophia.

" Oh, I was thinking how infinitely odd this party would look to anyone who might be standing on that bank at this hour, a hundred years—over a hundred years—hence."

" What a monstrous queer fancy ! Is it possible the world may go on for over a hundred years after us ? But if it does, I do not see why we should look strange. They will probably be just like us."

Sophia's tone was a shade petulant. She did not want the world to continue, dancing and talking and laughing, for over a hundred years after she was dead and forgotten. Forgotten ? Was it possible ? By everyone ? Even by her handsome, dull, agreeable, tiresome, devoted cousin, Vesey Clare ? But Vesey would be forgotten too, and everyone she knew. Brr !

She dismissed the tedious subject with a shrug as Mr.
Pangrie joined them. What a conquest Juliana had
made of him! Certainly she looked as lovely as an
angel to-night, thought Sophia, trying hard to repress
an inward sigh of jealousy. Well, there was always
Vesey. And she had a vast deal more spirit—she had
heard that Mr. Bolsover had called her a spirited creature. And who would care if she or Juliana were the
greater beauty, a hundred years—over a hundred years
—hence?

Juliana moved back to the dance on Mr. Pangrie's
arm. Their pale and shining shapes were clearly dis-
cernible in the minuet among the darker forms, whose
rich colours had deepened and grown indistinguishable
in the summer night. And Juliana (as though she were
outside her own body, as she had once dreamed in the
library armchair) found herself watching from a little
distance—it might have been from the river shore—two
silvery ghosts that moved among a group of shadows,
touched hands, bowed, curtsied, advanced, withdrew,
to the rhythm of a music that she could no longer
hear.

It lasted but a moment. The next, the sweet and
piercing strains of the fiddles were ringing in her ears;
she was there, dancing among the group and nowhere
else; Mr. Pangrie had taken her hand to hold aloft as
they made their three paces to the side, and certainly it
was no ghost nor shadow that held it in that warm and
living, that very close, firm grasp.

They did not arrive home at Chidleigh till after one
o'clock. The three girls yawned and chattered over the
cake and wine that was brought them, while Aunt Emily
unavailingly tried to hurry them to bed. Sophia rallied
Juliana on her fresh conquest, and suggested a host of
others, young men, old men, and palpable absurdities,
that her incomparable, invincible coz might add to her

train. She could be a really tiresome tease, and meanwhile Charlotte, talking louder and louder to drown her sister's persistent, restless chirping, bragged how she would get Mr. Ramshall to buy a place on the river, and they would have a regatta and bet vast sums on the boats.

At last the cousins embraced each other goodnight and retired to their rooms. Immediately after doing so, Sophia stepped suddenly out of hers and flung her arms round Juliana's neck as she stood in the darkness of the corridor.

"You looked as beautiful as an angel to-night—everyone was saying so, and Mr. Pangrie could not look at any other of his partners," she said in a determined whisper as if in obedience to some firm resolve.

"Oh, my Sophia!" exclaimed Juliana in a rush of glad gratitude—for the welcome information, certainly, but more, far more, that her own dear Sophia was the same to her as she had always been and would always be. And how unkind she had been to her in her thoughts of her and Lucian! She murmured shamefacedly "There is no one worthy of you—*no one*." It was true she was sure it was, of the dear, generous, warm-hearted girl.

They embraced again tenderly. Juliana stood in the doorway and watched her cousin go back into the lighted room and seat herself at the dressing-table and take off her earrings, leaning back in her chair with a long contented sigh. Sophia's new maid, a tall, trolloping girl, awkward but pleasant, came forward and threw a wrapper round her shoulders and began to take down her hair.

"Betsy—my slippers," said Sophia. The girl was stupid not to have thought of that first, but she would learn. Betsy kneeled down and took off the satin and gold-braided shoes and put on a pair of velvet slippers

nto which Sophia snuggled her small feet with a cat-like
purr of satisfaction. Betsy, kneeling with the discarded
shoes in her hands, her honest face filled with admiration
for the pretty things, might have been a *dévote* worship-
ping the relics of a saint. But a slight frown gathered
on the saint's fair brow, she glanced about her in
annoyance.

" Betsy—my comfit box."

Betsy rushed to find the carved silver comfit box, and
Sophia was all satisfaction again as she offered it to
Juliana and popped a comfit into her own mouth and one
into Betsy's.

Juliana remained by the door while the maid took
her place again behind her young mistress' chair. Behind them was the great bed, hung with blue, forming
a background like the curtains in a playhouse. The
candles, in their tall, flowered china candlesticks, shone
full on Sophia's sleepily smiling face. How pretty she
looked, thought Juliana, as her curls fell about her
shoulders, a white and misty cloud arising from the
disturbed powder.

Sophia took off her rings and dropped them slowly,
one after the other, with a faint tinkling sound, on to the
polished table. They lay there in little pools of light
cast by their own reflections. An army of china pots of
unguents and pomades and powders stood scattered
about the table—what a quantity she had brought for
this one night !

It was foolish to linger thus in the shadow of the doorway watching every detail of the familiar room as though
she were never to see it again.

" Goodnight," she said, but still lingered. What
else was there to say ? To-morrow—what would they
be doing to-morrow ?

Oh, yes, she knew now.

" To-morrow," she said, " Vesey wants us all to go

205

fishing in the stream before dressing time. He neve
wishes such a thing except when you are here."

" La, my poor freckles ! " exclaimed Sophia. " An
I have got three new ones after to-day. I positivel
must wear a mask to-morrow, as Grandmamma used t
do—'tis the only way to keep off the sun."

She picked up her hand-mirror, consulted it in a long
intent silence, then dropped it with a great yawn, an
laughed and said :

" What happy dreams we shall have to-nigh
Goodnight, sweet coz."

She kissed her hand to her. Juliana shut the doc
behind her and was outside in the dark corridor.

She knew her way too well to need a candle as sh
went to her own room. She passed the staircase leadin
down to the hall, and stopped at the head of it for a
instant. She thought that she heard voices below her—
a sharp exclamation, a cry, quickly stifled. They wer
not voices that she knew. Were there strangers
perhaps robbers, in the house ?

As she stood, peering down into the thick darkness c
the hall below, she could just distinguish two figures a
the foot of the stairs, and could hear, quite distinctly,
thin, ghastly, whispering voice that fear had transforme
to something hardly human.

" There ! Don't you see it ? All in white—leanin
over the banisters——"

And the answer, low and hoarse :

" Stuff and nonsense. There's nothing there I tel
you—nothing but a patch of moonlight."

She turned and fled back down the corridor to he
cousin's room.

" Sophia ! " she cried, flinging open the door.

No one answered her, and the room was in darkness
She called again. But there was no one in the room.

In the vague half-darkness of the summer's night, sh

saw that the great bed was not there. The room was almost empty, and it smelt musty and cold. Two narrow, empty beds, bare and uncurtained, stood near the closed but unshuttered windows. The only thing that was the same was the polished dressing-table, but that, too, was bare ; empty of all Sophia's pots and jars and sparkling rings, and covered only with a thick coating of dust that showed a dim, grey glimmer in the faint light from the windows.

CHAPTER XX

THEY said it was the heat, that it was unwise to go fishing without a parasol. They said it was the water-party, it had been too long and fatiguing. They said she could not have slept well for she had come down early, although they had been so late the night before, and had been writing at her journal for some time before breakfast. And she had not answered when Sophia had asked her at breakfast what dreams she had had of their joyous adventures. Sophia had thought it odd of her not to answer.

Now she lay in a dead faint, and though they had cut her stay-laces and slapped her hands and fanned her head and administered hartshorn and strong waters she had not yet come to herself.

They put her to bed in the small four-post bed in her room. Nurse was sent for, and arrived running with a basket of phials, a verbal volume of prescriptions, and little William clinging to her petticoats like a frightened cherub caught up and swept along in the ample robes of an agitated Madonna. Having heard that his darling Miss Julie was ill, nothing would induce him to leave his mother till he had seen her.

They were all in the room and round the bed, Sophia sobbing excitedly, Charlotte gaping, Aunt Emily darting in and out to fetch things that nobody wanted, Lady Chidleigh very still and composed, her high colour much abated, so that in her cherry-coloured wrapper her cheeks

vore an odd purplish hue. Vesey had ridden to Reading
or a surgeon, swearing that no servant could be trusted
o ride as fast as he, and George had vanished
mysteriously after the first alarm. Their absence,
however, was amply compensated for by the crowd of
servants huddled round the door.

Little William, frightened by all these bustling people
round that still, white face on the pillow, so different
from the Miss Julie he knew, burst into a loud roar of
crying.

Juliana opened her eyes and whispered, " What, have
you all come back ? " and then shut them again.

She was wandering, of course. William was removed,
but not unkindly, for it was felt that he had rendered a
service. It was less alarming to have her wandering
than in that dead passivity.

Juliana heard them say she was wandering. She
wanted to ask how far she had wandered and if she would
do so again, but she did not feel strong enough to ask yet.
She remembered that she had looked everywhere for
Lucian last night, knowing that if she could find him all
would be well. She must have forgotten that he had
left Chidleigh.

That was all she could remember of her wanderings of
last night as she lay now with closed eyes. She had
forgotten them altogether when she had waked early
this morning and rose at once so as to write the full
record of the water-party in her journal before breakfast.
She had forgotten them until Sophia asked her at breakfast what dreams she had had of their joyous adventures,
and then an obscure recollection of those " wanderings "
had floated disturbingly back upon her.

She opened her eyes once more. It surprised her to
see all those people round the bed, so full of life and
bustle. Last night the house had been empty of them.
At any moment they might disappear again.

209

The surgeon arrived, breathless at the rate at which Vesey had brought him. He bled Juliana and then pronounced that she had fallen into a health-giving sleep, thanks to his efforts. But in the health-giving sleep she continued so white and still, her breathing so scarcely perceptible, that all grew alarmed.

Vesey had returned with a strange new agitation on him. A dozen times he had begun to speak and then broken off, staring at the doctor or the servants with restless impatience. He left the sick-room to look for George, but George was nowhere to be found. Feeling wretched and awkward, he had ridden off to a bear-baiting, and left no word of where he had gone.

Vesey came back from his fruitless search just as the surgeon had declared that Juliana was no longer in a health-giving sleep, but unconscious, and was proposing to bleed her again. Vesey broke out at him in a roar. He was an ignorant quack, a dolt, a blockhead. His sister had lost too much blood already, or she would not be so white—" so white." He repeated the words in a sort of choking breath, almost a sob. He would ride to London and fetch the best doctor that could be procured ; he would not have his sister practised on by ignorant country quacks.

The man tried faintly to expostulate, but at his first words Vesey seized him by the collar and flung him out into the passage. One of the maids screamed, Lady Chidleigh protested, scandalized by such an uproar in the sick-room, yet half-pleased by his unwontedly energetic methods. Everyone was amazed at the change in the sleepy, phlegmatic youth. Grandmamma Chidleigh, who had entered the bedroom a few minutes before, nodded approval. For once he was showing himself like his father.

Vesey was showing it to the extent of turning all the maids out of the room. He would not have the silly

ussies there, gaping at him and screaming. When he
ad shut the door on them he turned and faced his
mazed relatives with blank eyes that did not seem to
ee them, did not even notice Sophia's pretty upturned
ace.

"I must ride or send to London," he said in a lower
oice. "Don't let that fool bleed her again. They're
ll fools—all fools and charlatans. It's not only that.
'he news is out in Reading. It will be all over the
ounty in a few hours. We are disgraced——"

Again he stopped on that half-choking breath, and his
yes now sought his mother's. He seemed to find speech
ifficult, but after a moment he brought out the next
vords stolidly enough.

"Madam, they are going to try my brother, Chidleigh,
or the murder of the French duke."

Juliana could not hear what they were saying. She
ad heard a loud, angry voice that seemed familiar, then
. quick scuffle and a scream. Then she heard that voice
gain and knew that it was Vesey's, that it was saying
omething she must hear. Her eyelids lifted a very
ittle, and through the fringe of her eyelashes she could
ee Vesey standing against the door in his red riding-coat,
is face flushed dark red.

Everyone was speaking, exclaiming in horror. She
nust hear what they said. It was something of impor-
ance—of danger—yes, of danger to Lucian. And now
he heard what Vesey was saying; that it would certainly
)e proved that Lucian had killed the Frenchman.

"What—his guest!" exclaimed Lady Chidleigh, on
. shocked, incredulous, tragic note. So might Lady
Macbeth have uttered her "What, in our house?" on
he morning after Banquo's murder. She would not
)elieve such a thing. It must have been a duel.

But Vesey replied that there had been no seconds, no
vitnesses, nothing to prove that Lucian had not killed

his man in cold blood. There was also the damning fact that Lucian had owed him large sums of money, and the extent of these had only lately been discovered. There was no doubt but that he would be proved guilty. Chrysole, that damned, sneaking, lying toad of a valet, had been working in the matter. The family of Saint-Aumerle were moving heaven and earth for revenge. They had appealed to the King; there would be no chance for Lucian except to flee the country, and doubtless he would do so on the instant he had his warning. No, there would be no chance for Lucian if they took him. He was known to have killed a man before in a slightly irregular fashion.

"Then they will hang him," said Grandmamma Chidleigh. "They hang for murder now, even those of rank. But a silken rope is granted to a prisoner of noble birth."

Her hooked chin sank trembling on her breast. For the first time, her changeless, immemorial antiquity, as of an inanimate object, gave way, and she appeared feeble and weary, a poor old woman.

Juliana saw them all very small and far away as though she were looking at them through the wrong end of Mr. Hilbury's telescope. She had understood that Lucian was to be tried for the murder of Monsieur le Duc. She thought she knew how he had died, but she could not remember. If she could remember, she might clear Lucian. But she could think of nothing. Her eyes moved vaguely round the room, though her head did not stir.

They fell on the stripe of sunlight between the curtains, drawn to keep the light from her eyes, on the picture she had painted of a noble youth, as graceful as a maiden, consulting a hermit in a lonely grotto, surrounded by savage mountains.

Her glance wandered to her clothes, left in disorder from the time when they had hurriedly undressed her that morning, her India muslin falling over the back of a chair as though it too had fainted. And there were the shoes she had taken off last night, they had not been put away either. They lay where they had been thrown down, creased and dusty after so much dancing on the deck of Mr. Bolsover's barge. " They have a dissipated air, have they not—positively exhausted ? What were they doing last night do you think, while you were asleep ? " She could remember Lucian's ludicrous questions. What was it she could not remember ?

She continued to gaze at the shoes, hearing nothing but a buzz of voices that seemed a long way off. Then, as she gazed, she thought she saw them, not dropped there on their sides on the rose-and-grey rug, but placed primly together on a dark floor lit up by a patch of moon-light. She thought she heard Monsieur le Duc's high, monotonous voice.

" But yes," he was saying, slowly and distinctly, " I can see very plainly the little green and silver shoes there in the moonlight."

With that, slowly and distinctly, all that had followed that night in the library came back into her mind. How could she ever have forgotten ? But Lucian had told her to forget ; she remembered that also, now. It was Monsieur le Duc who had attacked Lucian, had lunged at him before he had even drawn his sword. Yes, she knew how it had happened, exactly, every detail. She had only to speak and Lucian would be cleared of this preposterous charge of murder.

Her eyes opened wider, she saw all the occupants in the room clearly and near to her, and she saw that they were looking at her. They had noticed her eyes open, they were talking much more quietly and about her, and someone began to try and make her drink some-thing out of a cup. It was very strong and made her gasp and choke, but she drank what she could.

" Vesey," she said. " Is Vesey there ? "

He plunged forward, throwing himself down on his knees beside the bed so as to bring his head near hers, for she had spoken in a very faint whisper.

" I'm here, Julie. What is it ? What do you want ? "

His massive, red-coated shoulders seemed to heave over her, his flushed face, so unwontedly eager, was very near hers, he smelt of horses and wine. It was as though she were being crushed by him, although he was not touching her. Her head swam, she found it difficult to think what she was going to say.

" Dear Vesey," she began timidly, and was astonished herself to hear how low and far-away her voice sounded.

He flung his arms round her and she felt a great hot tear splash on her face. Vesey was crying for her ! He must think she was going to die.

" Vesey, dear Vesey, but I am quite well, really," she contrived to say, though with some difficulty. " But it is Lucian. Listen. Lucian did not——"

" She was conscious ! " exclaimed Mamma's voice in that pause. Juliana was making a supreme effort to collect her thoughts ; whatever happened she must not wander now, she must not be absent. She fixed her eyes upon the stripe of sunlight on the floor as if to fix her attention. It had moved a little since she had looked at it last.

" He attacked Lucian," she said. " He had drawn first."

There was a scurry of low, breathless voices.

" What does she say ? "

" She says he attacked Lucian—that he had drawn his sword first."

" What does she mean ? How can she tell ? "

" She cannot know anything of it. She must have been dreaming."

" She must be wandering."

They had drawn closer round the bed, but she did not speak any more. They pointed out to each other that she must have lost consciousness again, but this was not exact, for she could see them very well.

But she could also see herself, quite clearly, as though she were someone else, standing at a little distance.

She could see her face, still and white, on the pillow, and Vesey's great arm flung across her as though he were holding her fast to him. But he could not hold her, for she was not there. She looked at herself lying in her own bed, and remembered how she had once seen herself in the library armchair, herself, leaning forward, with the silver inkpot in her hands, her head bent, looking down at it, and a long curl at the back of her head drooping forward on to her neck.

It had been the worst dream of all, a nightmare, and now it had come true. She was absent and she could not come back.

CHAPTER XXI

LUCIAN was in his house in Soho. The room was almost dark, but the candles were not yet lit, and he sat in a spindle-legged armchair before a fire, his dark, purple silk breeches showing now black, now ruddy in its light. The evening was chilly, for summer, and Lucian hated to be cold.

Sunk in his chair, his hands dropped lifeless on its arms, his dull eyes fixed motionless upon the chimney-piece, he appeared an inert, almost lifeless figure, and in some way shrunken. At first glance, one would have taken him for an old man sitting there before the fire.

Less than ten minutes ago, private information had been brought him that by to-morrow morning there would be a warrant out for his arrest on the charge of the murder of Monsieur le Duc de Saint-Aumerle. He had little doubt of the way in which the evidence would go. Juliana was the only witness he could produce in his favour, and he had no intention of using her name in that curious story of the events that took place one evening in the library at Chidleigh. Also, he was certain that in the light of such a story, her evidence would be considered as worthlessly blind and partial.

His only chance was flight, and, thanks to his informant, he had several hours' start. He had given his orders, the horses were being saddled, Bartelmy was looking out what ready money he had and making all the preparations. He would ride to Dover with

Bartelmy only. It was quicker than coach or carriage, and they could change horses on the way.

Meanwhile, he had meant to consider his plans, but found himself giving more attention to the warming of his chilly legs, and the consideration of his high carved chimney-piece, of Robert Adam's work. He had reflected that this was probably the last time he would see those delicately moulded grapes and vine leaves, and regretted it, for he had been particularly well pleased with that chimney-piece.

It was unlikely that he should see England or France again for an indefinite period, perhaps for the rest of his life. " The rest of his life " was a tedious phrase. What in the world was he going to do for the rest of his life ?

Italy would not be very safe, since the family of Saint-Aumerle had many connections there. He had better make a start by going to Spain and then on to the East, perhaps—Constantinople, and see the Grand Turk—possibly even India. He yawned prodigiously. He had not the slightest desire to resume his travels, which had seldom succeeded in interesting him.

Most of the realities of his life had, in fact, failed singularly in this respect ; the vacant, or harsh realities of his sluggish, brooding boyhood, of his coldly ferocious pursuit of pleasure in early manhood, of his contemptuous rejection of ambition which could bring him nothing he had not already got.

His position had been secure and prosperous, as was the position of the whole country, apparently certain of equal security and prosperity in the future, a position which admitted no necessity and no desire for change. He thought of his past actions, his follies and excesses, possibly his crimes, without distaste or regret, merely with lack of interest. None of them had been what he desired nor how he desired them. Those preposterous debauches at Medmenham Abbey, when he had been

head of that ridiculous society, the Hell-fire Club—
" childish " was his word as he thought of them now.

" Lord, how dull it's all been," he murmured, and
thrust the poker into the fire to raise it.

No, there had been nothing in his life to interest him
as much as a certain odd fancy he had had for years, of
a girl that he had never actually seen—except for that
one instant, outside the library window, the night he had
killed Saint-Aumerle. And she had not looked pretty
then, he reflected, her face distorted in terror and her
mouth open as though she were shrieking to them,
though not a sound could be heard. When he had
rushed after her into the moonlit garden, there had been
neither sound nor sight of her. His dreams of her had
often ended so.

His account to Juliana of those dreams in boyhood
had been true enough. They were less frequent as he
grew older, but quite as vivid. As he grew older, his
visitor did too, though her dress remained as odd and
formless and her expression as smilingly frank and open
as when she had been a child. He began to welcome
and even seek for her, who had formerly been a teasing
intrusion into a world of monstrous or splendid shadows.
Now she appeared the only living figure in that world,
which he still sought as relief and escape from a life that
had grown less harsh but scarcely less tedious to him.

She was like no women he had met in life, she had not
their mannerisms, their way of speech, not even, it
seemed, their way of thought. She was fearless but not
bold, of a direct simplicity in speech that he found odd
and charming, and very far removed from the simplicity
of a fool. But in general they spoke little, though he
delighted to pay her compliments, which she received
with a child-like pleasure, as if, instead of the stale
currency of talk between a man and woman, they were
something rare and strange to her.

He called her " Incognita ", after the heroine of the late
Mr. Congreve's novel ; she called him the " Gentleman
Unknown".

She did not enter his world now, whether of fancy or
reality ; he went with her through a world he did not
know. They wandered through streets, and jostling
alien crowds, through gardens equally crowded, that he
had never seen.

Once or twice they loitered beside a miniature lake
and lawn, shut in by railings, where rabbits fed
undisturbed by the passing stream of people. One
foggy autumn evening they came down a dark street to
high iron gates that enclosed a tiny courtyard garden
where a statue stood above an empty fountain ; and
stayed there long, not speaking, until suddenly she
moved, her face upturned, her eyes glowing ; and he bent
to catch her in his arms, and woke.

So it had always ended, she eluding him, but with no
coquetry nor intentional inflaming of his desire. Rather,
she seemed to call to him, to try persistently to come to
him. Sometimes he had stood aside and watched those
monotonous crowds in his dream troop by, all alike, with
white, inattentive faces and unfamiliar dark clothes ;
and had seen her pass among them, looking quickly now
and then to right and left—looking, he knew, for him.
Sometimes he could join her, but he could never catch
her, never possess her, not even in a dream.

The desire of it had entered into him, giving the only
vivid and consistent purpose to his cold existence. It
had prompted him to the society of the strange company
of magicians, alchemists and hypnotists, such as Saint-
Germain, Cagliostro, Mesmer, whom Paris welcomed
with the fantastic delight of a city that had been wearied
by its long period of crisp and elegant death of the
emotions. He found that it was impossible for him to
be sent into a trance, or " mesmerised " as it was begin-

ning to be called, just as it was impossible for him to b
affected by wine. On the other hand, he discovere
considerable hypnotic powers in himself, and that h
could send messengers where he could not follow. H
had tried several, among them Monsieur le Duc de Saint
Aumerle, last of all, Juliana, the only one that had me
with any success for his purpose.

Yet he could hardly have told what he wished for i
success. If his dream could be embodied and possesse
would it be anything more than the repetition of a
experience he had had so often that he was wearied t
death of it ? To reverse Æsop's fable, he was droppin
the shadow to snatch at the substance, but, unlike th
dog in the fable, he could not be sure that the shado
had not after all the greater quality.

It was certainly an egregious piece of tomfoolery,
preposterous notion to try and match Dr. Donne'
fantastic commands :

> " Go and catch a falling star,
>   Get with child a mandrake root,
>   Tell me where all times past are———"

The last words arrested his attention. He leane
forward and took the poker from the fire, repeating them
this time aloud.

" Tell me where all times past are." The poker wa
hot to his hand and the end of it white hot. He ha
lately been reading that song in John Bell's new pock
edition of the Poets from Chaucer to Churchill :

> " If thou be'st born to strange sights,
>   Things invisible go see."

An alluring invitation !

What was it that, very rarely, but from time to time i

he excellently judicious family of the Clares, prompted
hem to such insane pursuits as these mentioned by Dr.
Donne? There had been the religious and poetic
frenzies of the hermit who had cut such an incongruous
figure in the time of Charles II; the beauty at King
James I's Court who had been tried for sorcery; and, in
he far distant past, a figure that he did not know if he
had heard of as a child or actually dreamed of, so vividly
had he appeared to see it—the figure of an old woman
with terrible gleaming eyes and mouth twisted with
curses, being hurried to a pond by a crowd of jeering,
shouting villagers.

He had been idly contemplating the white-hot end of
the poker in his hand, and how quickly it turned to red,
and now, as he thought of that savage witch-ducking, he
began to pass it along the pattern at the side of the
carved wood chimney-piece. Since he was not again to
enjoy that pattern, he would deface it, and the upturned
corners of his lips curled into a definite smile as the hot
iron seared and blackened the leaves and grapes and
exquisite tendrils. The solid rams' heads supporting
the chimney-piece on either side with an air of such
peaceful, almost divine responsibility, continued to stare
solemnly down at the growing destruction.

Would they not show their opinion of this wanton
sacrilege? The poker followed the twisting curls of a
pair of horns, then suddenly stabbed and blasted the
placid eyes between them.

"Tell me where all times past are," he repeated softly
in a whisper, again and again, as though he spoke to the
hissing wood.

Times past, times present, or times to come, were they
not all one, if he had the power to make them so?

A sudden breeze stirred the branches of the trees
outside into a hurried, whispering sound, and was as
suddenly hushed. Within the house, out in the street,

there was now a silence as deep as on the Chidleigh lawns at night.

Lucian stayed motionless with his hand suspended. His mouth was drawn up in a sharp curve, like the mouth of the stone satyr on the terrace ; his head was bent slightly to one side, which gave him the appearance of one who was listening intently. Yet the silence was as dead, as breathless as before.

Then again there came that light, whispering breeze, and a rush of rain drove suddenly against the windows with a noise like the beating of kettledrums. Lucian laid down the poker, rose to his feet with a quick, deliberate movement, and walked to the window. His breath came sharply between his shut teeth, his head was erect, his eyes shone with extraordinary brilliance. The indolent, quiescent figure seemed suddenly to have been quickened into an unnatural life and activity, a radiant expectancy.

He flung open the window. The room was on the ground floor, about a man's height above the street. The evening was not yet quite dark, a long stripe of stormy red sunset still hung over the houses of Soho. It had been fine and clear all day, but now the rain came down with the torrential violence of a thunderstorm, rushing down the gutters and quickly flooding them, the great drops splashing and leaping up into the air again like a myriad tiny fountains. As they fell past Lucian's eyes, against the stormy light of the sunset they appeared red, for one instant, like drops of blood.

Farther down the street, to the right, my Lady Gag was holding a reception. He could see a coach g rumbling and splashing through the mud, the dim form of the footmen huddled forward on their box, crouching from the rain. There was a blaze of light on the step as the hall door was thrown open, and the brightly l figures of a lady, in a towering head-dress and spreading

oops, and a dapper little gentleman went into the house.
The lady was hurrying from the rain, but the gentleman,
in spite of his pale coloured satin coat, walked behind
her with elaborate nonchalance, lightly brushing the
raindrops from his sleeve.

A sedan chair came sharply round the corner and
down the street towards my Lady Gage's. The men
were running and breathed in heavy, stertorous gasps,
while a lady's thin, screaming voice issued from within
the chair in some command, inaudible to Lucian.

Suddenly the rain diminished and seemed about to
ease, though the darkened sky had not yet grown
nearer.

" Bartelmy is an unconscionable time," he said softly,
but the words were uttered without thought or intention,
and he did not move from the window. His still form
seemed to be charged with some exterior force that gave
it life and power beyond the human. Conscious of it,
exulting in it, he stood there, waiting.

A slight, dark figure, not unlike that of a link-boy, but
carrying no lantern, came round the corner on the left
and down the street, went past his house for a few steps,
then turned sharply, came back, and stopped just
beneath his window, looking up at him. He saw the
dusky white oval of a girl's face in the dim light, and
knew it for the face he had seen so often in his dreams.
The eyes were dark, and wide with an expression he could
not fathom, her lips parted a little in an eager wonder—
was it also delight ? She stood there in the lightly
falling rain, in a straight coat with up-turned collar
buttoned to the chin, a close-fitting cap on her head,
which reached to a little below the window. Neither
moved nor spoke—he did not know for how long.

It was the supreme moment for his impossible desires.
He was awake and conscious, and he saw her there before
him, a few feet away from him, no longer in a dream, but

223

living, breathing a little quickly, her cheeks warm and fresh in the rain. Through Juliana, he had at last succeeded in bringing her to him.

He should not have thought of Juliana. It vaguely troubled him, intruding something that he did not wish to admit at this moment—a disturbance, a fear.

He shook it off and leaned towards the window. The girl below raised herself on tiptoe as if to approach him more nearly, she seemed about to speak. Her lips parted, moved quickly, he heard a clear voice speaking low, with eager pleasure. But he could not hear what she said, for he could not attend. Some other sound was clamouring for his attention, the sound of his own name, called urgently, beseechingly, in Juliana's voice. He tried not to listen, but the whole air seemed full of that terror-stricken cry.

She was in extreme danger and she knew it, or she could not have called like that. Furiously, he tried to deafen himself to it, to hear only the voice of the girl in the street below, to remember only that the moment he had wished and worked for so long was his at last. But the small, pale face upturned below him, the clear eyes shining through the dusk, were growing blurred by an image that would rise before it, the image of Juliana' face upturned to his, and wet, beseeching eyes that shone suddenly into smiles as he promised her that he would not let her be too much afraid.

He was losing his moment. Some power that lay in him and beyond him was slackening its force through his divided attention. Though awake and conscious, he had to struggle with himself, as one struggles not to awake when in a dream of ecstatic pleasure. For that actual and living being before him was not now as actual nor as living as the memory of his sister's face.

Through Juliana, he had brought her to him. Was he now to lose her for Juliana's sake? He flung from

224

the window, and in a leap was down the stairs and at the door.

There was no one outside the door, nor any figure moving in the street. He stood there for a little time, waiting, watching in the falling rain. The coach in front of my Lady Gage's house had driven off, and he could still hear the clatter and rattle of harness growing fainter in the distance ; the street remained empty.

He went back into the house and called the servants. An hour later, he was riding out of London with Bartelmy beside him.

At the cross-roads he turned his horse's head towards the road into Berkshire. Bartelmy spurred after him.

" My lord, my lord, the road to Dover lies straight ahead. At this pace we shall make it by the morning."

" I ride to Chidleigh," said my lord.

CHAPTER XXII

JULIANA opened her eyes. She was lying in bed and
Lucian was kneeling beside it, holding her hands, his
face very near hers. The curtains had been pulled back,
the windows opened wide, and the morning sunlight was
full on his face, showing it more grey and drawn than she
had ever seen it. It looked as though something had
been drawn out of it, some life, some power, that would
not return.

" You called me," said Juliana faintly.

" I have been 'calling' you for more than three
hours," he answered.

He let go her hands, rose slowly and fetched her
something in a glass which he made her drink. His
movements were like those of a tired old man. She saw
that there was no one else in the room.

She found it easier to speak after the drink. " I tried
to come before," she said. " I was looking for you. I
knew that without you I could never come back."

" No," said Lucian. " You could not have come back
without me."

He drank a glass of wine, then came back to the bed
and knelt beside it again. But it seemed that he was
more tired than Juliana, for he did not speak but
remained looking at her with his head resting on his
hand.

She remembered now that when she first knew that
he was calling her she had thought that she was drown

226

ing. She had tried to struggle upwards through deep waters to him; it was difficult, it was agonizing, she could not rise.

At last she had seen his eyes looking down on her through huge gulfs of water that were now clear as glass and then swept over her as black as ink. She was used to looking into water, glass or ink until other faces looked back at her; now it seemed that she had slipped in where those faces swam, and sunk far down, so far she could never come back. Yet slowly, painfully, she had to rise towards him, until she was floating upon the water, and always it was his eyes that drew her up to him, two steely points, motionless, devoid of light and colour.

She knew that before that time of drowning she had been wandering in an alien world, trying to find him. She did not want to remember that. She wanted to stay there quiet with Lucian looking at her, but she wished he did not look so tired. They stayed so for some time.

There was, however, something that would persist in disturbing her, that she must remember and tell him. And when the full memory came over her it was so terrible that she clutched at his hand.

"Lucian, the rooms, the gardens—nothing is the same."

"What is not the same?"

"Nothing is precisely the same." She hesitated and could only whisper it. "Nurse's cottage is not in the drive. And the drive—they are cutting down all the trees in the drive."

Lucian roused himself as with an effort and took both her hands in his again.

"That was a dream, when your senses were wandering. I rode down the drive this very morning when the dawn was breaking and the dew lay thick and white on the ground. The trees were all there, each one, they looked

227

huge and grey in that cold light, they were like the rugged columns of some ancient temple.

" Very soon, when you are stronger, you will walk down the drive and see that all the trees are there, and call at Nurse's cottage for a gossip. Her garden was looking very neat and pretty as I passed, all the flowers glistening in the dew as though their faces had just been washed." He took her face between his hands and looked intently into it. " The gardens, the park, the house are all the same—all precisely the same. You have been dreaming, my pretty one, but very soon you will forget your dreams, even those that were the most strange and enthralling—yes, you will forget them altogether."

His voice was coming with a little more strength and life in it. Suddenly he caught her to him and covered her face and hair with kisses. " My sweet, you have come back, you have come back. I thought I had sent you away for ever, but you have come back and you shall never wander again. No, never, for it was I who sent you, and I will never send you again. Do you understand, Juliana ? You are safe of me."

She clung weakly to him, scarcely comprehending, but glad to know that she was safe, though his words troubled her.

" Safe of *you*, brother ? "

" Yes, safe of me. Try to listen, for there may not be much time. You have asked me often enough what use or amusement you were to me, what it is that we share. It is this—that you were the most exquisite instrument to play on that I have ever known. You were sensitive to the slightest impression, responded to the lightest touch. I could do what I wished with your spirit ; I did it, and all but broke it. I did not think at first that would trouble me to break it, but when I found that was breaking, then I knew. Ah, do not try to understand, I only want you to know."

" To know—to know——? "

" That I love you," he cried, and kissed her again.

" But—dear Lucian—indeed, I have always known that."

" And had reason to, you hussy, for who would not love this fair face ?   Oh, you can well afford to triumph ! You—who were to be my instrument—my delicate plaything—have tricked me at the last into loving you more than my own purpose. It is you, my sweet fool, who have the laugh of me. Why do you not laugh ? "

" Brother, you talk so wildly. Why should I laugh ? Why are you laughing ? "

" To remember that there are others who love you and not to hurt, and that you will love them the better when I am gone."

" Gone ?   Lucian, you are not going ? "

" Yes, I am going and this house will be the happier for it. I have no place in it, nor in this country, nor, perhaps, in this whole age, but what of that ?   I shall rig about and fit into odd corners here and there and find new things to amuse me."

" But oh, brother, why must you go ? "

As she asked the question she remembered that Vesey had said Lucian was to be tried for the murder of Monsieur le Duc. And that there had been something he could do or say.

Exhausted as she was, she withdrew a little from his arms, and leaned back upon the pillows, trying hard to think.

" I remember now. I was there. It was in the library. You did not murder him. He attacked you and you fought. It was a duel. I was witness."

" So you once told me," said Lucian coolly, " but you were not there when I had the misfortune to kill my good friend, Saint-Aumerle. That was one of your strange dreams. Do you not remember my telling you so ? "

"No, no, it's true—I remember—" her voice rose sharply. "Look at my shoes—the green and silver shoes on the rug. They were there. Do you not remember—' the little green and silver shoes there in the moonlight ' ? "

He laughed softly.

"What a madcap mind yours is ! Would you bring the little green and silver shoes into court to bear evidence in my favour ? Why, it was I who spoke of their running through the house when you were asleep, dancing by themselves in the library in a pool of moon-light ! And then when you had that odd, life-like dream of my fight with Saint-Aumerle and his death, you heard him say something of the sort in his voice—it is the way of dreams. And would you tell that pretty fairy tale to a judge, my charmer ? "

"Oh, Lucian, do not laugh ! If I cannot bear evidence, who can ? I do not think it *can* have been all a dream—part, perhaps—the shoes—I do not know——'

He leaned forward and his face was serious again ; it wore indeed an expression of almost terrible earnestness.

"And if it were *not* a dream," he said, " if it were true that you had been there and seen it all (as it is not true) I would not, for anything that life or death can offer have your name brought into such a business. Should we tell the justices, the twelve honest men and true of the jury, pursy, staring grocers, of the odd undertakings that brought us down to the library after midnight when all the rest of the household were in bed and asleep ? Your evidence would do me little good in such circumstances, nor would they regard it for a moment.

"So you may satisfy yourself that not only is it an unreal fancy, but better that it should be so."

He was looking close into her eyes, and he did not speak again for some time. He seemed to be waiting, summoning his strength for some great effort. Sh could see herself reflected in the pupils of his eyes, and the sight gave her a quick fear, but she soon regained her composure. Lucian's eyes told her there was nothing to fear.

"It was a dream," he said at last, "which you will forget like the rest. You had forgotten it for some weeks, you know, and then Vesey's words and the fear for me brought it all back. But you will forget it again as you will the rest. Already, you are forgetting it. Forget it all—yes, *all.*"

"Forget it all?" she repeated. Those had been Mr. Daintree's words to her, down in the drive. Was it possible the same words should sound so different? Lucian's eyes were receding from her until they were mere motionless points. Forget? What was it that she would forget?

A very faint, dull sound came through the open windows. Lucian heard it, for he turned his head quickly, and, as he did so, Juliana heard it too. It was the sound of horsemen riding down the drive. From her high bed she could see the trees and the stone bridge over the stream. She saw a company of men come riding out from the trees and cross the bridge in the sunlight.

Suddenly she knew that they were the men who had come to arrest her brother.

"Lucian—quick!" she cried.

He, too, had been looking out of the window, and now as he turned his head to face her his eyes had all their old brightness. He snatched her up in his arms, half lifting her from the bed.

"You are my dear, sweet, pretty little sister," he said very fast and gayly, "and when you are married to your widower, your grandfather, and shut up in his great country house, you will not quite forget me, whatever else you forget. Nor shall I quite forget."

231

" Oh, brother, shall we not meet again ? "

" What—have you forgotten our promise ? To meet sometimes and walk upon the terrace ? Now, or a hundred years ago, or a hundred years hence—it is all one. I will not forget."

He was laughing as he kissed her, laid her gently down again upon the bed, and sprang to the door.

Most of the household were in the hall as he came down the stairs. Few of them had been to bed that night. They had been watching by Juliana who had not shown a sign of consciousness since noon the day before, when she had tried to speak of Lucian and Monsieur le Duc. By evening, the doctor had declared that she was sinking fast and there was nothing to be done.

At daybreak, Lucian had amazed them all by walking into the room.

They had thought he would be at the coast by now— they exclaimed and questioned—George told him his neck was in danger, Vesey told him he must ride like the devil. Lady Chidleigh, stupefied and exhausted, could only stare at him as though he had been a ghost.

Lucian had replied that he intended first to bring Juliana back to life. There were more questions and expostulations, but his only answer was that he must have the room to himself and at once, as there was no time to be lost. He drew back the curtains, opened the windows, and ordered the company out of the room.

" You can watch through the little window into the passage if you fear my methods," he said, " but no one is to enter the room or try to interrupt."

George said something about devil's quackery and danger to Juliana, and refused to leave the room.

Lucian answered, " I would remind you, brother, that I am not yet hanged, and you are not yet Chidleigh."

232

George gave an inarticulate growl between his teeth,
t left the room with the rest.

Mr. Daintree had arrived late in the evening before,
hearing of Juliana's condition, and had stayed all
ght. He urged the family now, since the doctor had
'en up all hope, to let Lucian try what he could do,
impeded, and it had been his entreaty that had helped
em to yield the quicker. He hardly knew what had
pelled him to it, and the frantic, unreasonable throb
hope that he had felt on seeing Lucian. But the two
:asions on which he had lately seen Juliana in the
rk had made him wonder whether Lucian were not in
ne mysterious way connected with Juliana's illness,
l that what he may have helped to cause he might now
able to cure.

For over three hours the household had drifted in and
t of the hall, up and down the stairs, looking anxiously
the door, from which no smallest sound emerged.

George, who insisted on looking in once through the
:le passage window, declared that Lucian was doing
thing in the world but holding the girl's hands and
ring into her face. The fellow was mad, he always
ew it. He seemed, however, a little disturbed, for
n, and did not look in again.

Now, after three hours, Sophia had stolen to the top
the stairs and come down declaring that she had heard
ices in the room ; yes, she was sure she had heard her
n precious darling's voice as well as Lord Chidleigh's.
ey all quickly gathered in the hall, debating whether
y should now go up to the room. On that instant
y saw Lucian come running to the top of the stairs
d down it in great leaps.

" Tally ho ! " he shouted. " Gone away ! George,
ll you get my brush ? "

He dashed through them, through the open doors, out
o the courtyard where Bartelmy had waited all this

time with two fresh horses, ready saddled. Both wer
on horseback in a moment and galloping out through th
archway.

It was at that moment that the constable and his me
emerged from the drive in a straggling, widespread line
and were suddenly charged by horsemen who cam
through the archway and through their line like
thunderbolt. None of the parties had time to load an
fire their clumsy pistols. Lucian's sword was out, an
he dealt a swinging backhander as he plunged throug
cutting one of the men from his horse. He and Bartelm
were clear of them in an instant and galloping furiousl
down the drive.

" Gone awa-ay," shouted Vesey from the steps, ma
with excitement, " Gad, he's a Clare after all ! "

He dashed out through the archway, and began pullin
up the fallen man's horse. Another horse had gor
down in the scuffle and its rider was pulling it on its fee
again, amid wild confusion and scurry. Only one ma
was riding after the fugitives. He had waited to loa
his pistol but was now riding hard.

Vesey had got the horse on its feet and swung himse
into the saddle. He had no whip nor spurs and pricke
it with his sword into a gallop, shouting to the man i
front of him to stop. But the man turned a stupi
staring red face for one instant and then rode on.

Juliana had heard the shouts and scuffle and clash
steel outside the courtyard, but it was not under h
window and she could see nothing. She heard th
beating of horses' hoofs again in the drive, a furious thu
thud that was now going up the drive instead of dow
Lucian, then, had escaped ; Lucian was riding awa
She heard a shot, but the thud of the hoofs continue
Whoever had fired must have missed.

Then she saw him come out of the drive, followed clo
by Bartelmy, on to the stone bridge in the open sunligh

But he rode strangely, swaying in the saddle, and as his horse's hoofs rang clear and hollow on the bridge she saw him suddenly roll over sideways and fall to the ground.

Bartelmy pulled up only just short of that prostrate body. She saw him dismount and run to his master, then Vesey came riding out of the trees and dismounted also, running towards Lucian. He shouted. Others came. There was soon a huddled crowd on the little bridge where she had seen the boy king sitting in the sunlight.

She could not see what they were doing, she could not hear what they said. Now they were all coming back down the drive to the house again, coming very slowly, or they were carrying something. Would no one come and tell her ?

She raised herself from the pillows ; she found that she could move, she could even get out of bed. She crossed the room, unsteadily, but still she reached the door. Down the corridor to the stairs, and there she stopped, clinging to the banisters, unable to go further. Down in the hall, people were crying out and running about distractedly. Lady Chidleigh had fainted in a chair and maids were attending to her. She heard slow, heavy steps coming up into the hall from the courtyard, the low murmur of men's voices.

" Lucian ! " she wailed. " Is he dead ? "

A figure detached itself from the little group now in the doorway, and dashed up the stairs to her. She was caught up and held tenderly and very close.

" Is he dead ? " she whispered.

" Yes, he is dead," said Mr. Daintree's voice, " but you—oh, Juliana, my love, my angel, you are alive."

TIME WILL BE

EPILOGUE

ON a Saturday evening early, in September, Donald Graeme came down for the week-end to Helen's cottage at Barton. Jan had come down the night before, more than two months after she had returned from her long holiday at Barton to her work in town. She had not seen Donald just lately as he had been away from town on a job and had now come down into Berkshire direct from it.

They had an early supper to leave time after it for a walk, and Donald reminded Jan of her promise to show him Chidleigh. They would be able to go all over the gardens and grounds now that the Harrises had left and the new owner had not moved in. Jan agreed, but without enthusiasm. She put on a brown leather hat that " went with " the old brown coat-frock she had been wearing all the summer, and thick brown shoes.

She found herself striding along interminably beside Donald, the light of the setting sun in her eyes so that her eyelashes were full of rainbows. She saw him through a yellow haze that made him seem dark and remote from her, a shadow stalking beside her rather than a living companion.

He had been talking for some time. She knew he had something to tell her from the moment when she had seen him come very fast up the village street and pull open the tiny garden gate with an energy wholly out of proportion to the amount required. She must attend more closely to what he was saying. She had not found it so difficult since she was at school, a bored, home-sick child whose mind in lessons was apt to grow more and more blank.

Whenever she thought of school she thought of a long, dark room, the walls covered with old books, where a boy sat alone at a large table, his head resting on his hand, his face hidden. He had books in front of him but he was not reading. The memory of that motionless figure was always slightly disturbing. She had wondered if it were an illustration to some ghost story she had read at school and forgotten, or possibly some dream, half nightmare, that she may have had there more than once.

And now she had seen that room.

She turned her head restlessly, and told Donald it was splendid news. She had heard him say he had been offered a job in America and now began to ask questions. Yes, it was a good job and it should lead to something bigger in the future. He would have to start in a few months. He was looking at her. He would soon be asking her if she would marry him and go out with him to America in a few months. She must think what she would say. She had felt so much alone just lately; would she be less alone if she married Donald and went to America ?

She used not to be alone. When she had walked through the parks or down the same old streets where she went every day, she had felt that she had walked there lately with someone, she had not known whom, but she had known that the touch of his sleeve under her hand was soft and velvety.

239

She used often to wake feeling happy and excited as though in her dreams she had been with some companion more delightful than anyone she had met. She could never remember her dreams, but often and often in the daytime she had been just on the point of remembering what that companion was like. She would find herself looking at the people who passed, in happy expectancy, as though she hoped to see and recognize that unknown face among all the other blank white faces in the street.

And now she had seen that face.

Donald was talking of American architecture, the sole architecture now to show any individual quality. He spoke his admiration for its dignity, its spaciousness and restraint.

Jan was attracted by the words. Perhaps in this, too, as in Donald's job, lay a promise of " bigger things " in the future. Donald advanced into technicalities. All that he said sounded so real and solid, she wished she could catch on to it. No doubt, if she could, she would find it all very dull, but then nothing could be more dull than this empty solitude.

She tried hard to think of American architecture. She saw wrought iron gates three times her height ; a high red wall, and behind it the slender tops of cypresses twisted chimneys, irregular roofs, and a white turret that might have imprisoned a princess in a fairy tale ; a window into a low, pleasant room where three girl laughed and chattered, in dresses that were out of date a hundred years ago.

She had never been able to get away from the house Whenever she had gone out for a ramble by herself she had always found she was turning in its direction, and again and again she would come through woods on to the drive when she had not realized that she was anywhere near it.

On the last evening of her holiday she had resolutely turned in the opposite direction, climbing the steep hill above the farther road, some way behind the cottage, toiling up a dark, open sweep of field that stretched up to a pale and luminous sky ; and there at the top had been surprised by the sight of the house far below. From above, it appeared to be closely surrounded by the trees of the park and drive.

She had stood and watched that straggling cluster of roofs and towers grow gradually more dim among the trees, and imagined it as the palace of the Sleeping Beauty, rising above the dark encircling grove of its enchanted forest.

It had been impossible to believe that the Harrises lived there, that the maids were probably at that moment turning down the beds and putting hot water cans in their washstands. What she had believed was that she was wanted down there ; that she must go down and see what was happening ; that there was danger, to herself, perhaps, but far more to some person in that half-hidden house among the trees.

She had laughed at herself, shaken it off, and gone home to bed. And then, after she had fallen asleep——

But no, she did not want to remember that night. She must have been asleep and dreaming or else stark mad.

She wished Donald would not look at her so thoughtfully ; did he see any change in her ?

But Donald had seen more than one change in Jan since her holiday. On her return from Barton he had thought her abstracted, and he had once or twice surprised a scared look in her eyes. This had changed gradually to an air of suppressed and hardly natural excitement ; she seemed positively to dance as she walked, her eyes full of a secret, laughing expectancy whose cause he could never fathom. Then quite suddenly she had become dull and lifeless, frequently irritable, as though some pleasing light of fancy had died out within her and left her empty. It was so that he had left her and now found her again.

They were going now over the fields by the short cut that Jan knew so well to the woods by the drive. Their eyes were dazzled by the setting sun, but the long grass where they walked was already in shadow. In another moment the sun had set, and the golden scene to which they had grown accustomed looked suddenly cold and strange. The last time she had gone that way had been when the moon was up.

That last evening of her holiday, she had stood and watched the house from the hillside until the sense of dread and mystery that had assailed her proved so strong that she turned and ran down the hill back to the cottage.

She had gone to bed very early for she was tired, but she could not fall asleep at once, and as she lay, uneasily dozing, she thought that she was called and sprang fully awake on the instant. She could not, however, be sure that she had heard her name ; and now as she considered, she was sure that she had not. Yet she had been called, she knew that, and she knew also that she was wanted now, and with terrible insistency. She must go to the house, and without telling anyone she hurried on her clothes and went.

An enormous moon was rising over the fields as she took the short cut across them, through the little wood, and was soon in the drive. The drive was striped and chequered with a confusing maze of shadows and white patches that looked like living forms ; it was familiar, and yet so alien, it seemed to be on another planet ; moreover, it appeared to be waiting for her.

She came to the gates and stood there, clutching the

cold bars and looking through them at the house, staring at the windows. They were all lighted. Mr. Harris had said they hardly used this side of the house, but perhaps they were having a house party at last. She noticed that it was a soft, yellow radiance, quite different from electric light ; perhaps the Harrises were showing how " feudal " they were to the extent of hundreds of candles. But though she said all this to herself at the time she did not believe it.

The lights in the rooms below went out, and presently those above went out too, and Jan found she was still holding on to the gates and shivering, though she did not feel cold. She walked on round the gardens until she came to the side of the house and saw there a lawn enclosed by massive yew trees, and behind it three long French windows that showed a very dim light. She climbed the low wall, and walked softly by the yew trees up to the house until she stood in the shadow, close to the first of the three windows, and stood there a long time, afraid to look in. Her fear was not of being seen but of what she might see. There was no breath of sound from within. At last she looked in, looking down at the floor.

It was a huge room and very dark. For a little way on the dark floor the moonlight lay in three paths from the three French windows, and just at the end of the centre path, it shone on a very small pair of green and silver shoes. Jan looked at them and wished there were nothing else to be seen in the room but those tiny, gleaming shoes.

Then she looked up and saw that the shoes belonged to a figure that sat in the shadow beyond the moonlight, a small greyish figure with erect head. Behind her the room was less dark, for a candle, screened from the windows, stood on a large table. The figure of a man stood in the shadow between the shaded candle and the

243

moonlight. He was behind the seated figure and was as motionless as she.

Jan could see quite clearly the pale outline of his head, the powdered hair tied back by a ribbon at the neck, against the dark panelled walls. He wore a coat of some light colour that gleamed with silver here and there. She knew him, though she knew she had never seen him before, and she could distinguish nothing in his face but his eyes ; they were looking not at her but at the figure in the chair, and they were very bright. She found she could not look away from those fixed and glittering eyes.

She watched them until they appeared to change, and she saw them, not as eyes at all, but as pools of bright water reflecting the figure in the chair. She then saw that that reflected figure, though erect and motionless, was of a girl that was being slowly drowned.

She tried to cry out, to appeal frantically to the two figures in that room, but, as in a nightmare, no sound would come, not even when she beat her hands against the closed window. They did not seem to touch the glass but to be striking out aimlessly at nothing. She found that she was standing there, her gaping mouth dry and parched, staring into a room which was empty and unlighted except for the three paths of moonlight from the windows. There was nothing at the end of the centre path, and no one in the room. She remembered now that she had seen this room before.

It was here that the boy had sat alone, his head resting on his hand, his face hidden.

She ran most of the way home, and all the time she was telling herself, " I'm real—real—— It was those others that were ghosts."

She saw Donald beside and a little ahead of her, looking straight in front of him, his head thrown back He was talking and she heard all he said.

244

With an obstinate pride that would not allow him to plead again for what he considered he had asked too often, he spoke little of themselves but more of his plans and prospects in America. At last he blurted out, " Well, will you come ? " and then in the pause that followed, reverted to the more impersonal subject.

Jan answered him as she got over the stile into the wood, and sat on it for a moment, cross-legged, laughing suddenly at what she was saying. It sounded solemn and pompous to be giving her gracious acceptance at last like this.

Donald drew away the hand that had been helping her over the stile.

" You tell me you will marry me, and you laugh," he said. " I have not much sense of humour, and I do not see why it is funny that you should be my wife."

She looked into his face, which was on a level with hers where she sat, and the dull pain and resentment in it filled her with a sharp sense of humility.

" Oh, Don ! " she said. " It's only because I saw what a conceited fool I'd been, and am, not to know all along what I should have in having you."

" Are you sure," he said, " that you know what you would have ? "

His anger seemed only to have deepened. He took a step nearer to her, and she thought as she had thought before that " crossness became him." But it did not please her that he should still be cross after her ample amends. It did not occur to her at that moment that the dark flush on his face was not of anger only, and that the abrupt movement with which he turned from her without helping her down from the stile had in it more of enforced restraint than of boorishness.

She hurried on ahead through the wood, feeling dissatisfied with both herself and Donald. They were always getting on the wrong side of each other—they certainly could not be meant for each other. But, then, for whom or for what was she meant ? Was it for nothing but a fancy, for a face that she had seen only once and knew she would never see again ?

She had seen him standing in the unlighted window of a house in Soho one evening when it was not quite dark, and she was hurrying home through a shower of rain. He was looking out into the street, a man in a dull purple coat, his face showing dark against his powdered hair. It was the man she had seen in the library at Chidleigh. This time she could distinguish his features, the slanting eyebrows, a little like a monkey and more like a satyr, the upturned corners of his mouth, and near it a patch, cut in the shape of a crescent, above all the brilliant eyes that were fixed on her. She recognized him as the " Gentleman Unknown."

They stood and looked at each other, it may have been for a minute. Then it appeared that the room round him was growing darker, and she could not see him so clearly. She spoke to him, begging him to stay, to speak to her ; and this time it seemed that he at least heard her voice. He was straining forward as though to see and hear her the more clearly. Suddenly he flung away from the window. She thought he was coming down to her, and waited a little, but he did not come.

Presently she noticed that the house was the restaurant where she and Donald had dined the evening before she had gone away for her holiday. She looked up again at the window and saw that the room was lighted, and that a waiter was passing to and fro, clearing the tables. Yes, it was the room on the first floor where she and Donald had sat by the chimney-piece and examined the burnt carving.

The moment she had always been waiting for had come and gone. It had been lost through something there that was stronger than herself ; stronger, even, than the will and desire of the man at the window. He had waited for her, she knew it now, as she had always waited and watched, unknowingly, for him.

Since then, as she walked to and from work, or through the city in the lunch hour, it no longer seemed worth while to look at the faces as they passed, in search for the face she wanted. She knew now what she had sought ; it was the sideward turn of the head, the quick, bright glance of the " Gentleman Unknown." But with that knowledge had come the certainty that she would never see him again. She had wondered some-times if it were because he had sought her and now had ceased to do so.

Donald heard a sharp cry. He hurried after her, ducking under the barbed wire and jumping the ditch, and found her standing, white and startled, as though she had that instant received some shock.

" There—there's no drive," she stammered in a low voice, speaking to herself, not to him ; and then, " They are cutting down all the trees in the drive."

For one terrifying, ridiculous instant, Jan had actually thought she had been transported as in a fairy tale to some unknown place. Now she looked on either side of her at the huge fallen trees, at the few that still remained standing in stark isolation.

Donald said something and though she did not hear what it was, she heard his voice and knew it was not the voice she was wanting to hear. It should have been low and quick in tone, reassuring, comforting, yet with the faintest tinge of mockery in it like a subtle and surprising flavour in a sweet, cool drink.

She sat down on one of the fallen trees and spoke in a sudden rush as though the words were flung out of her.

" It's no good, Donald, I can't marry you and go to

America and pretend any longer that real things matter most to me. They don't. I know I'm a silly fool, I'm all the more a fool because I've lost it, and yet I can't turn to and say ' That's all over like playing with dolls and now I'll be sensible and real.' I've been trying to, but I can't forget it. It's only left a gap."

He stood beside her, waiting. She twisted round on the mutilated tree-trunk and said in desperation, " You don't want me to marry you, do you, just because I'm dull and empty and want something to fill up a gap ? "

" You can marry me for any reason you choose, as a clod of earth to stop a hole if you like. I'll not engage to remain that clod."

His voice was not pleasant. Jan felt the more disturbed ; but perhaps if they quarrelled it might be a quicker way of ending it. But she did not want to quarrel with Donald, and she certainly owed him an explanation, if only she knew how to explain. She said at last, " I've always known there was someone, I didn't know whom. I know now it was the man in that picture I found at school—I told you about it. I laughed at you once for being jealous of a ' Gentleman Unknown '—well— you can laugh at me now. But he's not there any longer, he's gone away."

How like a block he stood ! But it was not surprising while she gibbered out such nonsense. She must try and make it clear.

" You can call it softening of the brain. I expect it is. I used to think about that picture at school, and somehow he was always coming in. Everything I liked reminded me of him. But it was later when I'd left school that I began to feel there was someone there, someone who liked me—who—— And it was funny it began then because I wasn't thinking about unreal people any more after I started work in town, everything was much too full and interesting and exciting and I was just enjoying myself all I could. But—I don't know how——"

Her voice dropped, her expression had grown abstracted, she was talking more easily, and to herself rather than to him. " The real people were never quite as exciting or as interesting as one thought they would be. I was always expecting something a little different, other words, or another way of saying them; something that would make them just right instead of just wrong. When I thought I was really beginning to be in love with anyone, the ' Gentleman Unknown ' would look at me and laugh as I put out the light, and I would wonder how he would have made love to me, and if I should ever meet anyone who would do it as he would."

Donald Graeme stirred a little on his feet, but did not speak, and when at his movement she glanced up at him in question his face looked as hard as ever. The sullen, tormented pride in it dismayed her.

" Don, don't look like that ! What can all this nonsense mean to you but that I'm a fool that's not worth having ? "

" Go on," he said.

" What's the use ? It only hurts you. Can't you take it that I'm no fit body for real life or a real wife, as I believe you once told me in a rage. Well, you were quite right."

" I ask you to go on."

She wondered a little at his harsh gravity. Most men would surely be laughing at her by now, telling her she was a silly, crack-brained child that had never had the sense to leave off crying for the moon. She had told herself so often enough.

She went on.

" It's as though I never even knew I had it till I lost it. And what ' it ' was—a companion I suppose. Yes, I knew that, for I used to find myself looking at all the

249

people who passed, fancying that I might catch sight of someone whom I couldn't quite remember and was always hoping I should meet. Sometimes I have thought he was just beside me and then when I turned round it was someone quite different."

" I have known that," he muttered, but she was too intent now on her thoughts to notice the almost inaudible tone.

She had put her hands over her face and was speaking in nervous, stammering desperation.

" Oh, Don, I'm stupid, but you do see, don't you, it's no use ? I wish it were, I wish I could, but I can't. It was only a silly make-up game I suppose, but it's gone, and nothing else will ever make up for it. If I married you it would still be the same. I like you, I admire you—no, it's more than that, for sometimes, when you're there, I feel very much in love with you. But I should still be wanting something else, something different, something I know I can never have—but that doesn't make it any better, either for you or me."

She was looking at him now and thought that her words had been thrown against a wall. What was the use of trying to explain ? He did not even pay attention to what she said. Oh, yes, he was a fine figure of a man ; she had frequently felt an involuntary thrill of admiration when she looked at him, but now she saw him as a shadow, dark and remote from her, rather than a living companion.

He might still want to marry her, he probably would, for he was of a dogged disposition. But he had not understood, or rather had not wished to do so, for she could not expect anyone to understand such an insane chimera. And if she gave in to him she would be alone, always, with someone who would always ignore or half unconsciously resent the thing that had mattered most in her life. She had lived in the company of a dream ;

it would be better to live on the memory of it than look forward to so empty a future.

She watched him in a dull wonder while he, with a slow and rather awkward movement, knelt beside her and put his arms round her crouched and shivering body.

" Why, what's all this to-do ? " he was saying in an unwontedly gruff voice. " Why do you put yourself to such pains to explain to me ? I thought you had more to tell me ; perhaps you will, some time. I have always thought you had the second sight, Rose Janet. I have felt that you were away—with someone else—when you were close beside me. I don't say it doesn't hurt—it does. But it doesn't hurt as much as to see you suffer like this. I wish you were not shivering so. My lass, don't cry like that."

It was a long time before she could speak again, and then stammered out, " Don—is it because you're half Highland ? That you take it so naturally, I mean. I've been wondering if I were going mad, or had been so all along—to have had my chief happiness in something that doesn't exist."

" Why should that surprise you ? It's the reason that fills the theatres and cinemas. Any servant girl who longs to be a duchess, anyone who has dreams of success-ful ambition, finds their chief happiness in something that doesn't exist. All artists do. Perhaps most lovers do also."

His slow smile with this delighted Jan. She must have been very stupid to think he had no sense of humour.

" And what is it that doesn't exist in me that gives you your chief happiness ? " she asked.

His answer was not given in words, nor was it, apparently, to something that did not exist.

She tried to remember that it was impossible for her to marry Donald and go out to America, that she would

251

only be wanting something else, something different. But for the moment, at any rate, she did not want anything else but Donald's arms round her, with the knowledge that he knew and understood, that he was not even much surprised.

They talked little. She did not wish to look ahead. Donald, she felt, was impatient, eager for the future ; soon, no doubt, she would be also. Life would begin again for her, it would " come real," so he assured her. It would always be so. Not in the present time but in some time just ahead would lie their chief happiness, and, still more, their chief security in happiness.

The approach of a gardener's wife recalled them sharply to the present. The gardener's wife was tactful and would have hurried past, but Jan wished her to show them the private chapel, and to that intent entered into conversation with a question about the old drive.

The gardener's wife replied that the new owner was selling the timber. Mr. Harris, he'd always said it should be done, as the old drive had been useless a long time now, but for her part she thought it a shame, all those fine old trees—her father had planted some of them himself, he had. Yes, he had been gardener here a many years ago. There was a tumble-down cottage and garden in the middle of the drive then, and they had cleared it all away and planted fresh trees there.

She consented to show them the chapel, though it would be too dark inside now to see it properly. On the way there, they asked if she had ever heard of the place being haunted and, with deprecatory giggles, she was induced to impart the usual vague, unsatisfactory things that one hears of any old house. A housemaid this summer had said she had seen a white figure at the top of the stairs, and had hysterics in the kitchen, but the butler had declared it was only the moonlight.

The library had not been used for a very long time and

people had got nervous of going into it. She *had* heard
tell that if you sat there at night you saw a little man in
a blue gown and a sort of turban come into the room
carrying a candle, " and he looks all round to see who's
there and then disappears." But she had never known
anyone who had seen it.

" It's so futile, anyway," Jan said to Donald. " Why
should ghosts always do such meaningless things ? "

" It may once have had some meaning to the little
man himself," he answered.

She was silent, thinking of the two figures she had seen
in that room. She would never know what meaning
they had had for each other, and for her.

They had reached the chapel by now. It had been
badly " restored " in the nineteenth century, and the
plaster, damp with the chapel's long disuse, was dis-
coloured and unsightly. It was impossible to see it as
a whole in the half darkness. The Vicar had told Jan
that the family of the Clares had died out by about 1800,
when the house was sold, with most of its possessions, and
had frequently changed hands since. She was looking
for the name at the beginning of the funny old diary he
had lent her, written by some girl who had lived at
Chidleigh long ago—a rather dull diary, kept only for a
few months ; nothing had happened in it, and he had
bought it for sixpence at a sale at the house. But there
was one thing in it that was strange ; a rough drawing of
a figure that had a distinct resemblance to Jan herself in
her straight coat-frock and leather hat.

It was some time before she found a small marble
tablet which informed her that Juliana Daintree, of
Crox Hall, youngest child of Robert Clare, Lord
Chidleigh, lay buried in Baring churchyard. She had
died in 1797, after eighteen years of wedded life, leaving
a son and two daughters. It was stated, as in a post-
script, that her husband, Richard Fawcett Daintree,

Esq., had died the following year, and beneath his name
and the dates of his birth and death, this epigram was
quoted :

> " She first departed ; he for a little try'd
>   To live without her ; lik'd it not, and dy'd."

" The young lady's found something to interest her,"
said the gardener's wife.

" One moment," said Jan. " I'll follow you in a
minute." She was reading again the inscription beneath
Juliana's name. It was more distinctive than most of
the epitaphs :

> "   She was
>   In manners elegant and interesting,
>   In disposition tender and affectionate,
>   In temper gentle and amiable,
>   In religion truly pious,
>   In life by all beloved,
>
>   And in death by all regretted.
>   She lies buried, not forgotten.
>   Obiit February 1st, 1797.
>   Ætatis suæ 35.   "

Jan thought of the ending of another epitaph :

> " But beauty vanishes, beauty passes,
>   However rare—rare it be.
>   And when I crumble, who will remember
>   This lady of the West Country ? "

There could be none now left to remember Juliana.

Donald found Jan grave and abstracted after they had left the gardener's wife. They had secured permission to go through the gardens, as the house was empty, and were now wandering through them in the increasing dusk. This time he was not prevented by pride or shyness from asking her what she was thinking.

She did not answer, but demanded presently, " Does one live only as long as one is remembered, do you think ? I have heard that that is all the immortality one can hope for. And when all who remember you are dead, then the last trace of your spirit also passes away."

He contested the point. It argued that memory belonged only to the living, and he saw no reason to suppose that.

She stood still, looking round her at the empty house, its darkened windows, at the gardens that already showed their neglect, at the few isolated trees where the drive had been. Even a place like this could be so quickly changed and forgotten. Juliana, who had lived here, had laughed and danced " till 3 o' the Clock " in one of those empty rooms, lay buried and was now forgotten. And so soon would she, too, pass away and be forgotten.

It may be that Donald felt something of that chill sense of loneliness that passed through her, for suddenly he clutched her to him and kissed her again and again with an urgency that was not mere passion but rather fear. When at last he set her down he shook himself and said with the strongest relapse into his native speech that Jan had ever heard in him, " We are juist twa silly bairrns to be afraid of the dark. I ken weel I'll remember ye and I'll no let ye forget."

He walked on very stiffly after that as though ashamed of his outburst, but kept tight hold of her hand. A thin new moon had risen, and the white roses growing sprawlingly round them shone dimly through the summer dusk.

255

Her hand slipped from Donald's into his arm and lightly stroked his rough tweed sleeve.

They were walking by a box hedge as tall as themselves at the end of one of the grass terraces. Then they went slowly down the terrace, the moon behind them. Faint shadows stole out before them, and she, looking down at the milky ground, saw that they were the shadows of a hooped skirt and a sword, of a bent head, ribbon at neck, and a head upturned to meet it, under a high-piled tower of hair.

THE END